Engaged to be married?

Phoebe squeezed her eyes shut, wishing, hoping, praying to disappear. Somebody was going to look very foolish in the next minute or two. Most likely, that somebody would be her.

"Phoebe," Tommy said, "why don't you come on up and let us introduce you to the good people of New Skye?"

She opened her eyes and looked for Adam, who had left the speaker's stand and moved nearer to where she stood. Holding out his hand, he waited for her to join him. He had decided to go along with Tommy's lie.

If she protested, denied the engagement, Adam's campaign would end today, this minute, his credibility with the voters destroyed.

"Phoebe?" Adam's voice came to her...a question, a plea.

She couldn't resist.

Turning to the crowd, he held her close to him with one arm and waved with the other, grinning wildly.

Tommy announced, "The future Mrs. Adam DeVries."

To Phoebe, the words sounded like the clang of a heavy iron door...the door to her new prison cell.

Dear Reader,

Often, writers will say that their characters "talk" to them. I've been known to sit my characters in a comfortable (if imaginary) chair and treat them as a psychotherapist might, asking leading questions and saying, over and over again, "How did you feel about that?"

With this particular book, I had more trouble than usual interviewing the hero. Adam DeVries doesn't talk much. When he does, he says as little as possible...because Adam stutters. No amount of coaxing can get him to ramble on about his childhood, his background, his family. He doesn't want to discuss his failures or his successes— he simply wants to get things done. Adam is a decent, honorable man who puts himself on the line for his beliefs. Though he's the last person you would expect to enter politics, with its endless campaigning and public speaking, that's what his ideals lead him to do. Sometimes the only way to conquer your weakness is to face it head-on.

And sometimes you need a little help with that task. Phoebe Moss loves to help, which is why she became a speech therapist in the first place. Adam's goal, and his gallantry, involve her deeply in his campaign, in his life. These two ride into battle very much like knights-errant in the old, old days, only to discover that the fight ahead may require more sacrifice than either of them can bear.

The Last Honest Man is the third book in my AT THE CAROLINA DINER series for Harlequin Superromance. I hope you enjoy Adam and Phoebe's story, and that you'll let me know what you think.

Happy reading!

Lynnette Kent
PMB 304
Westwood Shopping Center
Fayetteville, NC 28314
or lynnettekent.com

The Last Honest Man
Lynnette Kent

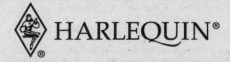

HARLEQUIN®

TORONTO • NEW YORK • LONDON
AMSTERDAM • PARIS • SYDNEY • HAMBURG
STOCKHOLM • ATHENS • TOKYO • MILAN • MADRID
PRAGUE • WARSAW • BUDAPEST • AUCKLAND

ISBN 0-373-71147-6

THE LAST HONEST MAN

Copyright © 2003 by Cheryl B. Bacon.

Visit us at www.eHarlequin.com

Printed in U.S.A.

To Laura,
with admiration
and gratitude

CAST OF CHARACTERS

Adam DeVries: Mayoral candidate and owner of DeVries Construction

Phoebe Moss: A speech therapist

Cynthia DeVries: Adam's mother

Preston DeVries: Adam's father

L. T. LaRue: A corrupt businessman

Curtis Tate: The mayor of New Skye

Kellie Tate: The mayor's wife

Tommy Crawford: Adam's campaign manager

Samantha Pettit: Reporter for the *New Skye News*

Dixon Bell: A songwriter and friend of Adam's

Kate Bowdrey: Dixon's fiancée

Charlie Brannon: Owner of Charlie's Carolina Diner

Abby Brannon: Charlie's daughter, who keeps the diner running

Jacquie Archer: A farrier, Phoebe's neighbor

Erin Archer: Jacquie's daughter

Teresa DeVries: Adam's sister

Tim DeVries: Adam's brother

Jenna Franklin: Phoebe's business partner

Pete Mitchell: A state trooper and Adam's friend

Mary Rose Mitchell: Pete Mitchell's wife

PROLOGUE

HEADED DOWNTOWN ON A SWEET May morning, Adam DeVries whistled as he waited through the stoplight at the top of the hill, enjoying the warm breeze that reached inside the open window to ruffle his hair.

One second—one classic double take—later, his world started spinning in the opposite direction.

He let his jaw drop as he stared at the ravaged parcel of land to his left across the street. All the newly leafed trees he expected to see there had vanished, not to mention every last blade of spring-green grass. And the old stone chimney, a landmark of sorts, was gone.

The traffic signal above his truck turned green, red again, then green, and a honk from behind prompted him to get out of the way. Adam swung left at the next corner, wheeled into the first driveway he came to and backed out just as fast. He paid lip service to a stop sign, pulled out onto Main Street and headed up the hill. Approaching the traffic light from the other direction, he turned right on red and screeched to a stop beside the razed lot. Once out of his truck, he strode around the front end but then pulled up short, his stomach constricting and his knees suddenly weak. The sight before him was even worse than he'd imagined.

One of the most beautiful pieces of land in all of New Skye, North Carolina, had been reduced to an ugly square of brown dirt, pitted and peaked by truck tires and bulldozer treads. A two-legged wooden sign lay flat on the ground, informing those who stood over it that this site had been rezoned for commercial use. Coming soon was a Speedy Spot convenience store and gas station, built by LaRue Construction.

Adam swore loud and long. Then he mourned.

Mourned for the childhood hours he'd spent here under the magnolias and poplars and oaks, some of them more than a hundred years old. When the 1880s house on the site burned down in the 1950s, the Brewer family had moved to a newer, safer home, but they'd cleaned up the lot, leaving the sturdy chimney standing among the trees. All the years since, they'd kept the weeds and grass mown for kids—like Adam and his brother and sister and his best friend Tommy—who'd brought balls and bats, books and games of make-believe to play in their special place. Teenagers sometimes hid under the trees in the dark to make out, though the police tended to keep a close eye on this unofficial "park" at night. Sunday afternoons, a family might wander down with their dog and their baby in a stroller, just to take in the fine weather and the view of downtown New Skye.

Adam could enjoy that view from where he stood now—not at the edge of the slope on the back of the lot, but on the street side—because the trees were gone. To his right, Main Street descended the Hill, as they called it, to the green circle of lawn that separated the grand old Victorian courthouse from traffic. Beyond the courthouse, the street with its new brick pavers stretched between tall crepe myrtle trees and giant planters filled with colorful flowers, which stood in front of renovated shops and offices. Anchoring downtown at the far end of Main were the new town hall and police department buildings.

There the trouble lay. Being in the construction business himself, Adam closely followed the rezoning notices for New Skye and the county. This case, though, had flown in under his radar. He'd missed the motion, the discussion and the vote that changed the use of the Brewer land from residential to commercial, forcing the owners to sell. Had he been sloppy? Or had the whole transaction been camouflaged to avoid public notice? A number of powerful people in town would have protested the conversion of this property...if they'd been informed.

"I s-spent an hour in the r-records office yesterday afternoon," Adam told his best friends during breakfast the next morning. After a couple of hard and fast hours of basketball, they were settling in for a decent meal at Charlie's Carolina Diner, where they'd been coming for more Saturdays than they wanted to remember. "M-Mayor T-Tate slipped the m-motion into a city c-c-council m-meeting with no prior notification to the p-public."

"The council went along without a whimper, no doubt, 'cause they're his buddies." Tommy Crawford shook his head. "I bet L. T. LaRue sat there the whole time, just grinning. He got what he wanted out of the deal—another building site."

"Kachink, kachink," Dixon Bell added. "All that scumbag ever thinks about is money."

They all stared glumly at their plates. "It'd be nice if they mayor and the city council gave some thought to the ordinary people in this town," Pete Mitchell said after a minute, "especially when there are real problems to be addressed." As a highway patrolman, Pete ran an after school program for juvenile offenders; he knew the hardships imposed by funding cuts. "I suppose that gas station will increase the tax base, but if it makes the town a less desirable place to live, then people won't move here and the tax base'll go down..." He shook his head. "I'm not sure there's a solution."

"We could murder the incumbents," Dixon suggested, with a wicked lift of his eyebrow.

Pete shook his head. "I don't want to go to prison on account of Curtis Tate and L. T. LaRue."

"The solution," Tommy said, pointing with his knife, "is to get some honorable people in the government, men and women who'll care about what's right, not what'll make them rich."

This was the very conclusion Adam had drawn late last night, when he made his big decision.

Tommy glanced around the table. "This is an election year, gentlemen. We've got the chance to make a change. So which of us is gonna run for mayor?"

Amidst the muttering of the other guys, Adam took his stand. "I w-w-will. I'll r-run f-for m-mayor."

Tommy looked at him with raised eyebrows. "De-Vries?"

In the silence, Adam looked at each man in turn—the boys he'd gone to school with, the friends he counted on when he needed help. "Wh-what d-do you th-think?"

Their hesitation lasted for a blink of an eye. Then they were all over the plan, giving advice, predicting success. Mounting a campaign would require money—they'd be sure he had enough—and time, which they offered freely. To hear them talk, the votes had already been tallied, the outcome secured.

Only when the others had left the diner and Adam sat alone with Tommy did the real impediment to their plan come up.

"So..." Tommy rolled his iced tea glass between his palms. "You're gonna run for mayor. You don't have a wife or kids to worry about. That's convenient. And you're the perfect candidate—good looks, good reputation, good family, everything we could want.''

''B-but…'' Adam didn't have to ask what Tommy was thinking. He had no problem putting every aspect of his life on the line in order to be the mayor of New Skye.

Every aspect but one.

Before he could eject Tate from the mayor's chair, Adam would have to abandon his closest companion of more than two decades.

He would have to learn to speak without the stutter.

CHAPTER ONE

"MR. DEVRIES?"

At the sound of his name, Adam looked up from the news magazine he'd been pretending to read.

Across the waiting room, a woman whose long hair was the color of natural ash wood smiled at him. "Good morning. I'm Phoebe Moss."

His heart began to pound against his ribs. He put the journal aside and got to his feet, pretending his palms weren't sweaty, his throat hadn't closed down completely. The receptionist, a grandmotherly woman with unlikely red hair, smiled at him as he passed by. Though he tried to return the favor, he doubted he'd been successful.

Phoebe Moss looked up at him when he got close—she was almost a foot shorter than he—and tilted her head toward the hallway behind her. "This way, please."

With every step, Adam's resistance mounted. He didn't want to be here, would rather have been just about anywhere else on the planet besides this place, this morning. Walking down the hall felt like pushing against an incoming tide. In the middle of a hurricane.

"Come in and have a seat." She ushered him into a north-facing office with a couch and an armchair, a desk positioned in the corner between two windows, and an assortment of assessment machines with which Adam was all too familiar, thanks to past experience. His strongest impulse was to run…as far and as fast as he possibly could.

But when Phoebe Moss sat in the chair in front of her desk and turned to face him with a clipboard in her lap, Adam lowered himself into the armchair.

She pushed her gold-rimmed glasses up on her nose and settled down to business. "What can I do for you, Mr. DeVries?"

"Y-you're a s-s-speech th-therapist." He clenched his fist, hitting it against his leg. Bad enough to be here, without having to explain why.

"Yes." The word definitely held a question. Waiting for his answer, she wrote briefly on the paper held by the clipboard.

"A-as y-you c-c-can hear, I s-s-stutter."

Nodding, Phoebe Moss scribbled something else. "Fairly badly."

"I w-w-want to s-stop."

Her gaze lifted to his face. "Why?"

This was even worse than he'd expected. "W-why do you think? Talking this w-w-w-way s-s-sucks."

Another notation. "I understand. Have you tried therapy before?"

He nodded, his lips pressed tightly together.

"Did it work?"

"Obv-v-viously n-n-not."

"Not even for a brief time?"

Adam shrugged. "If I c-concentrate," he said, very slowly, "I can g-get th-through short s-sentences. But that's n-not e-enough."

"Has something changed in your life to prompt this new attempt?"

He gripped his hands together, studying his thumbs.

The answer to her question was straightforward enough. Yet he dreaded her reaction.

When he didn't answer, she cleared her throat. "What's changed?"

After staring a little longer at his linked fingers, Adam lifted his gaze to her face again. Her eyes, he saw in that instant, were the dark gray of a stormy ocean.

"I'm going into politics," he said, using the exaggerated drawl he'd been taught. "I have to be able to talk without stuttering." He finished the sentence and winced. God, he hated the sound of his voice.

His worry over her response had been justified. Phoebe Moss stared at him, her mouth open in astonishment. "Politics? You're going to run for office?"

He nodded. "M-m-mayor of N-New Sk-Skye."

"That's an ambitious goal for anyone." Looking down at the paper in her lap, she tapped her pen on the edge of the clipboard for a moment. "When were you thinking about running for office?"

"Th-this y-y-year. I-I've al-already f-filed."

Her startled eyes met his. "Aren't elections in November?"

"Y-yes. B-but the c-campaign w-w-will s-s-start by L-Labor D-Day."

"You expect to stop stuttering in less than three months?"

"Y-yes."

"Mr. DeVries—"

"C-call me Adam."

"Adam, do you realize how much you're asking of yourself? Curing a stutter can take many months—years—of practice."

He shrugged. "I'll j-just h-have to work hard."

She leaned forward, bracing her elbows on her knees

and clasping her hands together, maintaining eye contact. "I can't make any kind of guarantee on your progress. Not in three months, or six or twelve."

"I c-can d-do it."

"Why are you so sure, when the past hasn't shown success?"

"Th-that w-w-was for…for o-other p-p-people." Adam took a deep breath. "This time is for m-me."

"I…SEE." STUNNED, impressed—and, to be honest, a little scared—by Adam DeVries's resolve, Phoebe sat back in her desk chair. A glance out the window to her right showed a white pickup truck, with the red-and-blue DeVries Construction logo on the door, parked next to her lime-green Beetle. Now that she thought about it, his company's signs were posted on building projects all over town.

"You're obviously a successful businessman." She gestured toward the truck. "Why worry about the stutter? Let the voters accept you as you are."

"G-good p-p-point," he said, without the rancor she'd expected. "B-but I have to be able to make my ideas plain." For the first time, he smiled. "At a speed g-greater than the average snail's p-p-pace." His words were clear—though very, very slow—and his tone was distorted, due to his prolonged speech pattern.

But that smile… Seeing it, Phoebe couldn't get her breath. The aristocratic planes of his cheeks softened, and his bright blue eyes crinkled at the corners as his firm lips stretched wide—Adam DeVries's smile was like the return of the sun after an eclipse, all the more valuable for being rare.

After a shocked moment, she gathered her wits to speak. "As I said, I can't make any guarantees."

"I-I und-derstand."

"We'll need several sessions every week."

"N-no p-problem. C-c-can w-we sc-schedule at n-n-night? I-I can't s-s-spend so m-many m-mornings away f-from w-w-work."

Phoebe frowned, not so much at him as at the frantic beating of her heart. What was she thinking? "I-I have responsibilities after work. And I live thirty minutes out of town."

"Oh." His dark brows lowered as he considered.

That was when she gave in to a truly crazy impulse. "I could see you at my home in the evening—if you wanted to drive that far."

Adam thought for another moment, then nodded. "Th-that w-w-would w-work for m-me. Wh-wh-when?" As he had during the whole interview, he clenched his right fist and pounded it on his thigh, as if the motion helped him get the words out.

That gesture would be one of their first points of change, when they began their sessions *at her house.* Phoebe got to her feet, not really believing she'd agreed to this situation, let alone that she'd suggested it to begin with. "Thursday night? Seven-thirty?"

"S-s-sounds g-good." He came to her at the desk with his arm extended. "Th-thanks, M-Miss M-M-Moss. I-I'll see you th-then."

"C-call me Phoebe," she said faintly as they shook hands.

For that, Adam gave her another one of those heart-stealing smiles. "O-okay."

She managed to remain standing as Adam DeVries left her office and headed down the hall toward the reception area. As soon as he was out of sight, she let her shaking knees give way and dropped back into her chair.

What was she thinking, inviting a man she didn't know to her home? No smart woman acted so carelessly these days.

The DeVries family itself was well-known in New Skye, of course, with a history dating back to before the Civil War. Preston DeVries, Adam's father, was a respected surgeon at the local hospital, while Cynthia, his mother, worked with the most prominent charity and volunteer groups. Phoebe had moved to North Carolina only a year ago, but she'd seen the DeVries name in the newspaper often enough to be curious. Her friends who'd grown up in town had filled her in on the details, which made Adam less of a stranger, surely. Less of a risk.

Then her first glimpse of him across the waiting room this morning had set her pulse skittering. Tall, broad-shouldered and lean-hipped, with a workingman's hands and a poet's sad, farsighted gaze, Adam DeVries embodied the sum of all her romantic fantasies. His thick, neatly cut brown hair, his smooth, tanned face and strong chin, belonged on a movie poster...or a campaign flyer. How could she say no to a dream come true?

And there was that smile...

Still, had she allowed her physical and emotional reaction to a client to overwhelm her professional good sense?

No, she concluded, *I didn't.* The smile hadn't caused her to bend the rules. Her decision resulted from the moment *before* the smile. The moment when he'd said, "This time is for me."

Phoebe knew exactly what he meant. She'd spent years trying to meet the expectations of other people, only to fail time and time again. Not until she'd begun to live for herself had she succeeded in dealing with her own stutter.

She wouldn't deny Adam DeVries his chance to accomplish the same miracle.

And she wouldn't consider the notion that he…and she…could possibly fail.

TUESDAY NIGHT, ADAM MET Tommy Crawford in the parking lot outside the Carolina Diner. "Th-thought you w-were g-gonna be l-l-late."

Tommy shook his hand. "Me, too. My last client decided not to come out in the rainstorm to discuss insurance. These elderly Southern ladies do have certain…peculiarities."

"D-don't I kn-know it. T-try b-building a h-house f-f-for one of th-them." Adam held the door and let Tommy go in ahead of him. "The rain s-slowed us d-down, too. I s-sent most of the c-crews h-home early." Combined with his late start, that meant not much work got done today.

Tommy turned a hard right and slid into Adam's usual booth. Just as Adam settled in, Abby Brannon appeared with two glasses of iced tea.

"Hi, guys. Isn't the rain great?" Abby's dad, Charlie, owned the Carolina Diner, but everybody in town knew that Abby was the real engine running the place. She flipped to a new page in her order book. "Tonight's special is porcupine meatballs, and I baked a red velvet cake yesterday. You want to think, or you want to order?"

Since they'd been eating here since they were teenagers, along with most of the other kids who attended nearby New Skye High, neither Adam nor Tommy needed a menu. They both ordered the special. "With green beans," Tommy said, "and macaroni and cheese."

"I'll h-have o-okra and ap-p-ples. L-looks like you're g-gonna b-be b-busy t-tonight."

Abby glanced around at the rapidly filling tables and brushed her brown bangs off her forehead with the back of her hand. "Rainy nights tend to bring folks out to eat. Unlike some people," she said to Adam as she grinned and punched him lightly on the shoulder. "Some people eat out every night."

"S-some p-people don't c-cook."

She winked. "You oughta find a nice woman who'll solve that problem for you."

He winked back. "I d-d-did."

Abby rolled her eyes and walked away. Tommy laughed. "So why don't you marry her and then you wouldn't have to drive out for breakfast?"

Adam looked at his best friend. "M-me? M-marry Abby?"

"Why not?"

"B-because..." He narrowed his eyes and thought. "There's always s-something Abby h-holds b-back. You kn-know? Y-you c-can't qu-quite r-r-reach her."

"She's a busy lady." They watched her bustle from table to table, serving drinks, clearing plates, taking orders. "But she'd be a sweet armful."

"S-so y-you m-marry her."

"Yeah, right." Tommy shook his head. "I'm too much of a wiseass for Abby. Give me a woman with a good suit of armor. That way we won't kill each other."

"Campaign meeting, gentlemen?"

Adam looked up to find one of his worst nightmares standing beside the table—Samantha Pettit, reporter for the *New Skye News*. Surprise made words impossible. He glanced at Tommy.

His friend took over smoothly. "Hey, Sam. How's it going? Sit down and have a drink."

"No, thanks. I'm meeting an interview in a few

minutes. But I saw you two sitting here and figured you must be planning election strategy.''

Adam had pulled himself together. "Election?"

Samantha flashed him a mocking smile. "I saw you'd filed papers for the mayor's race, Adam."

Tommy stepped in. "You just can't keep a secret in this town. You want the first interview, Sam?"

"Yeah, I do."

"Well, when we're up and running, I'll give you a call."

"You're the campaign manager?"

"Who else?"

The reporter nodded. "I'll remember. Keep me up to date on your schedule." Behind Adam, the bell on the door jingled. "Gotta go."

As she walked away, Tommy swore under his breath.

"W-what?"

"Her interview. She just sat down with L. T. LaRue."

Adam's gut tightened. "I g-guess they're t-talking about him w-winning th-that public housing p-project." The official announcement had only been made Monday, though the grapevine had predicted the city council's decision several weeks ago. "D-d-dammit, I really w-w-wanted that c-contract for D-DeVries C-Construction. We would have d-d-done a g-g-good j-job for the p-people of this t-town." He bounced his fist off the Formica tabletop. "LaRue will throw up s-something cheap and let s-somebody else d-deal with the hassle when the p-p-place starts f-f-falling apart."

Tommy shrugged. "You don't play footsie with Mayor Tate and the rest of the city council like L.T. does." He kept an eye on the table across the room. "Don't take 'em to dinner, pay for their golf rounds. Don't cut 'em in on your deals, put an extra ten grand or so a year in

their pockets. If you won't play the game, son, I d[ ]
know how you expect to get the prize.''

''J-just s-s-stupid, I g-g-guess. I thought a g-good plan,
a low b-b-bid and a reputation for honest d-dealing would
b-be worth s-something.''

''Your mistake. Meanwhile, it looks like LaRue and
our Brash Female Reporter are having a grand old time
together.'' Jaw clenched, Tommy glanced down at the
napkin he had shredded, then wadded the paper and
pushed it to the side.

Adam risked a glance over his shoulder. ''N-not for
m-much l-longer, if I have anyth-thing to s-say about it.
When I g-get elected m-mayor, you c-can damn well be
sure th-things are g-gonna change in this t-town.''

His best friend and campaign manager reached over to
shake his hand. ''I'm with you, buddy. All the way.''

Abby brought their plates, and they allowed good food
to distract them from the jerk and the journalist on the
other side of the room. Rain fell steadily outside the
plate-glass windows and the bell on the door rang almost
constantly, until there were only a couple of tables in the
diner left empty. Much as he liked Tommy's company
and Abby's teasing, Adam wished he'd taken fast food
home tonight. In a place as small as New Skye, where
most people knew him and his family, this kind of crowd
almost invariably meant running into somebody who
wanted to chat. And Adam really didn't do chat.

As a prospective candidate, he was realistic enough to
admit that running for mayor invited the intrusion of a
whole town of people into his life, people who would
believe they owned his time and attention. His goal was
to clean up New Skye government, and if that was the
price he paid, so be it. Let him get the stutter under control and he'd talk all day long.

Tonight, he just wanted to eat in peace.

A hand fell lightly on his shoulder. "Hi, Adam."

He nearly groaned aloud. Then he looked up from his slice of cake and barely kept his jaw from dropping. Phoebe Moss?

"H-h-hi." Somehow, he'd never expected to see her out in the real world.

But here she was, smiling at him, and then at Tommy. "This looks like the place to eat tonight. Jenna and I thought we'd have it all to ourselves." She nodded toward the tall blonde beside her. "This is Jenna Franklin, my business partner. Jenna, Adam DeVries."

"Hi, Adam." Jenna smiled as she shook his hand.

"J-J-Jenna, g-good t-to m-m-meet you. Th-this is T-T-Tommy C-Crawford."

Tommy nodded. "Nice to meet you. Enjoy your dinners—Abby's cooking is some of the best."

Phoebe's eyes widened at the obvious dismissal. Her smile disappeared. "Um…it was good running into you. I'll see you—" Tommy shook his head, and she stopped for a second, then cleared her throat and glanced quickly at Adam. "I'll see you around sometime. Enjoy your cake."

The two women moved away, and Tommy went back to his dessert.

Adam nudged his friend's plate with the tip of his knife. "Wh-what k-kind of b-brush-off was that?"

Tommy took a bite of deep red cake frosted with buttery icing. "You want to be seen talking to your speech therapist in front of the whole diner? Especially with L. T. LaRue and a reporter for the newspaper just across the room? We picked Phoebe Moss to begin with 'cause she's new to town, can't know all that many people. But if you start having dinner together, I can see the headline now—Mayoral Candidate Seeks Therapy Before Election Bid. What a start for the campaign.''

"R-running f-for mayor means b-being r-rude?''

"Winning the mayor's race means being careful.'' Then he shook his head in mock sorrow. "Though I do admit, I hate giving a cold shoulder to women as pretty as those. Just goes against the laws of nature, you know?''

"P-pretty?'' Adam had been so tense this morning, Phoebe Moss could have had two heads and he wouldn't have noticed.

His friend stared back at him. "When'd you go blind?''

Looking around, Adam found Jenna Franklin first, at a table almost directly in his line of sight. Phoebe sat across from her, in profile to his perspective. Studying her now, he found details from this morning coming back to him, characteristics he hadn't realized he'd noticed. She reminded him of the woman on the cameo brooch he planned to give his mother for her birthday tomorrow, with that wonderful hair drawn back into a knot at the base of her neck, a high forehead and straight nose, a slightly stubborn chin. Her skin was pale and smooth, her mouth soft pink. He remembered, with perfect clarity, her kind gray gaze.

"Y-you g-got it almost r-r-right,'' he told Tommy.

"What do you mean?''

"Ph-Phoebe's not p-p-pretty.''

"Not?''

Adam shook his head. "She's b-b-beautiful.''

"DeVries!''

He gave Tommy a wry smile. "And r-r-right n-now she's all that st-stands b-between me and t-total humiliation.''

To himself, he said, "And I hope to hell I can justify her effort."

AFTER A HARRIED DAY SPENT trying to catch up with the work he'd missed on Tuesday as well as cover Wednesday's quota, Adam arrived only ten minutes late for his mother's birthday party at the Vineyard Restaurant.

Named for the grape arbor still maintained in back of the house, the elegant restaurant had only recently been converted by DeVries Construction from one of the town's older homes. Adam took great satisfaction in the lustrous interior woodwork and, especially, the sliding pocket doors he'd installed to separate the front and rear parlors on both sides of the entry hall. To accommodate the sixty or so people attending tonight's dinner, the two south parlors had been combined into one large room, where white-draped tables, fresh flowers and a violinist playing classical music set the refined tone that characterized every event his mother planned.

As Adam surveyed the crowd from an unobtrusive position near the bar, his brother clapped him on the shoulder with one hand and offered a glass of whiskey with the other. "I was beginning to wonder if you would show," Tim said. "You and mom are usually the punctual ones in the family."

Smooth as silk, a long sip of Maker's Mark went down Adam's throat. He lifted the glass in a belated toast. "Here's t-to architects who ch-change their m-m-minds h-halfway through a p-p-project and then w-want to argue about who...who p-pays the c-cost of st-st-starting over."

Tim returned the salute with his martini. "And to physicians who believe practicing medicine is a nine-to-five career, making life hell for the rest of us who know the truth.''

They stood with their backs against the wall, nursing their drinks until Tim spoke up again. ''I heard on the news that LaRue won the housing project bid. Sorry about that.''

''Yeah, well.'' Adam shrugged. ''He c-can't w-win all the t-time.'' *And he won't, once I get to be mayor.*

His brother eyed him sharply, but took Adam's unspoken hint and changed the subject. ''Trust Mother to turn her sixtieth birthday party into a royal reception.'' He brushed a hand through his sandy hair, always worn a little long because he forgot to take time off work for a haircut. ''You'd think she was the queen of England. Somebody needs to remind her about that little disagreement we had, back in 1776.''

''Sh-she l-looks the p-part.'' Tall and graceful, with thick silver hair in waves around her face, Cynthia DeVries had been beautiful all her life, but never more so than tonight. ''And she d-does l-love the sp-spotlight. N-n-not to m-mention the g-glory, admiration and p-p-power that g-go w-with it.''

''Hence her involvement in every volunteer organization the town offers since as far back as I can remember. How many hot dog suppers did we eat as kids because dad was at the hospital and mom had a meeting?'' Tim drained his drink. ''She's been president so often, she should run for political office. We could be talking about Senator DeVries. Or, hell, even President DeVries.''

Their sister joined them. ''I'm afraid I must decline the nomination, being too young—thank God—to accept the office under current constitutional standards.'' Theresa clinked her glass against Adam's. ''Good evening, boys. Are we having fun yet?''

"Aren't we always?" Adam took another sustaining swallow of bourbon as he looked his sister over, from the top of her short, stylish dark hair to the red high-heeled shoes that matched her suit. "You l-look g-great tonight. As always."

"Thanks, sweetie. You sure do know the right thing to say." She kissed his cheek, giving him a whiff of expensive perfume, then moved to stand on his right, surveying the candlelit tables and chattering guests. "I am happy to celebrate Mother's birthday. And a free meal at the town's best restaurant is an opportunity not to be missed. Your guys did a superior job on the renovation."

"We d-do our b-best."

"You would have done a great job with the public housing project, too. I'm sorry to see LaRue get his way again." Theresa shook her head in disgust. "Makes me ashamed to work for the city, watching people cave in to his bribes and threats."

"Th-there's an election c-coming up. M-Maybe th-things will change." He had yet to tell his family about the campaign. Until his meeting with Phoebe Moss yesterday, he hadn't known if he could actually go through with therapy. Even though Phoebe hadn't promised success, she'd made him feel hopeful. The commitment to meet at her home was such a remarkable gesture, Adam felt certain she believed they would succeed.

"Maybe." Theresa drew a deep breath. "There sure are a lot of people to smile at and talk nonsense with." Straightening to her full height, as impressive as their mother's, she tossed back the last of her wine and handed Tim the glass. "I guess I'll get to work. I just might want these votes one day, when I run for district attorney."

Tim put her glass next to his own on a nearby tray, then turned back to Adam, arms crossed, one shoulder braced against the wall. While Adam and Theresa resembled their mother and each other, Tim was the spitting image of their dad, right down to his lazy posture, sleepy gaze and slow, genial smile. "Fortunately, I don't have to solicit votes for my job. When you're having a heart attack, the cardiologist's opinions, political or otherwise, don't matter a damn. Want another drink?"

Before he could accept the offer, the clink of silverware on crystal heralded his dad's suggestion that everyone find their seats for dinner. Adam checked the seating chart and winced when he found himself trapped between his aunt Diana, who always talked to him with a raised voice as if he couldn't hear, and his dad. Not the recipe for a relaxing meal.

"I heard on the radio that you lost that public housing contract to LaRue Construction," Preston DeVries said as their salads arrived. "Couldn't expect much else, I suppose."

Adam concentrated all his will on the one word. "No."

Aunt Diana put a hand on his arm. "Will losing this project ruin your business, dear?" Conversation around the room ebbed as everyone waited for the answer to the question they'd all heard. From a distant table, Theresa sent him a sympathetic frown, but there wasn't much she could do to help.

Again, Adam made the supreme effort. "Not at all. I've g-got p-plenty of work to d-do." Out of the corner of his eye, he saw his dad's grimace. The slightest hesitation in his speech, the smallest repetition or block, was always noticed. And regretted.

Talk resumed in a buzz, but Adam put his fork on the edge of the plate and pushed his salad away. Aunt Diana turned to talk with the person on her right, which was a relief, but when Preston directed all of his attention to the teenage cousin on his other side, Adam understood quite clearly that he'd failed. Again. The folks on the opposite side of the table gently ignored him, no doubt thinking to spare him the shame of having to stutter across the flower arrangement. Some kind of chicken dish arrived, but he barely touched the food. Knowing that he was a disappointment to his father destroyed what little appetite he'd arrived with. The party bubbled around him, but he might as well have been marooned on a desert island. Hell, he might as well not have come to the party at all.

Finally, the tables were cleared for dessert. Getting to his feet, Preston motioned for the cake to be brought in. "Cynthia, honey, happy birthday!" Then he looked at Adam. "Son?"

Adam had been hoping to avoid this particular tradition tonight, with so many people listening. No such luck. But this, at least, he could do right.

He drew a deep breath. "Happy birthday to you," he sang to his mother, aware of every face in the room turned his way. The words were perfect, the pitch true. The words he couldn't speak, he could sing. So he sent birthday wishes to his mother in a song.

He'd sung solos in church choir since the age of five, and stuttered since he was eight, but that talent had never influenced his speech, no matter how many years of choral practices he endured. He only hoped Phoebe could change the pattern. In less than three months.

When the verse ended, Preston gestured to the crowd and they all sang another round as Cynthia DeVries smiled and delicately wiped tears from her eyes. More champagne circulated with the servings of cake.

Since his chair faced the doorway, Adam had a chance

to watch the arrivals and departures of other diners in the restaurant. About nine-thirty, he looked up from the cake he was moving around his plate to check out the commotion going on in the entry area…and then wished he hadn't.

L. T. LaRue had come to the Vineyard for dinner. The mayor stood next to him, with an arm around LaRue's shoulders, every few seconds patting him on the back. They'd come in through the bar in the back of the house, because they already had drinks in their hands. The hostess approached and led them to their seats—not in the rear parlor, of course, but in the front room directly across the hall from the banquet room where Adam sat.

During the next hour, when he wasn't watching his mother open her gifts and smile at the toasts made in her honor, Adam watched LaRue celebrate "winning" the housing project contract. The word should be "buying," of course—a fact confirmed by the arrival of several city council members who joined the mayor's party with every evidence of satisfaction at a deal well made.

Preston DeVries leaned across the corner of the table. "The only way we're going to get this town cleaned up," he told Adam, "is to elect a new mayor." He pushed his chair back and got to his feet as guests prepared to take their leave. "I wish to God there was an honest man with the guts to take on that crook and give him a run for his money."

Adam swallowed hard. After setting an appointment for speech therapy, then actually showing up, this was the hardest moment he'd had to face since the day in the third grade when his dog died. "D-Dad?"

"Yes?"

"We've already g-got that m-man."

"You don't say? Who is it? I'll be damn glad to write a check for his campaign, help get those crooks evicted."

Standing, Adam faced his father eye to eye. "M-make your ch-check out to m-me."

"You?" Preston's eyebrows drew together. "I don't understand."

He took a deep breath. "I've already f-f-filed the p-papers. I'm running for m-m-mayor of New Sk-Skye."

His father stared at him, speechless, for a long moment. "Dear God, son," he said finally, too loudly. "Surely you're not serious! You wouldn't do something that stupid." His anxious brown gaze searched Adam's face. "Would you?"

CHAPTER TWO

TOMMY WHISTLED THE THEME song from *Goldfinger* as he crossed the parking lot on Thursday morning and entered the back door of the small building that housed his insurance agency. He wasn't a player in this town yet, though his family had been around forever and the Crawford name still meant something—mostly, a long line of men who let money run through their hands like water. But Tommy was going to turn that situation around, with a lot of smarts and a little help from his good buddy Adam DeVries.

He whistled his way to the front of the office, but there the tune died. Only one person sat in the waiting area. Her hair was shiny black, cut short in spiky strands that made her look like an elf…a very sexy elf. She wore a red suit jacket over a black top and a short black skirt that left a long, long stretch of excellent leg bare to his gaze. Tommy had no doubt who and what she was waiting for.

"'Morning, Sam." He fought to sound casual. "Long time, no see."

The reporter looked up from her magazine and gave him a wink. "I figured you would expect me to show up sooner or later, and that I might as well make it sooner." She came to her feet with a wiggle that had Tommy swallowing hard. "Can we talk?"

"Sure thing." He looked across at the reception desk,

where his cousin and sole employee stared at him with her mouth open. "'Morning, Bonnie. Let me know when my first appointment gets here."

"Your first…?" She might well be confused, since she knew damn well he didn't have any appointments today. But he lifted an eyebrow and she got the message. "Sure, Tommy. I'll buzz you."

He glanced back to Sam Pettit and smiled. "Right this way. Would you like some coffee? Bonnie makes a pretty decent brew."

"Sounds good." Her voice was deep, a little rough for a woman, and rubbed shivers over his spine.

"Sugar? Cream?" Tommy prayed the milk in the fridge hadn't gone sour.

"Black, thanks."

"That's easy." He poured them each a mug and put Sam's in her red-taloned hand, then led the way to his office across the hall. "Have a seat." His room was spectacularly neat, which might indicate a genius for organization but only represented, Tommy hated to admit, a lack of business. Shutting the door, he went to the chair behind his desk and sat down. "Now, to what do I owe the honor of this visit?"

Sam eyed him over the rim of her mug as she took a sip, which allowed him to concentrate on her light gray eyes framed by dark, thick lashes. Hypnotic, to say the least. "You know why I'm here, Tommy. Tell me about Adam DeVries."

"Nice guy. I've known him pretty much all our lives. We graduated in the same high school class—1989, New Skye High."

"And he's running for mayor."

"That he is." Her scent filled the room, a combination of danger and invitation that made his head swim.

"Why?"

Tommy sank back in his chair, letting the mug of coffee warm his palms, the steam fill his nostrils in defense. "I think it's a little early to put out position papers."

"But you can tell me what his motivation is."

"Why do you want to write an article on motivation?"

"Because, from all I can gather, DeVries is different from every other politician in town. Maybe the whole state. He's a dark horse coming up from behind. I think my readers will be interested in this race."

"So do I. But the flag hasn't dropped yet, Sam. We're announcing Adam's bid on Labor Day weekend with a big rally. I'll send you free tickets."

"The paper will give me tickets." She leaned forward to put her mug on his desk, and he got a glimpse of the curves of her breasts just underneath the top she wore.

His mouth went dry. A gulp of hot coffee did not help. Sam eased to her feet and adjusted the strap of her purse. "Well, if you're not going to deliver, then I'll let you move on with your day."

Tommy set down his own mug and joined her on the other side of the desk. "You don't have to pout."

She grinned and stuck out her red lower lip. "I will if I want to."

"Oh, I'm sure of that. You'll do anything you think you can get away with." They'd met a number of times in the year she'd been in town, and he was always amazed to realize she was shorter than he, even in high heels. Since he wasn't a big man—only five-seven—that made Sam Pettit, well, petite.

"Damn straight, I will." She turned in the open doorway and brushed back the spiky black bangs in her eyes. "Remember, Tommy. I never back off."

Watching her walk down the hall, noting the sway of

her hips in that short skirt, Tommy let his mind dwell on situations in which he would be thankful if Sam Pettit never, ever backed off.

"Whew." He went to pour himself a big glass of ice water, drank it all down, then poured another.

Bonnie came to the door. "Everything okay, Tommy?"

"Everything's fine, sweetheart."

"You sure? That woman looked like she could be real trouble."

Tommy took another long gulp of water. "Nothing I can't handle."

So he hoped, anyway.

SAM DROPPED INTO THE driver's seat of her Mustang, slammed the car door and revved the engine into the red zone before calming down enough to pull out into traffic. She had places to go, people to see who would actually cooperate when she interviewed them. But instead, she drove aimlessly around New Skye for a while, trying to get herself under control.

What did she have to do—proposition the man? Show up in a raincoat, garter belt and stockings and flash him in the reception area? Wouldn't that sweet little thing at the desk be shocked?

At the thought, Sam's fury gave way, and she laughed, hard and long. The only other choice was to cry. She'd met Tommy Crawford more than a year ago, at a chamber of commerce luncheon, and she'd been trying to get a date with him ever since. His skeptical, irreverent attitude, his wary eyes, his sidelong smile, had captured her heart from the first moment. She liked his compact build and his sandy hair, his scholar's slouch and his square, limber hands. She arranged to bump into him as often as possible, had exchanged her ordinary looks for a version of vamp, bought the most expensive perfume New Skye had to offer. Nothing seemed to work. The man remained oblivious. Or indifferent.

She pounded her fist on the wheel. No, that was not possible. He found her funny. He thought she was sexy—after that maneuver in front of the desk, she'd seen his eyes glaze over. For some reason, he simply wasn't connecting what he felt with the possibility that they could have a relationship. Sam knew Tommy Crawford was a smart man. So why was he missing the point?

Now he would be managing Adam DeVries's campaign—the worst possible news, as far as Sam was concerned. On the one hand, she'd get plenty of excuses to talk to Tommy. But her job as a reporter demanded objectivity. Even animosity, if that's what it took to get the facts. She and Tommy would be on opposite sides from Labor Day until the election. He'd be trying to present his candidate in the best light, and she'd be trying to find every single dirty detail to offer the public. Not a recipe for romance, by any stretch of the imagination. If she did enough damage, she might make an enemy of Tommy Crawford for life.

When what she really wanted was simply to marry him and live happily ever after. Was it too much to ask?

On a day like today, with yet one more rejection to her credit, Sam was afraid that the answer to her sad question would be a flat and final "You got that right."

THURSDAY NIGHT, ADAM followed the directions he'd received from Willa, Phoebe Moss's receptionist, and headed south out of town into horse country. When he arrived at the last turn fifteen minutes ahead of his appointment, he concluded that Phoebe must drive on the slow side. Or maybe, as his mother had mentioned on more than one occasion, he drove too fast.

No matter what the clock or the speedometer read, though, he hadn't failed to notice the sign announcing L. T. LaRue's latest triumph—the farmland he would use to build that low-income housing project for New Skye. Filled with trees and set on a gentle slope, Adam's site had been nearer to town and a bus route, for the benefit of those who didn't own a car. If LaRue operated true to form, he would no doubt simply mow down all the pine trees bordering the tobacco fields, pave the flat landscape and put up the most utilitarian building possible.

Shaking off what he couldn't—for the moment—change, Adam slowed down and turned his truck onto Bower Lane. Pines lined the road on both sides, their high branches casting shadows across the asphalt, making the evening seem almost cool. Behind the trees on the right, a herd of cows grazed a wide pasture, freshly green with yesterday's rain. On the left, comfortable ranch homes nestled in the piney shade.

Peaceful, pastoral. After a day spent standing in the hot sun on unshaded building sites, arguing with subcontractors and suppliers, Adam could appreciate why Phoebe Moss had chosen to live this far out of town. He'd look forward to coming out here…for any reason besides speech therapy.

The sign for Swallowtail Farm stood about a mile down Bower Lane on the left, just as the receptionist had said. The metal frame gate opened across a gravel drive. Adam followed the meandering track over the dips and rolls of the land to a small brick house. The front porch and windows looked out over the fields he'd just passed, with a barn off to the right in the back. He could see

Phoebe coming from the barn and across the grass in front of the house to meet him. To begin the session.

Trying to delay that moment as long as possible, Adam climbed out of his truck and walked to the pasture fence, where a group of horses cropped lazily at the short, wiry grass. The evening air still held the heat of the day and the animals weren't moving much, but all of them looked up as he approached. Their dark eyes surveyed him with interest for a moment, then the four heads bent to continue grazing.

"What do you think?" Phoebe stepped up beside him. Her head just reached his shoulder, which seemed to ease a little of his tension, for no sensible reason he could think of. She didn't meet his gaze, which also served to make him less nervous.

"I-I c-can't d-decide which is the m-most b-b-beautiful." Talking wasn't so hard, if he didn't feel he was being watched, being judged.

"I know what you mean. Cristal, the black filly, is young and spirited, a teenager you envy for her energy. Brady, the bay closest to us, is just an all-around great guy. Really laid-back. Robinhood, the red one—we call it chestnut—is at the height of his power as a male." She chuckled. "Even though he's a gelding, Rob thinks he's hot stuff. And Marian is simply gorgeous. That pale gray coat with the pewter mane and tail is terrific. You should see her gallop across the pasture. Like watching the wind."

Adam glanced at her and caught the curve of her smile. "H-have you al-always h-had h-h-horses?"

Still without looking at him, she shook her head. "I took lessons, because my parents thought it was the socially correct thing to do. But I never had one of my own until I moved here."

"The l-life s-suits you." Phoebe seemed a part of the landscape, as natural an element as her animals. Tonight, her long hair flowed freely, like the manes and tails of the horses, in a complicated range of colors from silver to maple. She wore a dark tank top that showed off muscular arms and a graceful throat, shorts that left her pale legs bare, and some kind of clog shoe that obviously did a great job of shaping the muscles in her calves. Adam was surprised to recognize the flicker of interest stirring inside him, a warmth curling deep in his belly that he could only call desire.

"I couldn't be happier," she said in response to his awkward compliment. She glanced behind him. "Do you mind dogs?"

He hesitated too long. "Uh…"

Phoebe's eyes widened, and she stepped quickly behind him. "Galahad, no! Gawain, Lance, no!"

Adam glanced over his shoulder to see three dogs bounding toward him, a Golden Retriever and two other breeds he wasn't sure of. As he turned and braced for the assault, Phoebe called, "Down, boys. Down!"

Like magic, the three dogs dropped to the ground, noses resting obediently on front paws, tails wagging wildly. Their eyes were eager and friendly.

"I'm sorry," Phoebe said breathlessly. "I should have asked you sooner. They wouldn't hurt you. But they can be too much. Especially if dogs make you nervous."

"N-no. N-n-not n-nervous." Though it sure sounded that way. If he tried to explain, she'd send him to a shrink. As his parents had when he was ten. And again at thirteen.

"Let's go inside and leave these three out." She opened the door of the screened porch on the end of the house. "You stay," she told the dogs. "Stay." The an-

imals stared pitifully at her, tongues hanging long in the
heat, but when she motioned Adam inside and then
stepped in herself, they stayed on the grass.

Moving across the concrete floor, Phoebe opened the
inside door. "Air-conditioning is a gift from God." She
led the way through a darkened laundry room to the
bright kitchen. "What can I get you to drink?"

"W-water's g-g-great." He looked around with interest. Phoebe kept an old-fashioned kitchen, with natural
oak cabinets, a big table with a scarred top, and a couple
of pie safes used for storage. Dried herbs hung from the
ceiling in front of the window looking over the pasture,
and wildflowers filled colorful jars on the windowsill
above the sink.

"There you go." She handed him a tall, thick glass
filled with ice cubes and water. "Let's sit down." Wav-
ing him toward a chair across the table, she pulled one
out for herself and sat. "It's time for us to get to work,
right?"

Dealing with the dogs would have been easy, com-
pared to this. Adam took a gulp of water and tried to
ignore the twist of fear in his belly. "Whatever yo-
s-s-say."

OVER THE NEXT THIRTY minutes, Adam's frustration level
climbed steadily. Phoebe had thought she was prepared
for the usual first-session difficulties. But somehow she
couldn't remain unaffected by this client's struggle.

Fifteen minutes before the scheduled end of their session, Phoebe pushed her glasses up on her nose and then
set her hands flat on the table. "That's good. You read
the whole paragraph with much softer consonants, and
your long vowels are improving. Let's stop on a high
note."

Adam shook his head. ''I-I d-d-didn't h-hear any imp-p-p-provement. I-I'll r-read it a-again.''

She took the card away from him. ''No, you won't. I'm the therapist and I call the shots.''

His mouth tightened even as he clenched his fist and punched the table. ''I-I d-don't h-h-have m-much t-t-t-time.''

Phoebe leaned over and placed both her hands over that rigid fist. ''Here's your first homework assignment.''

He lifted his eyebrows. ''H-h-homework?''

''If you want to move fast, you have to practice. Now, listen.'' Gently, she massaged his fingers, his wrist, the back of his hand. ''You tense up when you speak. You make a fist and use it to get you through blocks. I want you to think about relaxing this hand when you talk.'' As she continued to stroke and knead, his grip loosened. ''There doesn't have to be anyone else around. Say whatever comes to mind. Recite poetry, song lyrics, your grocery list. But think about keeping this hand open and soft.'' Finally, his palm was revealed, his fingers gently curved. Phoebe laid her palm gently against Adam's. ''Say something to me.''

He stared at her for a long moment, his brows now drawn together, his blue eyes narrowed with effort. His mouth opened and his fingers tensed.

''Relax.'' She stroked her fingertips over his.

Again he tried to speak, and again his fingers tightened. Finally, after several more attempts, he managed a sound. ''N-n-n…''

Phoebe waited, her palm resting in his.

''N-n-n…n-n-ni…'' Adam squeezed his eyes shut and drew a shaking breath. ''N-n-ni…n-nice.''

Smiling, Phoebe squeezed his hand with both of hers.

"Exactly. You don't need this hand as much as you think you do. So practice talking without it."

When she went to withdraw, though, his fingers caught hers. "Th-thanks," he said quietly, holding her gaze with his own.

Even without the smile, he was a mesmerizing man. She found herself lost in his eyes, all too aware of his skin touching hers. Suddenly, the air conditioner didn't seem to be doing a very good job of cooling the house.

The loud chime of the clock in the other room woke Phoebe from her trance. "Nine o'clock—you've definitely worked long enough for one day." She pulled her hands from his, got clumsily to her feet and took their water glasses to the sink. "Construction starts very early in the summer, doesn't it? Because of the heat?"

"S-sure does." He crossed the kitchen on the way to the screened porch. "I-I'll b-be at w-work b-by s-six."

"And you have such a long drive back to town." She followed him to the porch door, where Gally, Gawain and Lance waited patiently. "Um…let me take them to the barn. I'll be right back."

He held up a hand. "D-don't. I j-just haven't sp-spent any time w-w-with d-dogs for y-y-years. It's ok-k-kay."

Whether by instinct or intelligence, Gally, Gawain and Lance stayed still as Adam stepped outside. He didn't try to pet them, didn't even look at them as he walked by.

"Stay," Phoebe told them, as a precaution. Then she caught up with Adam on the driveway. "Are you sure this is a good time? I'm still building my practice, and I have open appointments almost any hour of the day."

The night was very warm, with a high humidity that carried a thousand different scents—grass and horses, the wild magnolias blooming in the woods, the roses she'd planted near the barn, and an indefinable accent that simply said "country."

Adam took his keys out of his jeans pocket. "N-no. I-if it w-w-works f-for you, I-I l-l-like this arrangement."

"Okay, then." Above them, stars had begun to pop out in a not-quite-dark sky. "I'll see you Monday? Same time?"

He looked across the pasture, and then his gaze returned to her face. "W-would I-I-I m-make m-more pr-progress if I-I c-came t-t-tomorrow, t-t-too?"

Her heart began to flutter. "I...well, I think you would. There are s-some intensive p-programs that go for f-five s-straight d-days. We c-could try." The thought of seeing him again so soon had started her own stutter acting up. Phoebe swallowed hard, trying to relax, to recover her self-assurance.

Her effort fell flat in the face of his wonderful smile. "G-good." He took a deep breath. "Th-this r-r-really is a n-nice p-place. M-makes m-me feel b-better, just b-being here."

She nodded. "M-me, too."

"S-smart w-woman." He gave her a two-fingered salute and headed toward the truck. "S-see you t-tomorrow night."

"Adam?" He turned back, brows lifted in question. "W-would you chain the g-gate closed when you g-get outside?"

His white teeth flashed in the dark. "N-no p-problem."

Watching him walk through the twilight, she allowed herself a moment of sheer gratitude for the beauty of a male body. She could imagine the pleasure of running her hands over Adam's strong, bare back, his tapered waist, his tight rear end. Her breath shortened as she visualized the glory of lying with him on soft sheets, in a dark room with only moonlight as a lamp to light their exploration of each other. Adam would be a wonderful lover, sensitive and considerate, powerful and yet gentle at the same time. His hands would be so warm on her skin....

Phoebe herself was warm by the time the fantasy had run its course. She blushed even hotter when she realized that darkness had fallen completely while she'd stood like a statue, lost in her erotic thoughts.

"Lance, Gally, Gawain? Let's go, guys. In the house." She led them inside, made sure their water bowl was filled, then proceeded through her nightly routine, deliberately blocking all thoughts of Adam DeVries from her mind. Tonight was Lance's turn for a brushing, which she completed while watching a dog show on TV. All three dogs got their teeth cleaned—good-natured Lance and Galahad the cheerful mutt didn't mind too much, but Gawain, a high-strung Weimaraner, fought her every step of the way, as usual. Finally exhausted, with a day of work ahead, Phoebe had no choice but to go to bed.

In the dark and quiet of a country night, her thoughts refused to be controlled any longer, and she pondered long after the canines had settled into their baskets, after the house cats, Arthur and Merlin, had curled up in their respective corners on the bed.

Her strong sexual attraction to Adam wasn't hard to explain. He was gorgeous, to begin with, and holding the session in her home created an unusual intimacy. She'd never before brought a client to her house, here or in Atlanta.

But she had worked with many handsome men, as colleagues and as patients. Dates hadn't been rare in her life until she moved to New Skye precisely to escape the social-climbing, influence-seeking connections that passed for relationships in her mother's world. She hadn't missed male company in the last year.

And I don't now. Turning over yet again, punching her pillow and rearranging the covers, Phoebe renewed her resolve.

Yes, Adam DeVries was an attractive man—an attractive man who planned to run for mayor. She did not want a life lived in the public eye. She'd moved from Atlanta expressly to escape that kind of stress. Her personal goals were privacy, peace and self-reliance. With or without a man to share her life.

Maybe if Adam lost the election...

No, she wanted him to win, because he wanted to win badly enough to put himself completely on the line. She admired his dedication to the goal, was proud to think she could help him achieve it.

Over in the corner, Galahad snorted, then started in with his usual gentle snore. She smiled at the sound and tried, again, to relax.

Adam DeVries would never be more than a client. Thinking rationally now, she doubted they could even be close friends.

How could she have any kind of real relationship with a man who didn't like dogs?

ADAM PARKED AT THE end of his parents' driveway late Sunday afternoon, took hold of his jacket and climbed out of the truck into the stifling heat. As he shrugged into the coat, his sister's black Miata slid to a stop just inches from his front fender. Theresa joined him on the walk up the drive to the house and asked the critical question of the day.

"Beef or chicken?"

Adam had already given the matter some thought. "I

th-think I'm in t-trouble. B-beef.'' He noticed his clenched right fist, imagined Phoebe's soft touch and loosened his fingers.

"What did you do now? Mom hasn't staged one of these mandatory Sunday dinners for a couple of years at least.''

He glanced sideways at his sister. "N-nothing.'' His hand stayed relaxed.

"Except, maybe, decide to run for mayor without telling anybody?''

"Is th-that a c-crime?''

They reached the front door and Theresa pushed the bell. "In this family? What do you think?''

Their father opened the door. "Come in, both of you, come in. Tim just called to say he'll be late and to go on without him.'' Theresa got a hug and Adam a hearty handshake. "Your mother's putting the finishing touches on the roast. She'll be out in a few minutes.''

Theresa frowned as they went into the living room. "I should've been a doctor,'' she muttered under her breath, for Adam's ears alone. "Tim's always sleazing out of dinner because of his patients.''

Adam grinned. "L-legal emergencies are k-kinda r-rare.''

"Maybe we could start having court sessions on the weekends.''

Their mother emerged from the kitchen. "Honey, how are you?'' She hugged her daughter, stroking a hand over Theresa's hair. "Have you had a hectic week?''

Adam found himself thinking of Phoebe, how the different colors of her long, wavy mane blew through and over one another as she stood with the horses in the pasture. He wondered if that amazing hair felt as soft as it looked.

"Son, I'm glad to see you." His mother offered him an embrace, a good deal more restrained than Theresa's. "Dinner is ready. Let's sit down."

The formal dining room, with its elegantly carved wainscoting, crown molding and woodwork, had inspired Adam's own building efforts. But the antique mahogany table and his assigned chair—immediately to his father's right—had been the setting for some of the most painful moments in his life.

He took his seat and dragged in a deep breath, glanced down and found his hand clenched on his thigh again. Phoebe's voice came to him. *Relax.*

Adam tried. "S-smells g-great, M-Mother."

Cynthia smiled. "Thank you. Your great-grand-mother's recipe for roast never fails." She looked down the length of the table to her husband at the other end. "Shall we say grace?"

The four of them bowed their heads as his dad prayed. Then there was all the passing of dishes and carving of meat to occupy their attention, but Adam knew his moment was coming. His mother arranged her battle plans with the efficiency of a four-star general.

Sure enough, she attacked halfway through the meal. "Adam, the news you gave your father Wednesday night was surprising, to say the least. You filed papers with the board of elections to run for mayor of New Skye?"

He settled for one clear word. "Yes."

"You didn't think this was a matter for discussion with your family?"

That answer called for more than one word. "I'm s-still p-planning, M-Mother. I w-wanted t-to w-wait until the s-s-situation was s-set." He was clenching his fist again, dammit.

"Your father says he suggested you reconsider. Have you?"

"N-no."

Cynthia gazed at him, then set her fork down and folded her hands together on the edge of the table. "Adam, dear, as your family, we are patient with your…difficulty. We love you and we understand. But how can you campaign for public office? What chance do you have of actually winning? You'll never be understood, or even listened to. As mayor, you would have many ceremonial public duties. How could you possibly execute those responsibilities, given your…challenges?"

In his head, Adam heard a line from an old TV commercial. He said the words almost in unison with the memory. "We th-thank you for your support."

"I think we have fully supported you in your endeavors. Your father loaned you the money to start your business—"

Preston held up a hand. "Which the boy has paid back. With interest."

His wife nodded. "Of course. I'm only concerned about the reception you'll receive from the public, Adam. Crowds can be most unkind. I hate to see you exposing yourself to that kind of ridicule when it's not necessary."

"I-I think i-it i-is n-n-necess-sary." Adam loosened his fist yet again. "D-Dad and I talked about this at your b-b-birthday d-d-dinner. This town n-needs honest l-leaders. I'm tired of c-c-corrupt g-government. S-since I'm the one w-with the c-complaint, I'm the one d-d-doing s-someth-thing about it." By the end of the speech, his fist was pounding against his thigh. He uncurled his fingers enough to pick up his napkin and place it on the table. "Excuse m-me, p-p-please. I have to g-go n-n-now."

The other three stood as he got to his feet. Preston put a hand on his arm. "Son, don't leave mad. Let's talk this over."

"Sit down, Adam," his mother commanded. "We haven't finished talking. I have not given you permission to leave."

But whatever his failings, he wasn't a little boy anymore and he didn't take orders, even from his mother. Adam shook his head and left the dining room. Theresa followed. "You can't leave me here alone with them," she whispered in his ear. "Mother will start on why I'm not married."

With the front door open, he turned back and gave her a sympathetic smile. "N-nobody's p-p-perfect." He leaned close and kissed her cheek. "G-good luck."

"Jerk." But she grinned as she said it.

By the time he reached the truck, he'd taken off his jacket and tie and rolled back his shirtsleeves. Without thinking too much about the decision, he put the engine in gear, abandoned the perfectly groomed neighborhood he'd grown up in and headed south. To Swallowtail Farm.

CHAPTER THREE

THE SOUND OF A VEHICLE coming up her gravel driveway startled Phoebe, since the only guests she expected were already here. When she recognized Adam's truck, she was doubly surprised.

They'd had another intense session Friday night, with Adam getting increasingly frustrated over what he perceived as a lack of progress. She'd battled her own frustration, as well, trying to maintain complete objectivity when it would be so terribly easy to step over the line between therapist and friend.

Or more. In fact, she'd been wondering if she should recommend that he see Jenna instead of herself for therapy. Happily married and the mother of a new baby, Jenna wouldn't be so sensitive to her client's every reaction.

Adam got out of the truck, and Phoebe met him halfway between the drive and the riding ring. The dogs stayed behind, in the shade of an apple tree, instead of following her as they usually would. They knew they would not be wanted.

"S-sorry t-to j-just d-d-drop in," Adam said, before she could even say hello. "I-I-I d-d-didn't r-realize y-you had c-c-company unt-til I-I'd almost r-reached th-the h-house." His face was tight, his fist clenched.

"I'm glad to see you, whether I have company or not." Taking a risk, Phoebe put a hand on his shoulder and squeezed gently. "We're just having fun with the horses. Come watch." She caught his right fist with her left hand and led him toward the ring, hoping the physical contact would help him relax. Or so she told herself.

As they got close, Dixon Bell eased Cristal to a halt in front of them. "Hey, DeVries, what brings you out? Good to see you." He leaned down and reached out to shake Adam's hand, which Phoebe reluctantly let go.

"You t-two kn-know each other?" Adam glanced at her in question.

"Cristal and Brady belong to Dixon. He boards them with me and comes out to ride most weekends." She looked from one man to the other. "Now it's my turn to ask…y'all are friends?"

"Went to high school together," Dixon explained, soothing Cristal as she protested having to stand still. "And every grade before that, come to think of it. Kate, too," he said, referring to his fiancé, who was bringing Brady slowly around the ring toward them. "DeVries and I play basketball together Saturday mornings with some of the other guys from our class."

"I g-give him s-some help remodeling his house f-f-from time to time. And p-plan to d-dance at his w-wedding." Adam nodded at Dixon. "F-from th-the way you handle th-that h-horse, I'd say you've sp-spent s-some t-time in th-the saddle in your day." His stutter had diminished a bit as he became more relaxed.

Dixon grinned. "An hour here and there." He had, Phoebe knew from Kate, worked on a ranch out west for a number of years before coming back home to New Skye.

Kate brought Brady to a stop nearby. "Hi, Adam, how are you? I'd lean down for a kiss, but I'm not sure my balance is that good."

He gave her his wonderful smile. "I'll take a rain check. Sh-show m-me what y-you can d-do."

For another thirty minutes or so, Phoebe and Adam stood at the fence to watch Kate and Dixon work. To be accurate, Adam watched the riders and Phoebe divided her time between the horses and the man at her side. He was now more at ease than she'd ever seen him, which meant he felt very comfortable with Dixon and Kate.

And me? Phoebe wondered, wishing she didn't care quite so much. What trauma had brought him this far out of town on a Sunday evening? Why in the world had he come to her, of all people?

She kept her questions to herself and the four of them chatted as Dixon and Kate untacked and cooled down their horses. The men brought flakes of alfalfa hay and buckets of grain rations to the pasture while Kate and Phoebe leaned on the fence to talk.

"New Skye can be a very small world," Kate said, watching Adam dump grain into the different feed dishes. "How did you meet Adam?"

Phoebe hesitated. Did he want even his good friends to know he was undergoing speech therapy?

Kate was quick enough to spare her the choice. "Ah…I understand. Never mind. I didn't ask. I'm glad to see him out here, though. He works too hard and spends too much time alone. I think you and your farm could be really good for Adam." Kate belonged to another of New Skye's prominent families, the Bowdreys. The Bells held a similar position, and Dixon was also related to the Crawfords, including Tommy, who was a cousin. Kate had explained some of the connections to Phoebe, along with tidbits about the DeVries clan.

"He does seem to relax when he comes out." She felt

better, having Kate's approval. "Would you and Dixon mind if I invited him to join us for dinner?"

Kate laughed. "You took the words right out of my mouth."

When asked, Adam tried to beg off, of course. "I-I d-don't want to intr-trude."

Dixon threw an arm around his shoulders. "Yeah, right. We're all just putting up with you to be polite. And your punishment is rabbit food."

Adam looked at Phoebe. "R-rabbit food?"

"Phoebe's a vegetarian," Kate said, with a severe frown in her fiancé's direction. "This is the one meal in a week I can convince Dixon to forgo meat."

"And, man, it's tough. But Phoebe fixes pretty good rabbit food, so I manage to make it all the way back to town before I need a burger."

Phoebe punched Dixon in the side as she stalked toward the house. "You'll eat those words. I guarantee it."

"No way."

"Want to bet?"

"Sure. What're the stakes?"

"If you aren't stuffed to the gills after this dinner, I'll grill you a two-pound steak next time you're out here."

Dixon grinned. "And if I am?"

"You have to sing for me after dessert."

He pretended to consider. "Mighty high stakes there, ma'am. But you're on."

As they sat on the screened porch after the meal, with a warm breeze occasionally tilting the flames of the candles on the table, Dixon groaned. "I give in, Phoebe. You win. I didn't know jambalaya could taste so good without meat."

She stuck her tongue out at him even as she reached

to the floor beside her chair and handed him the guitar waiting there. "Told you so. Now, pay up."

Dixon looked over to Adam. "What'll it be?"

"It's n-not m-my b-bet."

"Aw, come on, help me out here. How about 'Crazy'?"

Adam sighed and shook his head. "G-give m-me an intro."

Phoebe looked from one man to the other, not sure what was happening. Dixon played a jazzy set of chords, and Adam sat forward. The next thing she knew, Adam's voice eased into the twilight, crooning the old country song in a smooth, stutter-free baritone. Adam DeVries could sing. Boy, could he sing. She felt like a puddle of melted chocolate by the time he'd reached the final phrase.

Between them, the guys produced an amazing reel of tunes, from romantic to rowdy, while she sat and marveled at their combined talent. "You two are incredible," she said when the music came to an end. "I had no idea either of you was this good."

Adam shrugged and Dixon grinned. "Just a couple of good ol' boys, pickin' and hummin'."

"Right." Dixon wrote songs for a living, among them some of the most popular recordings on the charts. "Can I make a request?"

"Do we know it?"

"Doesn't everybody? I'd like to hear 'I'm So Lonesome I Could Cry.'"

Dixon started the chords, but Adam stirred in his chair. "That's a s-s-sad one."

Kate leaned forward to put her hand on his. "I've never heard you sing it. Please?"

With a tilt of his head, Adam gave in. On this song,

Dixon joined in with harmony. Phoebe felt tears gather, and fall, as the two men sang the day into night with Hank Williams's poignant words.

A long silence followed the final notes. Finally, Phoebe wiped her eyes. There weren't words to describe how she felt. "Thank you."

"Anytime." With a squeeze of Kate's fingers, Dixon propped his hands on his knees and pushed himself to his feet. "The kids will be home in about an hour, so I guess we'd better get there to meet them." Kate's children had spent the weekend with her ex-husband and their father, L. T. LaRue.

Adam stood, as well, evidently prepared to take his own leave. Phoebe smothered her disappointment. She'd been hoping he would stay for a while and give her a chance to ask what had been bothering him when he arrived.

By luck or by his intent, Adam did stay to see Dixon and Kate drive away and only then turned to her with his own goodbye. "I-it's b-been n-nice. Th-thanks for letting m-me stay."

"You're more than welcome. I wondered what h-had upset you. Why you c-came out." Her tension was bringing back her own stutter.

Adam didn't seem to notice. He shoved his fists into his pockets and looked away. "W-went to d-d-dinner at m-my p-p-parents', who are p-p-pissed that I didn't t-talk the c-campaign over with them f-first. They implied I was s-sure to lose, and I g-got p-pissed, too."

Phoebe kept her indignation to herself. "I would think so. There's no reason you can't win this election."

"M-my d-d-difficulty, as m-my m-m-mother calls it, w-will g-get in the way."

"So we'll work on that. I think you can do it." Phoebe

put her hand on his bare wrist, desperately trying to ignore the warmth of his tanned skin against her palm.

Adam brought his hand to her cheek. "Wh-when I'm out h-here, s-so d-do I. I g-guess that's why I came. You help me believe." He gazed at her for a long moment, and his touch lightened, as if he were about to step away. Suddenly, though, he tilted her face up with his palm and gave her a smile. "You're s-something sp-special, Phoebe Moss."

He was going to kiss her. That would be heaven…and a complete disaster.

She backed away from him, turning toward the pasture as if the horses had made a noise she had to check out. "The singing…you know, quite a large percentage of people who stutter can sing clearly."

"That's what I've read."

"You could use that as you practice—sing the words instead of saying them, gradually working to decrease the tune and simply talk." Keeping her own words clear was a challenge tonight—she felt herself falling into the stutter. Eyes on the horses, Phoebe focused on staying relaxed.

"I'll work on that."

"So you'll be here T-Tuesday night? Seven-thirty?" Still, she didn't look at him.

After a long silence, Adam cleared his throat. "C-count on it. I-I'll l-lock the g-gate." His footsteps crunched on the gravel drive, his truck door squeaked open and slammed shut.

At that sound, she felt safe to look over, and she watched until his taillights disappeared in the dark.

ADAM FIGURED PHOEBE WOULD have finished dinner when he arrived Tuesday evening, so he stopped by the

Carolina Diner for something to eat before driving out of town. Unlike last week, business was slow, and Abby came out right away with his iced tea.

"F-fried ch-chicken," he told her. "I'm f-feeling tr-traditional t-tonight. With m-mashed potatoes and gr-green beans."

"The perfect Southern dinner," she agreed. "You want white and dark meat, right?"

"R-right."

She nodded and made a note on her pad, then leaned her hip against the opposite side of the booth. "I hadn't heard until today that you'd decided to run for mayor."

"Y-you m-must've been the l-last one to find out."

Her brown eyes crinkled as she laughed. "Not easy keeping secrets in this town. I just wanted to say I'm proud of you. We could use somebody with a sense of decency running New Skye for a change." A car door slammed outside and she glanced through the window. "Damn. Speak of the devil. I'll get your meal. You—" she poked a finger into his shoulder "—stay out of trouble."

He wasn't sure what she meant until L. T. LaRue's hearty voice carried through the door. "Yessirree, got the steel on its way and the 'dozers headed out there tomorrow morning. I'm getting this show on the road."

The doorbell jingled and several people walked in. Seated with his back to the door, Adam didn't turn around. With any luck, LaRue and his friends would sit over on the far side of the diner, and he could ignore the fact they'd ever been here.

LaRue, however, was not a man to leave well enough alone. While the rest of the group sat down, L.T. appeared beside Adam's table. "Well, well, if it isn't our fledgling candidate. Eating by yourself, DeVries? That's no way to win an election.''

Adam relaxed his right hand. ''I-I'm n-not p-planning to f-feed the whole t-town t-to get e-e-elected.''

LaRue crossed his arms and propped his hip against the same place Abby had. ''That so? And just how are you planning to get elected?''

''B-by g-giving the v-v-voters an h-honest candidate and the opportunity to ch-choose a m-mayor who w-won't use his office to m-make m-money. I'll offer them a m-mayor who d-doesn't take kickbacks for st-steering city b-business to his f-f-friends.''

''You think that's what they want?''

''I-I do.''

The other man shook his head. ''I think what the voters want is a mayor who can deliver—deliver goods, deliver services, deliver the kind of life they expect to live in this town.'' He slapped his hand against Adam's table as he straightened up. ''Not to mention deliver a speech they have half a prayer of understanding. Enjoy your dinner, DeVries.''

Whoever had come in with L.T. enjoyed the joke. They were still laughing when Charlie Brannon rounded the counter at the front of the diner with Adam's plate in one beefy hand. The ex-marine set the meal on the table and gave Adam's shoulder a squeeze. He stopped for a second at the door, then made his way with his habitual limp to the table on the other side of the room. The group quieted down in preparation for placing their orders.

''I'll have—'' L.T. started.

''Sorry, folks. We're closed.'' Charlie's tone was polite, even casual.

''What do you mean? It's barely six o'clock. You can't

be closed.'' Adam didn't turn to watch, but he heard L.T.'s indignation.

"It's my place, I can close any damn time I want to."

"What's the problem, Charlie?" L.T.'s voice took on a wheedling tone. "We came in for some of your good home-style cooking. Just like DeVries over there."

"If you had half the brains or the manners of the man over there, I'd be serving you dinner. But you don't, and I'm not. We're closed until further notice. You want something to eat tonight, you'll get it someplace else."

Adam could hear the group shuffle to their feet, hear them muttering as they headed out the door. Just behind him, L.T. made his last stand. "You'll regret this, Brannon. I've got friends in the inspection department. I'm gonna bring them down on you like a plague of locusts."

Charlie let loose with his booming laugh. "You think you're the only guy with friends in this town? The only one with influence? You try putting me out of business, LaRue, and I'll have your butt on hot bricks so fast you'll wish you'd never opened your mouth. Now get out. We're closed."

LaRue slammed the door behind him. Charlie caught the bell to stop the noise and drew the blinds against the Closed sign. Then he returned to Adam's table. "You better eat before it gets cold."

"Th-thanks, Ch-Charlie. B-but I h-hate you t-t-to l-lose business b-b-because of me."

"I won't." He grinned. "We'll open up again in a little while. I just wanted LaRue off the property. He's always been scum and I put up with it for Kate's sake. She's doing good now, so I'm thinking I don't have to tolerate that jerk anymore." Turning, he headed back toward the kitchen. "Abby baked coconut cream pie last night. I'll bring you a piece."

Adam didn't protest. Instead, he finished the plate of chicken and vegetables, asked for seconds on rolls and enjoyed every bite of his pie. Once he announced his campaign, he'd have to get used to being accosted in public places, by supporters and opponents alike. He'd always kept a low profile, stayed in the background even when his family received attention for some charity event of his mother's or a hospital function concerning his dad. Now he'd called down the spotlight on himself. His stuttering had better improve, and fast. Or he would, as his mother predicted, look like a fool.

Heading out to Phoebe's, he wondered—as he had since it happened—whether he should apologize for that almost-kiss or just ignore the incident altogether. The impulse had felt right at the time, but almost immediately he knew he'd been out of line. She was his therapist. He needed her expertise to make his run for mayor a success. His impulse to take refuge at Swallowtail Farm had been a mistake, one he would have to avoid in the future. Neither of them could afford to complicate their relationship with emotions. Or even just simple physical desire.

Easier said than done, though, when she came out of her house barefoot, wearing a light linen dress that skimmed her curves—very nice curves—and left her well-shaped arms bare. Her hair hung in a braid over her shoulder, with curls escaping at her temples and behind her ears. Adam had a sudden vision of a darkened room and himself slowly unlacing that braid, running his fingers through her loosened hair, over the soft skin underneath…

But this was not that kind of therapy.

As he got out of the truck, he noticed the dogs were stationed under the apple tree again, watching his arrival but not coming any closer. Somehow, Phoebe had trained them to stay out of his way. He hated the idea of himself as a person who didn't like dogs or small children. And that wasn't the case, anyway—he did like dogs, as a species, and he wasn't afraid of them. He just didn't have room for them in his life.

"Good evening," Phoebe called. "Come on in."

As he got close, he noticed that her gray eyes were wary, a little distant. Her smile said "professional." Regret slapped him, then relief. They really did need to keep their interaction strictly business.

The session quickly turned into a disaster. He was too aware of Phoebe's caution, too aware of his own body language, and so his stutter became impossible to manage. Containing his frustration wound the tension to the breaking point.

"Read this one," she said, handing over another card of paragraphs specifically composed to twist his tongue.

Adam looked at the words, assessed the preponderance of *B*s and flipped the card across the kitchen table. "I d-don't think s-s-so, thanks." His chair scraped the wooden floor as he pushed back from the table. "I'm c-calling it a n-night."

SAM HADN'T INTENDED to put Adam DeVries under surveillance. The situation arose simply by accident. In a town the size of New Skye, you couldn't get through a day without seeing people you knew—at the grocery store, at the dentist's office, or at a stoplight somewhere on the streets.

So she wasn't surprised, late Tuesday afternoon, to find herself sitting behind Adam's truck as they waited for the light to change. She wasn't surprised to find herself going in the same direction—he had a building site on the south side of the city and she liked to get fruits and vegetables at a roadside stand nearby.

But Adam drove straight past his project without so much as slowing down. While puzzling over that, Sam missed the turn for the vegetable market. She shrugged and, out of curiosity, followed the truck at a safe distance. The evening ahead promised her a solitary dinner in front of the TV and, if she got really energetic, hours of research on the Internet. A country drive couldn't hurt.

She might have thought twice if she'd realized how far into the country he was going. The four-lane highway narrowed to two lanes, and still Adam drove on. Just past the new low-income housing project, though, he finally put on his turn signal. Bower Lane. Had he started a new project out here in the boonies?

A mile or so down the narrow little road, the white truck flashed another turn signal. This time he turned onto a private gravel drive, which left Sam grinding her teeth in frustration. Swallowtail Farm, the sign read. What was that? She couldn't follow him onto someone's property without a really good excuse. Simple nosiness wouldn't cut it.

She parked on the shoulder of the road, deciding what her next move should be. Just as she cut the engine, her cell phone rang. Her editor kept Sam on the phone for almost twenty minutes, going over changes for a story scheduled to run in the Saturday paper. All the while, Sam never moved her eyes from that driveway.

After hanging up, she gave in to her curiosity and decided to investigate. Dirt and gravel sifted into her sandals as she slipped down the lane, staying behind the trees that lined it as much as possible. The drive was much longer than she'd imagined it would be, and she hadn't come dressed for exercise. But a good story would more than pay for dry-cleaning the sweat stains out of her silk blouse.

She came up yet another rise and saw—finally—a house in the distance. Four horses grazed in the pasture in front of the house, watched by a man and a woman standing close together at the fence. Three big dogs lay under a tree nearby.

Dogs. Sam went cold. If they caught her scent, she'd be lucky to get out alive, let alone unseen.

Hesitating a moment longer, she looked back to the couple by the fence…and found them holding hands, staring intently into each other's eyes. The next moment, she was sure, would bring a kiss. And whether from sheer jealousy or an aversion to voyeurism, Sam wasn't about to watch.

This could be a real scoop, though. Adam DeVries had a girlfriend out of town. Who was she?

Thinking of sources for that information, Sam turned to go back the way she'd come and promptly turned her ankle over a rock hidden by the grass. She kept her balance, didn't fall, didn't say more than ''Ow.''

In that instant, all hell broke loose as the three dogs cried out the hunt. Sam heard them come after her, barking, whining, roaring, it seemed, as they streaked down the drive. She ran. They ran faster. She wasn't sure whether they had a greater distance to go to reach her than she had to reach the gate, but she had a feeling they would all find out.

The front fence came into sight as the dogs rounded the curve just behind her. Sam sprinted, grabbed hold of the heavy steel gate and pulled it closed just as the three hounds arrived within biting distance. Though the dogs could have slipped through the widely spaced bars, they were so excited they didn't think about it. They circled at the gate, still barking, panting and jumping on one another, while Sam put the chain through the bars and around the wooden post, linking the ends with the open padlock. Throwing a quick glance in each direction to check for oncoming traffic, she dashed across the road and slammed herself into the car. Only then did she dare to breathe.

And only when she'd driven farther along Bower Lane, with no real clue as to where she would end up, did she start thinking about the possibilities for her story. Summer was a slow time for news. A budding romance involving a mayoral candidate was sure to spark some interest.

She thought about Tommy Crawford and his insistence that nothing needed to be said until Labor Day and the official announcement.

"Sorry, Tommy." Sam drove through the country twilight, grinning at the prospect of a good story. "You've got your job to do.

"And—come hell, high water or everlasting love—I've got mine."

ADAM HAD ALMOST REACHED his truck when Phoebe caught up with him and grabbed his arm. He let her stop him, though he could have jerked free easily enough.

"You're confused about who's in charge here," she said. "I'm the therapist. I say when the session ends."

"Ph-Phoeb-be." He dropped his chin to his chest for a second. "I c-can't even s-say your n-name. L-l-let it g-g-go f-f-for to-night."

She softened her grip. "You c-can't leave d-def-feated."

Brows drawn together, he glared at her. "You w-wouldn't t-t-taunt me. You s-stutter?"

Phoebe nodded, gazing into his face, waiting.

"H-how d-did you st-stop?"

"I d-didn't, as you c-can hear." She drew a deep breath. "I've l-learned ways to minimize the problem."

He took her free hand in his. "T-tell me."

"Breathing, as you've practiced. Soft consonants."

"Th-that's it?"

"No." She looked past him to the pasture where the horses swished their tails at flies and bent graceful necks to nip at sprigs of new grass. "I live the life I want, with as little stress as I can arrange. I make my own decisions, regardless of other people's expectations. I stay calm and happy."

"C-calm and h-h-happy."

"Pretty much." His expression was skeptical. "Stuttering is a response, Adam, a way to deal with some person or event in your life. You used it long enough to form a habit you haven't been able to break. My job is to help you find ways to break that habit. Those are the ways I found to break mine."

He tensed, and she waited, hoping he would volunteer the details of when and why he had started stuttering. But the silence stretched, and she accepted that he wasn't prepared to share his secret.

"So." Phoebe realized that she still held his arm, as he held her hand. She backed up, letting go with reluctance, feeling his fingers holding on to hers.

And then the dogs went wild. They leapt to their feet and filled the night air with noise—Gally's frantic barks, Lance's excited yelps, Gawain's deep bay. Like hounds of hell, they dashed down the drive.

Adam stared after them. "Will they g-go out th-the g-g-gate?"

"I don't think s-so." She crouched to go through the

pasture fence, no mean feat in a long narrow skirt. "They never have."

Adam followed her. "Where are you g-going?"

"This is a shortcut." The horses had lifted their heads as the dogs went past, then went back to grazing as Phoebe walked by.

"You're barefoot. And the pasture is…"

She grinned at him over her shoulder. "Grassy. Just watch where you step."

They reached the front gate to find it closed, the ends of the chain drawn together with the unfastened lock and the dogs barking wildly as they jumped up and down at the barrier.

"None of them seems to have the brains to realize they could go through," Phoebe said, in between pants.

"S-Somebody has b-b-been h-here." Adam stood with his hands on his hips, staring at the gate. "I left this open b-b-behind me."

"They must have closed it between them and the dogs."

"Why were they h-here? Why not c-c-come in? Or why c-come in at all?"

"This is the country, Adam. I don't think they meant any harm."

He didn't look convinced. He didn't look too happy, either, as they walked back up the drive with Gawain and Gally and Lance gamboling around them, chasing sticks Phoebe threw.

She really wished he liked her dogs.

Back at the house, Adam took his keys out of his pocket, preparing to leave.

Phoebe tried again. "Do one thing for me before you go."

"What do you n-need?"

Touching him was a bad idea, so she clasped her hands together. "Come around the truck. That's right, to the fence." They stood side by side once again, staring at the horses. "Now, tell me what you see. Slowly, gently, calmly. Describe the scene."

He opened his mouth.

She held up a finger. "Deep breath, first."

"Okay." His shoulders lifted, and he blew out softly. "T-twilight above the trees, p-pink, p-purple, g-gold. P-pines, d-dark green and b-brown, stretching b-between grass and sk-sky. Horses white and b-brown and b-black, colors b-blurring in the gray light, b-beautiful and p-peacef-ful and s-safe." He looked over at Phoebe. "Are you s-sure you will b-be?"

She had to draw her mind back from his poetic description. "I'll be fine. You'll lock the gate again, the dogs and I will go into the house, and everything will be good until morning." Again, she had to stop herself from touching him. "I promise."

"Okay." Adam started toward his truck.

"That was lovely," she told him as she followed slowly. "You did a good job with your consonants. And the description. That's what I see when I'm here."

He looked around again, and then smiled at her for the first time all evening. "Yeah. I'm b-beginning to understand j-just how that therapy of yours w-works."

"I THINK WE'VE COVERED the agenda. Does anyone have questions or comments?" Cynthia DeVries glanced at each member of the fundraising committee, now assembled in her living room. "If not, then we'll close. Be sure to have another cup of punch and some more dessert before you leave."

A collective sigh preceded the polite bustle as most of

her listeners returned to the dining room. Cynthia gathered her papers together, rose from her chair and turned to find Kellie Tate, the mayor's wife, approaching.

"I knew you must be dying for something to drink. I thought I'd bring you some of that delicious punch." Kellie offered one of the cut-crystal cups she carried and sipped at the other. "Where did this recipe come from?"

"Thank you so much, dear." As the fruit drink soothed her dry throat, Cynthia felt the tension that had been holding her up through the meeting begin to drain. She hoped everyone would leave soon. "My mother got it from one of her bridesmaids. We served it at my wedding to Preston."

"Heirloom recipes are the best, aren't they?"

"That's quite often true." Moving nearer the front door, to be on hand when the ladies began to leave, she waited for Kellie to come to her point.

Most of the guests were gone, however, before she stated her business. "You know, Mrs. DeVries, quite a few people were surprised to hear that your son has decided to run for mayor."

Herself among them. Cynthia called up a thin smile. "I imagine they were."

"Curtis feels like he's done his very best for the citizens of New Skye. After running unopposed for four terms, he's…well, he's hurt, if you want to know the truth, that Adam wants to challenge his fitness to be mayor."

"I can see how that would seem like a personal slight."

"I know you must have a great deal of influence with your sons, Mrs. DeVries. Surely they know how fortunate they are to have such a respected and admired woman as their mother."

Through sheer willpower, Cynthia managed not to roll her eyes. "Kellie, dear, I'm not sure what you and Curtis think I could do to change Adam's mind. I can give him my advice, but I can't force him to resign from the race." A fact amply demonstrated by his tantrum on Sunday.

"Oh, of course not." The younger woman waved the idea away. "Curtis was just reflecting on how much the Botanical Gardens means to the city as a whole, and how impressed he is with the idea of the Stargazer Fundraiser. A dinner dance under the stars in the gardens—you were so clever to think of such a wonderful way to raise money."

She paused to finish her punch, and Cynthia waited for the punch line.

Kellie looked at her over the rim of the cup. "I expect Curtis could find some funding tucked away in the city budget somewhere that would be very helpful to the garden. He might even be able to match the money you raise with the dinner dance. Wouldn't that be a wonderful gift for the Botanical Gardens?"

"Yes, indeed." She said goodnight to the remaining committee members and walked into the dining room to set down her cup, relieved to note the housekeeper was beginning to clear the table. Kellie followed, not too obviously anxious, to grab one more lemon square and turn in her punch glass.

Cynthia placed a hand in the small of Kellie's back and eased her to the front door. "I do appreciate your husband's generosity and his willingness to assist in keeping the gardens at their very best. I don't know that I have nearly as much leverage with my son as you believe, but I'll certainly keep your ideas in mind when I talk to him about this endeavor."

Standing on the front porch, Kellie turned, her lips parted to make another attempt at persuasion.

"No, dear, really. I do understand." Cynthia held the door open just wide enough for her face to be seen. "I'll get back to you on this. I promise. Good night, and drive carefully." She closed the door, giving the mayor's wife no choice other than to go away. Finally.

The clock struck eleven before the house was orderly once again and Cynthia felt free to sit down with a glass of dry sherry and slip off her high heels. Kellie Tate had certainly provided her with food for thought. As the current president for the New Skye Botanical Gardens Auxiliary, she would be quite satisfied to leave as her legacy a sizable donation to the organization. She expected the Stargazer Fundraiser to bring in adequate money, but if the city provided a matching donation, then she would, indeed, have done her job well.

To achieve that goal, all she had to do was dissuade Adam from making a fool of himself and his family by continuing his run for the mayor's office. From earliest childhood, he'd been a stubborn little boy. Sometimes she thought his speech difficulty was just another attempt at defiance.

Rarely, very rarely, had she allowed him to prevail. Descended from a long line of those who'd withstood the assault of British troops, the Yankee invasion, the shame of Reconstruction and the desperation of the Great Depression, Cynthia did not doubt her ability to control her own son.

The DeVries family held an enviable position and enjoyed a sterling reputation in this town, thanks in no small part to her own work in the community. If Adam did not understand his role in maintaining the respect due his mother and father, he could be taught. He must come to his senses and withdraw from the campaign. Or suffer the consequences.

And Cynthia could ensure that there would be consequences.

CHAPTER FOUR

SAM DECIDED TO AMBUSH Tommy Crawford in his office again. Early morning seemed to be his vulnerable time. Besides, she liked seeing him as a way to start off her day.

This time, she brought breakfast. She heard the rear door of the office open and close and then a pause, as if he caught the aroma in the air.

"Bonnie, honey, did you bring doughnuts?" he called from the back. "There will be stars in your crown for that act of goodness." His footsteps came quickly down the hall. Sam loved how he moved, with a grace and precision that only looked slow. "I stayed up watching the Braves game and slept too late—" He came into the front room and saw her. "For breakfast."

"Great game, wasn't it?" Sam got to her feet, holding the familiar green-and-white doughnut box in one hand and a carrier of gourmet coffee in the other. "Could you believe that play in the bottom of the eighth? I thought for sure the Yanks were pulling away with that hit. Instead, the big boys from the South turned it into a double."

"Amazing. You're here for breakfast?" He didn't seem as surprised as she'd hoped.

"Most important meal of the day."

"Where's Bonnie?"

"She went to the bank. I told her I'd watch the front door."

He massaged his jaw with one hand. "Sure, let's eat. Come on back."

Sam hoped to confuse him, keep him off balance, because he was such a smart-ass, always knew the score, always got the last word. Sometime, though...sometime she wanted to see him serious, see him thinking, see him caring. About her, the way she cared about him. In a forever kind of way.

If, that is, Adam DeVries and his run for mayor didn't ruin her chances completely.

They settled in Tommy's office again with the doughnuts open between them. He chose chocolate-covered cream, as she predicted, and settled back with a groan. "No calories here, of course. No fat. No cholesterol."

"Just air," Sam agreed, taking a raspberry-filled bite. She licked jelly and glaze off her lips, savoring the tart sweetness.

Tommy choked, choked again, and went into a fit of coughing. When she would have come round the desk, he held up his hand and shook his head, then staggered out and across the hall to the break room. She heard the water running, and his coughs gradually died.

He returned, red-cheeked and wet-eyed. "Man. That bite went down the wrong pipe." He sat down again and picked up his coffee with both hands. "So what's the deal, Sam? Did you come specifically to choke me with a doughnut, or do you have a more sinister purpose?"

"Well..." She leaned back in her chair. "I did want to ask you about Adam DeVries's new girlfriend."

His eyebrows rose into the fringe of his hair. "Girlfriend? Not that I know about."

"Lives out in the country, works in town. Long, silver-streaked hair, drives a green Beetle. Speech therapist?"

"You mean Phoebe?" Tommy gave a one-sided grin and took a sip of coffee. "Girlfriend? Nah. They're just friends. Longtime buddies."

"She's only lived in New Skye a little over a year."

"Yeah, and Adam went to school in Atlanta, where she's from. Figure that one out."

She already had, damn it, but was hoping for more. After all, she'd seen them getting ready to kiss. "Maybe a long-distance romance grown closer? The people will want to know if there's a Mrs. Mayor in his future. Kellie Tate's pretty popular." Pretty enough to blind most folks to the shenanigans of her husband, the mayor. That story, Sam had never been able to crack.

Tommy shrugged. "Adam's been my friend since diaper days. I think he would've told me if he had plans."

"And you, of course, would tell me."

"I would tell you anything, Sam, honey, for dough-nuts."

The implication of bribery made her mad, all the more so because she knew it for the truth. Since she couldn't get him to tell her on the strength of their friendship—since *friendship* was too strong a word for what they had and not at all what she wanted from him, anyway—she'd brought food as a last resort. And even food didn't work.

"Well, then, enjoy." Teeth clenched, she got to her feet and deliberately tugged at her skirt, too tight and too short to be eating doughnuts in. The legs, the breasts, the face raved about by her past boyfriends didn't impress Tommy Crawford in the least. "I'll check back with you before the big Labor Day bash."

He followed her to the door. "You do that. Maybe I'll know something more by then."

Sam let her temper get the best of her. "Not likely," she told him with a whip in her voice. "You're just about the least observant man it's been my misfortune to know."

Tommy let the glass door close between them, watching until Sam had stalked to her car and peeled rubber as she headed for downtown. He'd noticed the red Mustang parked outside when he arrived, so he'd been prepared to face her. Or so he'd thought.

Something about seeing her always knocked him for a loop, though. She was fantastic, plain and simple. Full of fire. She'd come to the *New Skye News* from a paper in Illinois, having grown up in the Midwest. He couldn't imagine why, or that she'd be staying long. Big talents didn't tend to settle down in podunk towns like this.

No matter how much some of the podunk citizens would like them to stay.

Instead of daydreaming about Sam Pettit, though, he really should be tracking the candidate down, finding out what the hell could have given Sam the impression there was a personal relationship happening between Adam and Phoebe Moss. At least that interpretation was preferable to the real one. He'd managed to divert the reporter's attention by making her mad—it was always fun to watch Sam flare up—but he really didn't want the fact of Adam's speech therapy broadcast to the voters. Tommy planned to keep their one liability as low key as possible, which meant keeping Adam out of sight until Labor Day. And having as little to do with Sam Pettit, Brash Girl Reporter, as possible.

He clicked his tongue and shook his head. The sacrifices he made for his best friend. Adam would do the same for him, he had no doubt.

And then they'd drink their way through the long, lonely nights. Single, miserable, but together.

THE FIRST KISS HAPPENED by accident. Phoebe would have sworn to that.

One moment, she and Adam were standing at the edge of the pasture after his session, watching Brady and Rob frolic in the hot, windy July twilight while Cristal and Marian munched their hay. In the next instant, a sharp flash of lightning bleached the night, even as a slap of thunder whipped the horses into a breakneck race from fence to fence. Then the sky ripped open, shedding a torrent of needle-sharp raindrops.

Adam grabbed Phoebe's hand and dragged her to the nearest shelter, which was his truck. He pushed her into the passenger seat, slammed the door almost before her foot was out of the way, and sprinted to the other side, throwing himself in just as another bolt of lightning struck nearby.

"D-damn, that's s-some st-storm." He gazed at her across the cab, his brows drawn together, the raindrops on his face highlighted by the interior lights. "Are you okay?"

Phoebe nodded, taking off her water-spotted glasses and setting them on the dashboard. "I don't think I'll melt from a little rain."

"What about the h-horses?"

"They don't melt, either." She grinned at him, then turned to follow his gaze through the rain-sheeted windshield. The only horse visible through the dark was a ghostly presence under the trees. "Marian's the boss mare,'' Phoebe told him. ''She's calmed down, so I think the others have, too.''

''Sh-shouldn't we b-bring them in?''

''They're safer in the pasture, I think. Horses are meant to be outside in all weathers—they have good instincts for danger.''

''And the d-dogs?''

The question surprised her, warmed her. ''They're in the barn, I'm sure. They know how to stay dry.''

Just then, the interior lights shut off, leaving them truly in the dark, with rain drumming on the roof, gusts of wind rocking the heavy truck, and lightning dancing across the four corners of the sky.

With a sigh, Phoebe settled into her seat. ''I do love thunderstorms.''

''Wh-why?'' Adam knelt in the driver's seat and reached into the back seat, searching, rattling paper and plastic.

''I guess it's the idea of a force we can't contain, can't control, despite all our technology, all our building and mechanical expertise. A storm demands that you acknowledge your own lack of power in the universal plan.''

He sat down again, with some white cloth in his hand. ''That's n-not an idea I f-find c-comforting. I bought T-shirts today. Want to dry off?''

Laughing, she took the one he offered. ''You're sacrificing your new T-shirts?''

''They'll wash.'' In only a few seconds, he had scrubbed his face and hair dry. ''Not much we can do about our clothes. Unless you want me to turn on the heater.''

''Oh, no. It's warm enough.'' Phoebe sat up and pulled her braid over her shoulder, then began blotting water out of her hair from the top down. The process took a long time. And she could feel Adam watching her every movement, every moment.

"You have beautiful hair," he said finally, quietly.

The air in the truck seemed to be getting closer, heavier. "Thank you."

"Would it dry faster if you unbraided it?"

"Um…probably. But that's okay."

"Let me." Before she really knew what was happening, Adam had leaned forward and taken her braid out of her hands. The band slipped off and in the darkness she watched his tanned fingers weaving through her hair. The gentle tug against her scalp stopped her breath. The occasional brush of his touch against her bare arm seemed likely to stop her heart.

The braid began just at the nape of her neck. By the time Adam's hands came so close, she had closed her eyes, trying with all her willpower not to melt, not to fling herself across the seat and devour him. Her pulse thundered in her ears, in her fingertips, deep in her belly.

This was not the behavior of a professional therapist.

"Th-there." His voice was a whisper in the storm. He combed his spread fingers through the whole length of her hair.

Phoebe shivered. Her "Thanks" was soundless.

"Are you c-cold?" He reached back for another T-shirt. "C-cover up with this."

She didn't protest, because she couldn't speak. Somehow, in the process of draping the shirt across her shoulders, their hands met, clasped. His face was close, his blue eyes the only glint of light.

Then his mouth touched hers. Lightly, tenderly, almost tentative. She could have stopped him with no trouble at all.

Had she wanted to. Had she thought about it.

But Phoebe didn't. She thought about his taste, a hint of sugar from the ice tea she'd served, edged with lemon from the slice she'd added along with a mint sprig. Plus something much deeper, darker, richer…Adam. Parting her lips, she offered him more of herself.

After a second's hesitation, he answered. The kiss went deep and long. Around them, the air got hot, and the sounds of their sighs, their gasps, drowned out the rain. They faced each other across the barrier of the console, mouths fused, hands holding tight.

Phoebe thought, *More.*

With that word though, awareness spiked her brain. Breathing hard, she pulled away. "Adam…"

He let her go immediately and dropped back into the driver's seat. "G-God." He scrubbed his face with his hands. "I'm s-so s-sorry."

Phoebe reached out, then drew her hand back. "N-no. D-don't be." In the silence, she realized the rain had slowed to a patter. "B-but we c-can't do th-this again." She grabbed her glasses, opened the door and dropped out of the truck, right into a puddle. "Aack!"

Adam had come around to her side. "C-could th-things g-get worse? Are your sh-shoes r-r-ruined?"

"P-probably." She should have known better than to give in to vanity and wear her linen sandals, just because he was coming. "That's okay."

"I can carry you to the house."

Didn't that sound like a recipe for delight…and disaster? "D-don't b-be silly. I'll just take them off." She suited action to words, then faced the pasture, where the horses had become visible under a clearing sky. "See, they're all fine. They love the rain. And they love to roll in the mud," she added, as Brady demonstrated that particular horse behavior.

The sound of many paws riffling wet grass warned of the dogs' approach. "Watch out," she warned. And "Stay," she told them. But Gawain and Gally and Lance had decided never to bother The Man. They flopped on her opposite side, lolling in the wet grass.

Phoebe turned back to Adam. "So, everything and everybody is fine." More or less. "The rain will have done the pasture a world of good. If you'll lock the gate as you leave, we'll settle in for the night."

"S-sure." He stared down at the ground for a long moment. "I-I'm s-sorry," he said, when he looked up at her. "It w-won't happen again."

"It's okay. But…" Fingering her glasses, she drew a deep breath. "I think perhaps I ought to transfer you to my partner, Jenna. She can meet with you at the office in the evenings, when her husband is home to care for her baby. S-seeing you out here, at m-my home, is asking f-for tr-trouble. You're making pr-progress, I d-don't want you to stop your therapy. Jenna's wonderful, and—"

"N-no." Adam held up a hand. "That won't b-be n-nec-c-c…w-we don't have to d-do that. I'll m-meet you at your office d-during the d-day."

She didn't know whether to be relieved or worried. "Are you s-sure?"

He nodded. "I'll c-c-call your s-secretary f-for an ap-p-pointment. 'N-night."

Watching the truck's taillights diminish in the darkness, Phoebe understood his abrupt departure. His control was almost gone. Hers wasn't much better. They needed to separate, to reflect and recover.

To regret.

"N-NOTHING," ADAM SAID at dinner the next night at the diner. "N-nothing at all b-between Ph-Phoebe and m-me. Except…you know."

Tommy nodded. "I believe you. But Sam Pettit must have some reason for thinking you two have a thing going."

Across the table, Adam stirred butter into his mashed potatoes. "D-don't know what. I n-never s-see her except for s-s-sessions."

"She could put two and two together, if she saw you going into the office."

Adam shook his head. "I've b-been g-going to Phoebe's house."

"Her house?" Tommy leaned back against the booth. "That's cozy, isn't it?"

Staring out the window, his friend misunderstood the implication—deliberately, Tommy thought. "It's a n-nice p-p-place. But," Adam said, bringing his gaze back to the table, "I'll be g-going to the office from n-now on."

There was clearly more to that story than met the eye and ear—maybe Sam was right. "You need to tell me, DeVries, if there's something I should know. I can't be ambushed by anything in this campaign. You know how hard surprises are to deal with after the fact."

"I do know. Th-there w-won't b-be any s-surprises." He grinned and offered his hand. "D-double t-trouble p-promise," he said, using the words and the shake they'd created as kids twenty-five years ago.

"Must be serious," Abby said, arriving at their table with two servings of red velvet cake. "I haven't seen you guys use that sign for years and years." She set down the plates and blew a breath off her lower lip that lifted her brown bangs. "Lord, wouldn't you like to be that young again?"

Tommy pulled over a piece of cake, then looked at his friend. "I don't know—I kinda like being over the legal drinking age. And the women are easier to get when they're older than twenty-one. What do you think? Would you be a kid again?"

Adam shook his head. "N-not on your l-l-life."

"You've made remarkable progress," Phoebe said on a Friday at the end of August, as they sat together in her office. "Your blocks are way down, your repetitions significantly reduced. And your speed continues to improve." She showed Adam the charts from the recording and analyzing machines in her office. "I'm very impressed."

Adam pretended to study the papers. "That's g-good." She was happy to be doing her job well. He was happy to be making headway against the stutter. His mother called at least twice a day, trying to argue him out of the campaign. Two out of three wasn't bad.

"Has there been much of a problem at work?" She took back the file, then walked around to sit in her chair behind the desk, as if she needed a huge piece of cherry wood to keep him a bay. "Losing an hour three mornings a week must make a difference."

"It's n-not as if I'm indi-di-disp..." He shrugged. "I've g-got g-good foremen."

Phoebe nodded, still in professional mode. "I'm glad to hear you're relaxing about work. And your kickoff rally takes place next weekend, right?" She tucked a small curl behind her ear and smoothed it down.

Every time he'd seen her since that stormy night, she'd worn her hair pulled back tight in a knot on the crown of her head with hardly a wisp escaping. He supposed she thought the repressed hair made her unattractive, cooled his urge to seduce her.

What he felt, though, was a desire to take her by the shoulders and shake her until all the pins holding that knot fell out, and then kiss her until neither of them was thinking a single coherent word, much less saying one.

Of course, that wasn't why he came to see her, was it? "Yes. The c-c-campaign starts Labor D-Day."

"So now's the time to write your speech. When you come next Tuesday, bring the rough draft with you. We'll start practicing. Don't write with half a mind on whether you can say that word, or this one. Write what you want to tell the people who are listening. We'll work on getting the writing into spoken words."

"S-sounds g-good." He winced at the stutter, felt his fingers start to curl into a fist and deliberately relaxed them.

Phoebe stood up. "Excellent. You remembered to ease up. It'll become natural soon enough." She gave him that distant "time's up" therapist's smile. "See you Tuesday."

Adam still wanted to shake her. Instead, he nodded, without a smile. "Tuesday."

He did give Willa a grin on his way out. She was a nice lady, proud of her grandchildren and willing to talk about them with anyone who'd listen. Adam had learned to listen a long time ago. Now he had to talk.

Over the weekend, working with Tommy and on his own, he crafted his speech. He'd majored in engineering at Georgia Tech, and writing had always been easier than talking, so he knew his way around an effective paragraph.

Tuesday morning, he entered Phoebe's office and laid

the text of his speech in front of her on the desk. "Here's m-my homework."

She looked up with that damned professional smile. "Oh, good. Have a seat." Her rapid scan of the pages did nothing at all for his ego. In just a minute, she offered them back to him, along with a red pen. "Now, what I want you to do is underline the words you think will give you trouble. Every single one."

For a minute, Phoebe thought Adam would turn around and walk out of her office, never to return. He didn't take the papers, only stared at her with his brows lowered and his blue eyes sparking like flint. She struggled to stay calm, to keep her smile and her hand steady, while her heart pounded like the engine of a freight train.

Finally, he drew the pages from between her fingers. "Sure. N-no prob-blem."

The room temperature seemed to drop twenty degrees as Adam sat with his back to her at a nearby table, going through his speech. Phoebe attempted to work on another client's file, but the scratch of that red pen filled the silence and her thoughts.

When he gave her back the papers, every line of every page had been neatly underlined in red. "Adam!"

He shrugged as he sat down across the desk. "You s-said underline the words I thought would g-give m-me tr-trouble. I think any and all of them could tr-trip me up."

She slapped her hands flat against the desk. "You're b-b-behaving like a th-th-third-grader."

"You're acting l-like a third g-grade teacher."

At this moment, his stutter wasn't as bad as hers. How crazy was that? "I am tr-trying t-to d-do what you h-hired m-me f-for."

"You're so afraid I'm g-going to attack you, you c-can barely l-l-look me in the eye."

"That's r-rid-di-c…not true."

Adam folded his arms. "I think it is."

"I c-can't get involved with you. It's uneth-thical."

"Nobody's asking you to."

He might as well have punched her. Phoebe stared at the man across the desk for a silent minute. "G-get out."

"My time's not up." She understood his point—since that night in the storm she'd been careful not to let their sessions run over.

"Today it is." Standing by the open door, she held his speech in her hand for him to collect as he left. "R-read through this aloud at l-l-least five t-t-times t-tonight. We'll w-work on it again t-tomorrow."

Adam took the pages. "I might not make it tomorrow."

Phoebe shrugged. "It's your political c-career."

She heard him swear under his breath as he strode down the hallway and out the front door. Poor Willa at the reception desk didn't even get the usual goodbye smile.

Jenna stepped out of her office. "What happened? Clients don't often storm out of here."

Phoebe leaned against the doorframe. "We w-weren't m-making progress."

Her partner's eyes sharpened as she heard the stutter. "Are you okay?"

"I will be." She'd been through worse—much worse—with her family. Surely she could survive this, too.

He was, after all, just a client. Right? Not someone she cared about.

And a horse, she thought, going back to her desk, *is just a way to get from here to there.*

TOMMY WAS SITTING IN their regular booth when Adam got to the Carolina Diner Tuesday night. "Too bad Charlie doesn't serve anything stronger than beer. You look ragged, man."

"Thanks." Adam smiled at Abby as she set down his tea.

"You must have had a really bad day," she said, flipping to a new page in her order book. "Or are you coming down with that summer cold everybody else has?" She put the back of her wrist against his forehead. "You don't feel like you have a fever."

"I d-d-don't."

"He can't get sick," Tommy said. "He's got the big rally day coming up. Gotta make an impression on all those folks who show up for free food."

"I'm not s-sick. J-just tired." Adam rubbed his eyes. "I think I'll have a b-burger and fries, Abby."

"Make mine an Italian sub, warm."

"Coming right up." Abby hesitated, still staring at Adam. "You really do need some rest. When's the last time you took a day off?"

Tommy laughed. "When's the last time hell froze over?"

"That's what I thought." She nodded. "You'd better relax now, Adam. Once you're mayor, you'll be too busy to breathe."

"S-sounds g-great." He took a long draw on his ice tea as Abby disappeared into the kitchen.

When he looked up, Tommy was staring at him with a raised eyebrow. "As your campaign manager, I have to tell you that your enthusiasm leaves a lot to be desired. We're not winning this race with 'Sounds great.'"

"Like I s-said, I had a b-bad d-day."

"You don't have bad days. You're the take-charge, can-do, never-give-up DeVries Construction boss. That's why I'm your campaign manager." His grin said they both knew the truth.

Abby set down their food and put a hand on Adam's shoulder. "I brought you some salad, too. You need your vegetables—be sure it's all gone when I get back."

"There you go." Tommy gestured with a fat French fry. "You should marry her and eat at home." He reconsidered. "But then, where would I eat?"

"You think she'd s-stop working here j-just b-because she had a husband? Anyway, women are too much trouble."

"Oh-ho. Now we get to the point. You had an argument with Theresa?"

"No."

"Good. Your sister argues like a lawyer and you'd be sure to lose. The Ice Queen? I mean, your mother?"

"Phoebe."

Tommy's jaw dropped. "How'd you argue with Phoebe?" He'd come to a couple of sessions with Adam, to offer campaign-specific advice. "She's practically a saint already."

Adam gave him the look that comment deserved.

"Well, okay, not a saint. But she's sweet and friendly and patient and…and easy to look at. How could you argue with somebody so…so nice?"

Good question. Adam wasn't prepared to admit, even to Tommy, that the frustration of seeing Phoebe but not really being *with* her had driven him into juvenile behavior. He'd come to depend on the nights at her farm, had learned to need her friendship. He wasn't handling rejection well at all.

Then there were those kisses, and the honey taste of her mouth that he couldn't seem to get out of his mind....

"DeVries? You still with me?"

"S-sorry. It's h-hard to explain."

"I bet."

They finished their meals, though Adam had to divide the huge salad with Tommy and threaten to withdraw from the campaign if he didn't eat all of his half. Out in the parking lot, Tommy stood for a minute beside Adam's truck, flipping his key ring around his finger.

"You know, DeVries, that rally Monday really is a big deal."

"Yeah."

"Your speech—I mean, the speech you wrote—matters. A lot."

"Yeah."

"I'd feel better if I knew Phoebe had smoothed things out with you as much as possible."

Tommy had never once, in their childhoods, their teenage years, or any time since, complained about the stutter or teased him in any way. "I understand."

"So I think we need some intensive work this weekend. Lots of practice, so the words are automatic."

"I c-can d-do that."

"I think Phoebe needs to be there."

"T-Tommy…"

"Why don't we get her a hotel room in town, and you can spend time there off and on over the weekend, really buckling down on the big speech?"

"She's g-got animals to take c-care of. She won't l-leave them that l-long."

"Oh, yeah." He flipped the key ring again. "Okay. You can stay out there."

"No way. No."

"It's the answer, Adam. I'll come out, work with you both. We'll keep you out of sight for a couple of days, then you show up at the rally and bowl them over."

"Not p-possible. Phoebe won't ag-gree. I d-don't, either. For-get it. Think of s-something else. It's a b-bad idea, Tommy. A v-very b-bad idea."

Tommy grinned at him. "We'll see about that."

CHAPTER FIVE

"ABSOLUTELY NOT." Phoebe's tone was harsher than Tommy had ever heard it. "That won't be possible."

"Come on, Phoebe. You can see that Adam needs this time to get his speech down just right. You've helped him so much this summer. You can't quit just before you succeed."

"Adam has done the work. He's the one who will succeed. He does not—*does not*—need to stay in my house this weekend to accomplish his purpose."

He switched the phone to his other ear. "Can you stay in town for a couple of days? We'll put you up at the hotel downtown and you can work together there."

"No. I have animals to take care of. I can't leave the farm for all that time."

"What if I could get somebody to take care of them for you?"

"What part of 'no' don't you understand?"

"I'm an insurance salesman. I can't take no for an answer."

He heard her chuckle. "You are irrepressible."

"Does that mean 'pain in the butt'?"

"Pretty much."

"So which way do you want to do this?"

"I don't want to do it at all." But there was the possibility of surrender underneath the words. "Who would I get to take care of my farm?"

"Dixon and Kate said they'd be glad to stay at your place for a couple of nights."

"You've already talked to them?" A ticked-off pause. "Two nights?"

"Well, I figured you'd come in Saturday, stay the night, work Sunday. And then the rally is Monday, and I know you want to be there to hear Adam speak. Dixon said they'd get the animals taken care of Monday morning and then come in for the picnic."

"Does Adam know you asked his friends to do this?"

Tommy winced as she exposed the weak point in his planning. "He'll be okay with this."

"You know very well that he'll hate what you've done. He hates people going to any trouble on his behalf."

"As far as I'm concerned, DeVries has never had enough people making an effort on his behalf. He wants to serve this community in a concrete way, and I'm here to make sure that happens."

He waited through a long silence. "One night," she said finally. "I'll come in around dinnertime Saturday night, stay over and come back Sunday evening."

"I'll tell Dixon and Kate—"

"No. I can get Jacquie Archer to come over Sunday morning, make sure everything is all right. She lives just a couple of miles down the road."

Now he felt guilty. He was asking a lot, and the strain it caused her came over the phone line, loud and clear. "Are you sure? Dixon said they'd be happy to have a weekend in the country."

"Unless the weather looks really unsettled. Or somebody gets sick or hurt. With horses, you never know. But Jacquie's a farrier and experienced with my horses, so she's a good person to leave in charge."

"Okay, then. Thanks. This will be a good idea, you'll see."

"Tommy, you're going to tell Adam, right? You won't just open the door and surprise him with me?"

The woman was a danged psychic. "I'll tell him. He'll be glad you agreed."

Once he finishes tanning my reprobate hide, that is.

ADAM HAD NEVER APPROACHED a doorway with less enthusiasm. He was tempted to get back in his truck, hunt Tommy Crawford down and finish the tongue-lashing he'd started before he got too tangled up in his words to talk at all.

Instead, he would attempt to honor his best friend's good intentions. Pulling open the glass-and-mahogany-paneled front door of New Skye's Highlander Hotel, he crossed the lobby to the brass elevator panel and pushed the button. On the sixth floor, he took a deep breath and turned left, remembering to breathe out again when he got to room six-thirty.

Phoebe opened the door. "Hi."

"H-hi." They stared at each other for a few seconds. She looked as uncomfortable as he felt. Their last two sessions had been very polite, very impersonal. If the atmosphere was the same tonight, he might as well leave right now.

Then she smiled at him, the sweet smile he'd come to associate with Swallowtail Farm. "Come in."

He couldn't help brushing her arm as he walked through the door, couldn't help noticing her flower scent. That, too, reminded him of her farm and one stormy July night. His gaze lighted on the bed, and he swallowed hard. Tommy and his bright ideas.

"This is a lovely hotel," she said, following him. "I

didn't realize New Skye boasted such elegant accommodations.''

"The original b-building was a n-newspaper office. Sherman b-burned all the p-presses on his way through in '65. When rebuilding started, they put up a h-hotel. Then the r-railroad m-moved out of t-town and New Skye d-d-dwindled.'' He couldn't seem to stop talking, no matter how bad it sounded. "Ab-bout t-ten years ago, they s-saved this p-place, renovated and s-sold it to a m-major chain.'' The stutter got worse the longer he spoke, which didn't bode well for Monday. Adam glanced out the window, then realized he was clenching his right fist.

Damn you, Tommy Crawford.

"No, that's okay. Just relax.'' She sat down in one of the armchairs and motioned him into the other. "You started thinking about how much you'd said, lost your relaxation and your focus. Do you have a copy of your speech?''

He opened up the folder he'd brought with him. "One for you, one for me.''

"Good.'' She adjusted her glasses and looked at the pages. "Let's start at the beginning.''

Phoebe listened to him read through without a stop, though the process was far from pleasant. At the end, Adam flopped back in his chair and let the papers fall to the floor.

She waited to say anything until his breathing had slowed. "You're tense because someone is listening.''

"I'm t-tense b-b-because there will be h-h-hundreds of p-p-people listening on M-Monday and I'm going to look like a jackass. M-Mother kn-knows b-best.''

"Most people get nervous when they have to speak to a crowd. Especially when they have to persuade a crowd to like them, look up to them, vote for them.''

Eyes closed, he didn't answer.

"What's the worst that can happen?"

Adam blew out a deep breath. "I embarrass m-myself. M-my f-f-friends. F-family." He held up a hand. "N-no, wait, I've already d-done that. I g-give L. T. LaRue the opportunity to gl-gl-gloat."

"That's the worst?"

His lashes lifted, and his blue gaze sharpened. "N-no. The w-worst is that the p-political c-corruption in this town will go on and n-nobody will stop it."

"Exactly. So start again."

By the time the room darkened enough to need a lamp, the speech was going better.

"A c-couple m-more times through, and I'll h-have it m-m-memorized."

"That wouldn't be a bad thing." Phoebe took off her glasses and rubbed her eyes. "You'd probably relax more."

"I'm s-sick of the s-sound of my own v-voice."

"I'm not." She grinned at him. "But we can stop for the evening, if you want. Start again tomorrow."

"At least long enough f-for d-dinner. Where would you like to g-go?"

By focusing on stacking the pages of his speech into perfect order, she managed to avoid meeting his eyes. "You don't have to take me out. There's a sub shop just down the street."

"I d-don't want a s-sub."

The suspicion that he was deliberately being difficult crossed her mind. "Then let's call it a night. You have dinner at home, and I'll get a sub."

He stretched to his feet, leaned over and caught her hand, drawing her out of her chair. "I'm taking you to d-dinner, Phoebe. The qu-question is whether you choose where we g-go or I d-do.''

''Adam—'' His warm hand around hers weakened the resolve she'd worked so hard to build.

''F-fine.'' Keeping hold of her fingers, he pulled her toward the door. ''I'll choose. G-got your room k-key?''

SAM HAD LEARNED THAT SHE could keep track of Adam DeVries simply by checking in at Charlie's Carolina Diner every night about dinnertime. The man never ate at home. She had to wonder why he didn't marry Abby Brannon and get his meals for free.

And then he walked through the door on Saturday night with Phoebe Moss.

Sam sank a little lower behind the table of her back booth, thankful for the healthy crowd. Adam's preferred table was empty—maybe Abby kept it reserved for him until after his usual dinnertime. That spoke of an affection above and beyond mere friendship. Did Abby pine for Adam DeVries, suffer because he never noticed her? Would she be crushed to see him here with a date?

Or was Sam simply assigning her own misery to somebody else?

Though she'd come incognito—mousseless hair, barely any makeup, a plain shirt and jeans and sneakers— she kept her chin down as she watched the conversation at the table by the door. Getting caught spying would make future cooperation from the candidate hopeless.

Abby stood by the table for a little while, chatting with Adam and Phoebe. When she moved away, they faced each other self-consciously for a moment. Phoebe said something and smiled; Adam lifted his chin, as if laughing. From that point on, the meal looked very cozy, very comfortable…and as romantic as dinner in a diner could possibly be.

In Sam's opinion, dinner on a tree stump would be romantic with the right person to share it. But she refused to mention his name, even in her mind.

When dessert arrived, she decided to make her move. No sense waiting for them to find her. No sense skulking around any longer in case *he* came in.

She paid her check to Charlie at the cash register and turned, putting her change away in her purse. Just as she looked up, Adam reached across the table, where Phoebe held out the bowl filled with little containers of cream for coffee. They were laughing still, their gazes connected. Quicker than thought, Sam whipped out her camera and took the shot. No flash necessary—the diner's fluorescent lights effectively eliminated shadows.

With the camera stowed, she headed toward the door…but then jerked to a stop beside Adam's booth, as if she hadn't seen the occupants until this moment.

"Well, hello there, Adam. Building up your energy for the big political race?"

He wasn't glad to see her. "J-just eating d-dinner."

"This is a good place for it." She turned to Phoebe and stuck out her right hand. "Hi, I'm Samantha Pettit."

"Phoebe Moss."

"I understand you and Adam went to school together in Atlanta."

The other woman's eyes widened in surprise. She glanced at Adam, and then back to Sam. "Why, no. That is—"

"Where d-did you—" Adam started to ask, then stopped. He obviously knew the answer.

Sam nodded. "Good to talk to you both. I'm looking forward to the rally on Monday. See you there." Still smiling, keeping eye contact with Phoebe, she moved around the booth and reached for the door handle.

Only to have her hand land on Tommy Crawford's belt buckle, instead. His fingers clamped over hers and she looked into his brown eyes, saw the irritation sparking there. Along with the flicker of another emotion she might have welcomed more.

Swearing under his breath, Tommy grabbed Sam's hand off his buckle before she could snatch it away. Then he backed out the way he'd just come, taking her with him.

"Let go," she protested as he pulled her across the parking lot. "What do you think you're doing?"

They reached her car, that sexy red Mustang, and he backed her up against the driver's door, keeping her there with a hand on either side of her shoulders. She was even more petite than he'd realized. "I could ask you the same question. What the hell do you think you're doing?"

"I was talking to Adam and Phoebe. Where's the crime?"

Her dark eyes were bigger than he'd ever seen them. Her skin was fine and clear, and didn't need the makeup she usually wore.

He shook his head, trying to clear the distraction. "I saw you take the picture. What are you gonna do with it?"

She shrugged. "I dunno. It looked like a good shot. 'The candidate relaxing with a friend,' that kind of thing. Nothing for you to be upset about."

"I don't believe you." But he wanted to, damn it, almost as much as he wanted to taste those lush, bare lips.

"That's your problem."

"No, it's your problem, because if I find you're

harassing my candidate, I can and will make serious trouble for you on the job and just about everywhere else in this town.''

"Oooh, I'm scared." She pretended to shrink away. "Don't hurt me, Mr. Big Shot."

Her defiance pushed him past good sense. Tommy closed the space remaining between their bodies and took her mouth with his.

After a second's struggle, she was still. Her lips accepted his kiss but didn't return it. He wanted to sink into her taste, coax her to a response, see where this insanity would lead them.

Not more than he wanted Adam to win the election, however. And Sam Pettit was becoming a real threat to that win.

So he backed off, dropped his hands to his sides, set her free entirely. She stared at him, her eyes round, her breathing too fast.

He found his voice. "Are you…okay?"

The transformation took place in front of his eyes, from vulnerable to invincible in less than three seconds. "Sure," she said, and even without the makeup, the sexy clothes, she'd become Brash Girl Reporter again. "I drive guys crazy every day of the week." She opened her purse, gave him a glimpse of the camera as she pulled out her keys and unlocked the Mustang. "See you Monday."

He could've—should've—grabbed the camera. But he let her go. Touching her again would not be a good idea—he was still reeling.

And Tommy suspected he might never get his balance back.

PHOEBE WAS STILL WORRYING about Sam Pettit's comments when they got back to her hotel room. "What do you think she'll say in the paper? I guess it was pretty clear that I had no idea what she was talking about. Do you suppose she'll report that Tommy lied? Will that ruin your campaign?''

Adam dropped into the armchair, rubbing his tired eyes. "I d-doubt it. N-no way to know until it h-h-happens. T-take your own advice. R-relax.''

She sat down in the other chair. "I'd hate to cause you trouble.''

"You already h-have." He softened the truth with a grin. "L-let's m-move on.''

"Like you've been so easy to deal with, yourself. Are you going to read this again?''

"D-do I have to?" Her glare answered that question.

But three times through was as much as he could manage. "I'm d-done.''

"I agree. You must admit you've made a lot of progress. You've got the problem words down to mostly those starting with *B*s and *N*s. Maybe we can find synonyms for some of them, at least." She drew her chair closer to the table, laid the pages down and began to go through the speech again.

Adam groaned. "Phoebe. C-call it a n-n-night.''

"I will in just a minute.''

He closed his eyes. "Wake me up when you're d-done.''

Those were the last words he said for a long time. He opened his eyes once, twice, and saw Phoebe still working. The third time, she'd leaned back in the chair and put her glasses in her lap. Her eyes were closed.

"Phoebe," he murmured. Or thought he did. "I should g-go.''

The next time Adam opened his eyes, sunlight

streamed through the window. Church bells rang in a clear, bright September Sunday morning.

He'd spent Saturday night in Phoebe Moss's hotel room.

And all he had to show for it was a crick in his neck from sleeping in a damn armchair.

MONDAY DAWNED HAZY AND hot, as was usual for Labor Day in New Skye. Adam reached the rally site—the lot he'd planned to build the housing project on—at ten, but Tommy had been working since sunup, supervising the raising of tents, the arrangement of barbecue ovens, the placement of beer kegs and lemonade stands and ice cream carts.

"Hey, man," he called as Adam approached. "This is gonna be a terrific party. We'll get you elected on the taste of the barbecue alone."

"If the b-barbecue m-makes the d-difference, they should v-vote for the c-cook." Adam grinned. "You've d-done a great job, though. I like the balloons."

"So will the kids." He looked Adam up and down. "You look good. Folks will like the suit, and you can take off the jacket soon enough, loosen the tie—you'll come across as serious about the job, but just a regular guy like everybody else. Remember to kiss all the babies and give all the girls that killer smile."

"R-right." The thought of kisses reminded him of what he had to tell Tommy. "G-got a minute? We n-need to talk."

"Sure." As he turned toward Adam, a worker came running up. "Mr. Crawford, we've got a problem with the mikes. Ed sent me over to get you."

"Gotta have the mikes. I'll get with you later, DeVries."

"Tommy—"

He was gone before Adam could hold him back. From that moment on, events snowballed. Tommy didn't get another free moment before noon, when the crowds started showing up for free food, free drinks and live music from one of the most popular local bands.

Adam worked the crowd in good political style. He and Phoebe had practiced "Hey, how are you?" Sunday afternoon in between run-throughs of the speech. The button on his shirt gave his name so people knew him without an introduction. One of the cruelest jokes of his childhood had been having to say "DeVries."

"You've got a motley crew here." His brother joined him in the shade of an oak tree. "Have a beer."

"Thanks." Adam took a long, cold drink. "I'd say we g-got a c-cross-section of the city, more or less." He looked Tim up and down. "You're here as the Old S-South, right? S-straight out of Faulkner?"

Tim adjusted the set of his white Panama hat, brushed an invisible speck off his creased white pants. "Somebody has to uphold the family pride." When Adam didn't say anything, his brother winced. "Hell, I didn't mean that the way it sounded. Sorry—you do know I'm damn proud of you taking on the whole town, don't you?"

"Yeah." He hadn't expected his parents to show up, but he'd hoped. "Theresa here somewhere?"

"Haven't seen her. But who's that?" Tim snapped to attention.

Following his line of sight, Adam saw a petite figure in sinfully cropped shorts and a top showing more skin than fabric. "Walking tr-trouble, that's who. S-Samantha P-Pettit. A reporter."

"Excuse me. I have an important piece of news to impart."

Adam managed to get hold of his brother's arm before he escaped. "C-careful what you s-say. She's already n-nosing around, tr-trying to tr-trip me up."

Tim nodded. "Sure. I'm not planning to talk about you. Or talk much at all." He grinned wickedly and set off on his quarry's trail.

"That should be interesting to watch." Dixon Bell stood at Adam's shoulder. "The perpetual bachelor and an ambitious woman. My money's on her."

"I'm not a b-betting man." Tim had caught up with Samantha and engaged her in intense conversation—a conversation being observed carefully, Adam noted, by none other than his campaign manager. Tommy and the reporter? What a complication that would be.

"This is a nice site," Dixon said, looking around them at the grassy, tree-dotted acres. "You were going to put the housing project here, weren't you?"

"That was the p-p-plan."

"Seems like a good place for today's announcement, then."

Adam finished his beer. "S-speaking of which, g-guess I'll g-get to work."

Dixon clapped him on the back. "Good luck. You've got my vote."

"Thanks. I got your wedding invitation, too. Already mailed the reply card."

His friend's grin was the widest Adam had ever seen. "Three weeks and counting."

"You've b-been a p-patient m-man."

"Kate's worth every second of the wait."

Envying Dixon Bell more than he really should, Adam returned to campaigning. More handshakes, more baby kisses—and little-girl kisses, and not-so-little girl kisses—some with photographs, some not. The blazing

afternoon wore on and the starch steamed out of his shirt.
And he still hadn't found Phoebe.

At four o'clock, the speeches began. Judge Taylor, a
pillar of the community who happened to be the DeVries's
next-door neighbor, took the podium to speak about honesty in government. Pete Mitchell, a state trooper and
Dixon Bell's future brother-in-law, talked about troubled
teens and the need for community programs to keep them
off of the streets. Theresa, looking her usual cool, controlled self in a sleeveless blue dress, dealt with more personal issues, giving some of Adam's background, his
schooling, his career as a builder in New Skye.

Then it was his turn. Enthusiastic applause rolled over
him as he stepped up on the stage. A sea of expectant
faces spread out at his feet. His throat locked. He
clenched his right hand, and panic set in. This would not
work. There were no words in his head and the paper
before him blurred.

Then he looked down. Directly in front of him stood
Phoebe, with her smiling gaze fixed on his face, her
hands clasped lightly in front of her. Her marvelous hair
was drawn back by a band but hung loose around her
shoulders, with a strand or two lifted by the breeze. In
her gray eyes, he found the courage he needed.

Adam took a deep breath, and another. "G-good afternoon," he said, leaning a little toward the microphone.
"I hope you've had your f-fill of b-barbecue. If n-not,
b-be sure to get some more. There's plenty for everybody."

He stopped while the crowd whistled, shouted and
clapped hands. "Not to mention the b-beer. B-But
d-don't d-drive if you've b-been d-drinking. We will
have a couple of troopers on d-duty, checking folks out
as they leave, for safety's sake."

More noise. Adam held up his hand. "You've heard s-some g-good people talking about issues this town faces." He glanced down at Phoebe, who nodded. "Now let me tell you what I think about those s-same issues."

The stutter wasn't completely gone. He got through the speech, though, more smoothly than he'd ever have believed possible. Nobody heckled, like in his nightmares, and nobody walked away while he spoke.

"As a b-businessman, I want honest government," he told them finally. "As a resident of this f-fine town, I want responsive government. And as a citizen, I kn-know it's my responsibility to vote for officials who will accomplish my goals. That's why I ask you all to elect me, Adam D-DeVries, as mayor of New Skye on the first Tuesday in November!"

The applause was loud and long. Adam looked at Phoebe and grinned. She gave him the thumbs-up sign with both hands, grinning back.

Tommy came onto the stage, carrying another microphone. "Candidate DeVries is willing to take questions. Just form a line at this side of the stage."

Adam hadn't expected that addition to the program. The speech had gone well, though, so he felt confident enough to field at least a few off-the-cuff comments.

Police budget, schools, libraries…these topics he'd thought about, considered comments on. The dialogue with the audience went smoothly, as Tommy fielded the questions and repeated them into the mike for everyone to hear.

Last in line, though, was trouble with a capital *T*. Sam Pettit stepped up and, instead of allowing Tommy to announce the question, took the mike from his hand. Before he could grab it back, she stepped away.

"Candidate DeVries," she began, "the voters are always interested in the backgrounds and personal lives of their elected officials. You're unmarried, is that right?''

Adam remembered not to grip the sides of the podium, not to betray nerves. ''Yes.''

''Not planning to get married?''

''When I meet the right woman.'' He kept his eyes on Samantha, deliberately did not look at Phoebe. Or anyone else.

''Dating?''

''Running a b-business and running for mayor d-doesn't leave much time for d-dates,'' he said, and got a laugh.

''And yet you've been seen around town recently in the company of one woman. Ms. Phoebe Moss.''

A word crossed his mind that could not be said into the mike. ''She's a f-friend.''

''You visit her often at her farm out of town.''

''I l-like to get out in the c-country.''

Samantha Pettit paused dramatically. ''And this past weekend, you were seen entering the Highlander Hotel with Ms. Moss late Saturday night. You were not registered in a separate room. And you didn't leave until the middle of Sunday afternoon.''

The audience's gasp was almost comical, like a cartoon sound effect. Tommy's shocked face was not nearly so funny.

''While I realize these are personal matters,'' Samantha continued, ''the people of New Skye deserve to know what caliber of man wants to be their mayor. Do you have an explanation for these events, Mr. DeVries? Do you still maintain that Phoebe Moss is just 'a friend'?''

Adam glanced at Phoebe, saw her standing wide-eyed, stiff, with her hands held palm to palm and her straight fingers pressed against her lips. She had never bargained for such exposure.

"M-M-Ms. P-Pettit, I—"

"There is an explanation, of course." Tommy's voice drowned Adam's own. Adam faced him, wondering what the hell his campaign manager was about to do. They had agreed to keep the speech therapy as quiet as possible.

"And what would that explanation be?" Samantha turned to the man standing just above her.

"It's quite simple, actually." Tommy shrugged and grinned at the crowd, letting them in on the joke. "She's his fiancée. Adam DeVries and Phoebe Moss are engaged to be married."

CHAPTER SIX

ENGAGED TO BE MARRIED?

Phoebe squeezed her eyes shut, wishing, hoping, praying to disappear. Somebody was going to look very foolish in the next minute or two. Mostly likely, that somebody would be her.

The crowd noise had vanished, though whether due to the effect of Tommy's announcement or just the roaring in her ears, she couldn't be sure.

Impossible as it seemed, the situation then got worse. ''Phoebe,'' Tommy said, ''why don't you come on up and let us introduce you to the good people of New Skye?''

Yes, the fool would be herself.

She opened her eyes and looked for Adam. He had left the speaker's stand and moved to the steps nearest where she stood. Holding out his hand, he waited for her to join him. Adam had decided to go along with Tommy's lie.

If she protested, denied the engagement, Adam's campaign would end today, this minute, his credibility with the voters destroyed. His business might suffer, as well, once word got around of this deception.

But what about her business…her life? What kind of commitment would she be making?

''Phoebe?'' Adam's voice came to her…a question, a plea.

She couldn't resist. Waves of applause buffeted her as

she climbed the steps and joined him on the stage. He bent his head and kissed her—or so it would have looked to the audience. In reality, he brought his lips close to hers and whispered, "Thank you." Turning to the crowd, he held her close to him with one arm and waved with the other, grinning widely.

Tommy said, "The future Mrs. Adam DeVries."

To Phoebe, the words sounded like the clang of a heavy iron door…the door to her new prison cell.

TOMMY DIDN'T SUPERVISE the takedown of the tents, the stage, the sound system. Instead, he stood under a tree at the back of the lot as Adam's fury erupted over him.

Phoebe stood nearby. One part of her brain admired Adam's overall fluency. In the torrent of words, he stuttered only occasionally and suffered few actual blocks.

Another part of her brain—or was it her heart?—wondered what was so terrible about being engaged to her, especially since the whole situation was make-believe. As Tommy had pointed out, the engagement could be ended after the election when she "decided," based on the experience of the campaign, that life in politics was not her choice.

Nothing could be closer to the truth.

Adam, however, was not convinced. "Why the hell did you start taking questions, anyway? And why did you g-give Samantha Pettit an opportunity to n-nail me? You know that's what she wants, she's said so. She sat outside the hotel all night, stalking me, waiting to draw the worst possible c-conclusion. And you handed her the opportunity to dish it out. Are you so hot for her you c-can't keep your head on straight?"

Tommy straightened up. With his fists jammed in his pockets and his shoulders squared, he looked formidable,

even a little dangerous. "If I'd known there was something to hide—something else to hide—I would have
been on my guard. It helps to be informed."

"There isn't anything to hide. Let's publish the truth—
Phoebe's just a speech therapist helping me deal with the
stutter. Get it out of the way, get on with the real issues."

Just a speech therapist. Phoebe felt the words like an
arrow slicing into her chest. Much as she wanted to,
though, she'd already learned that she couldn't expect to
disappear from this situation.

So she let herself get mad. "I am not *j-just* anything,"
she told Adam, stepping between him and Tommy. "I
am not a p-problem to be solved, a l-l-liability to be dealt
with, or a secret to be h-h-hidden away somewhere."

Adam took a step back, his eyes wide. "Phoebe, I—"

"When you explained you w-wanted to k-k-keep your
therapy c-confidential, I agreed because my cl-clients are
nobody else's business. I p-played along with the stupid
charade this afternoon because I d-didn't want to be em-
barrassed. I d-didn't w-want anybody to be embar-
rassed."

She looked at Tommy, then back to Adam. "You need
to g-get your t-t-temper under c-control. The mistake is
made, and now the qu-qu-question is how best to handle
it, not whose fault it was. P-put your male egos b-back
where they b-belong and starting using your br-brains.
C-c-call me when you've figured out what you want to
d-do."

Marching back toward the parking area, she blinked
hard to keep the tears out of her eyes. How could she
ever have imagined her new life would hurt her this
much?

Getting involved, that was the problem. From the very
first, she'd sensed that Adam DeVries threatened every-

thing she valued, everything she'd worked to build for herself. Maybe he'd decide to tell the truth and dump her from the campaign effort altogether. They would never have to see each other again.

Heading out of town, Phoebe hoped this situation would work out for the best.

She just wasn't sure anymore what the best would be.

THE TWO MEN WATCHED Phoebe's green VW disappear into the twilight. Adam turned back to Tommy. "She d-deserved to b-be protected."

"Agreed." Tommy ran a hand over his face. "If I'd had the least idea Sam had that kind of ammunition, I'd have been more careful."

"We b-both screwed up. B-bad."

"We'll fix it." His natural Crawford optimism reasserted itself. "A little positive publicity will put us back in the driver's seat."

"I'm n-not talking about the c-campaign, dammit. We hurt Phoebe." Adam headed for his truck. "I'm g-going to talk to her."

"Good idea," Tommy called after him. "I've got someone to track down, myself."

He'd known Sam's address for several months now— a nice town house community built with Adam's usual attention to detail—but he'd never actually knocked on the door. Since it was after ten, he figured she would have filed her story and come home for the night.

The doorknob turned, and she peered at him one-eyed through the opening above the chain. "Tommy?"

"'Evening, Sam. Can I talk to you for a minute?"

"Um…sure. Let me get some clothes on."

Once, he might've told her not to bother. Tonight, he said, "I'll wait."

Five minutes later she was back, opening the door and inviting him in. She wore jeans, a baggy T-shirt and no makeup. Amazing how the woman looked sexy dressed up or down.

"Can I get you a drink? Coffee? A beer?"

"No, thanks."

She gestured to the couch. "Have a seat."

"No, thanks." He kept his hands in his pockets. "I just wanted to ask where you get off ambushing my candidate at his rally this afternoon."

She shrugged, avoiding his eyes. "My job is news."

"Reporting, that is. Not making it."

"All I did was ask a couple of questions."

"About things that weren't anybody's business."

"You wouldn't give me any information, so I had to figure things out on my own."

"By parking outside the Highlander all night?"

"Since that's what it took."

"What's your agenda here? Do you want to see Mayor Tate and his cronies using the city to get rich?"

"I want to be recognized for doing a good job."

"Why the hell didn't you go to Chicago, then? Or D.C. or New York—somewhere folks feed on the personal peccadilloes of their elected officials? Why come to a little Southern town to stir up trouble? We really don't need that kind of journalism down here."

"You're suggesting I leave town?"

"I'm suggesting we don't need brass-balls reporting in New Skye. Adam DeVries is an honest guy whose only vice is working too hard. If you want real meat, look into Tate's business dealings with L. T. LaRue. Look into city council members taking kickbacks for awarding contracts. Look at all the stuff Adam would like to change in this town. There's your story."

"Like I haven't tried? Do you know how far those stories get? Guess who Tate and LaRue have lunch with every Wednesday. Yeah, that's right—Ken Montgomery, the publisher of the paper. Kellie's dad, the mayor's father-in-law. I'm thinking the only way I'm going to break that news is to slide it into an article on your guy. So I'm keeping my eye on him. He's got my vote, if that helps any."

"Gee, thanks. One down, eight or nine thousand to go." He turned and grabbed the doorknob to let himself out.

"Tommy?"

"Yeah?" He didn't look back.

"Why did you kiss me the other night?"

"I don't know. I guess because you make me so damn mad."

"You're not going to tonight?"

"No."

"Why not?"

"Because I'm having enough trouble sleeping as it is." He slammed the door behind him on his way out.

Then he stopped on the porch and leaned against a post, fighting the urge to go back inside and kiss Sam Pettit until sleep was the last thing on either of their minds.

THE GATE TO SWALLOWTAIL Farm was locked when Adam got there. He sat for a minute and swore, though he would have been just as mad if he'd found it open. Then he locked the truck, climbed the gate and hiked down the drive, wondering if the dogs were coming for him. Would they tear him up, lick him to death...or just sit there and stare, as usual?

None of the above, because the dogs didn't show—

Phoebe must have brought them in for the night. About halfway to the house he stopped and stood still, struck by the quality of the darkness around him. An owl hooted at intervals, a whippoorwill called through the trees, there were frogs chirruping by the pond and crickets sawing in the grass. Stars swam in a black sky made hazy with heat and humidity. That same humidity carried all the smells of the country—grass and pine, hay and horse, plus a freshness that might just be the absence of too much asphalt, too many cars, too many people. After a day spent politicking, Adam really understood the need to escape.

As he started up the final rise toward the house, the thunder of hooves created an eerie counterpoint in the darkness. Marian, the white mare, galloped along the fence line to his right, followed by the darker figures of Brady and Robin. Last came Cristal, black moving against black; a stray beam of light flashed just as she kicked up her heels and gave a shrill, challenging cry. Horse voices answered from across the pasture, then the four of them joined forces, racing corner to corner, and again around the perimeter.

Adam stopped to watch, not sure if his presence had caused the uproar or if this was what horses did after the sun went down. Before he could decide, he heard the porch door open.

And then the ominous rattle of a gun bolt being drawn back. "Who's there?" She sounded calm. Deadly.

He put his hands in the air, turning slowly to face her. "Ph-Phoebe, it's Adam. N-no harm intended, I p-promise."

"Oh." Finally, she lowered the barrel. "What are you doing here?"

"I wanted t-to t-talk t-to you."

"You could've called."

"I...d-don't l-like ph-phones."

She sighed. "Of course not. I wasn't thinking." A long pause. "What did you want to say?"

"C-could we g-go inside? The m-mosquitoes have d-discovered m-my pr-presence."

Yet another hesitation. "Okay. Come in."

Phoebe stepped backward into the screened porch and Adam followed. Five pairs of eyes glowed beyond her in the dark, an animal army arrayed at her back. There was no hint of welcome in the air.

"I g-guess I won't worry about you out here anymore," Adam said ruefully. "You seem to have plenty of protection, starting with Mr. Remington, there."

She looked down at the shotgun cradled in her arms. "It has its uses. We see snakes, from time to time."

"Like m-me?"

The surprise in her glance changed to laughter before she looked way.

"For a s-second, I thought you m-might sh-shoot even after you knew who I w-was."

"I can't say I wasn't tempted." She opened the kitchen door. "Let's get inside where it's cool."

The three dogs and two cats trooped in at Phoebe's heels, leaving Adam behind, with a very solid impression of his rank in the pack. In the kitchen, a single lamp on the counter provided a soft light that glinted on the barrel of the gun lying nearby. Phoebe opened the refrigerator and brought out a pitcher of tea while the dogs disposed themselves strategically around the room. Without being asked, Adam took a seat at the kitchen table.

"What did you come to say?" she asked, pouring two glasses. Wearing a long white nightshirt, with her loosely braided hair and bare feet, she looked medieval, mysterious. Even a little magical.

Ice rattled as she set a glass before him. "Adam? What did you come to say?"

He shook his head. "I'm s-sorry. P-pure and s-simple. I m-made a lot of m-mistakes this weekend."

"Don't worry about it. The worst is over—you're on the way to being mayor. Today's mistake will get buried under the real issues."

"You m-mean our eng-gagement?"

"Mmm-hmm." She sat down across the table and sipped her tea, avoiding his eyes.

"You're b-backing out?"

That got her to look at him. "Of course. You don't need a fiancée to be mayor."

"It'll be tough to explain Tommy's announcement."

"Say I broke up with you after the rally. Blame everything on me." After a long pause, she sighed. "That really won't work very well, though, will it?"

"If that's what you want, that's what we'll do."

"But the voters will think…they already think…" She drew a deep breath. "They think we spent the night together at the Highlander."

"S-Samantha P-Pettit s-saw to that."

"If we end the engagement, they'll believe I'm a w-woman who w-would…s-sleep with a man one night and then call it off the next day."

"N-no one who knows you will g-give that a second thought" was all the reassurance he could muster.

"I suppose I shouldn't care, one way or the other. Except that I do. I don't want to be the 'floozy' who dumped New Skye's future mayor." She covered her face with her hands. "I-I c-can't bear the thought that tomorrow m-morning the whole town will be talking about my…our…s-s-sex life. I left Atlanta to get away from just this s-sort of s-situation."

"Your family was in p-politics in Atlanta?"

"No, but we knew p-people who were. I w-went to pr-private schools with their k-kids. Got teased by them, then when I g-got therapy and l-lost the stutter, they w-wanted to be w-with me because I w-was Dr. Moss's d-daughter—the famous plastic surgeon, who did their m-mothers' face-lifts and tummy tucks. Or because they thought my mother the math professor c-could help them g-get into Georgia Tech. Or, sometimes, because they thought I'd be so d-desperate they c-could g-get me into bed." She straightened up and sent him a small smile. "That was the g-guys."

"I f-figured." Now that her hands were free, he reached out and curled his fingers around hers. "I guess it's n-not f-fair to ask you to think about d-dealing with those k-kinds of people again. But c-continuing with the eng-g-gagement might be the b-best way to f-fight the g-gossip."

Phoebe stared at their clasped hands for a long time, then took a deep, sad breath. "I s-suppose you're r-right. Put on a br-brave f-face and d-dare them to stare us d-down."

"Exactly." He squeezed her fingers, then kissed her knuckles. "I'll m-make things as easy on you as I c-can."

"Thanks," she said, her voice breathless.

Adam got lost for a minute, looking into her wide, startled gaze. He fought the urge to draw her closer, to eliminate the table between them and take another taste of that pink rosebud mouth. Fought…and regretfully won.

"I'd b-better g-go." He loosened his hold on her hands and got to his feet. "I c-can't tell you how m-much I appreciate your help, Phoebe."

"I want to s-see you win, Adam. I'd hate to d-do anything else to hurt your c-campaign."

"Lock up," he ordered as he stepped through the outside door and turned to shut the panel.

"Yes, sir."

With the light off in the kitchen, Phoebe could see Adam walking along the drive, past the horses and down the hill, until he finally disappeared into the dark behind the pines. After double-checking the door, she got back into bed and lay facing the front window as soft canine snores once again punctuated the night.

She was well and truly caught now...engaged to Adam DeVries. The man who wanted to be mayor. The man she knew she could fall in love with.

The man who didn't like dogs.

SAM SAT AT HER DESK in the newsroom, regarding the front page of the Local News section with a jaundiced eye. Her picture of Adam DeVries and his fiancée rode high on the page, next to the headline Candidate's True Love. She'd argued over that one, but the editor always won in the end.

"Pretty good deal." Photographer Rory Newman leaned on the corner of the desk. "Above the fold and a headline, for a story on a first-time sucker sure to lose."

"DeVries is a big name in this town." She pushed the paper away and looked up at her favorite redhead. "You know that—you were born here."

He tossed one of the peanuts in his hand into the air and caught it in his mouth. "Yeah, yeah. My money's still on Tate. His reaction's a masterpiece of statesmanship." Rory found the printed response piece. "'I welcome all honest debate on my years as mayor of this fine town,'" the photographer quoted, parodying the mayor's heavy Southern accent. "'A democracy works best when all citizens are involved in the process. I'm sure Mr. DeVries and I will have a lot to say to each other over the next weeks.'"

Sam shook her head. "Standard politician bull."

"Exactly. A little romance will make the campaign interesting, at least. Last go-round, the challenger was over seventy and his hobby was Civil War relics. Bo-o-o-ring."

"I thought everybody down here was crazy about the War Between the States. Talked it breakfast, lunch and dinner."

"That's what all you Yankees think." He flipped another peanut, gave her a wink and walked off. "Some of us Rebs actually enjoy the twenty-first century."

"Sounds like a story waiting to be told," she called after him. Then she glanced at the photograph again. Adam and Phoebe appeared to be holding hands at the diner, laughing and gazing into each other's eyes. She'd deliberately caught them in a moment of intimacy. But she hadn't wanted to use it as an engagement announcement.

Tommy had forced her hand, in front of hundreds of people who would confirm his story. Now she had to go along with the fiancée angle, whether she believed it or not.

And, of course, she didn't. A glance at DeVries's face, at Phoebe Moss's horrified expression, had been quite conclusive proof. Neither of them had been prepared for Tommy's announcement, and not because they wanted to keep the secret. There simply wasn't an engagement to announce, until that moment. The speech-therapy angle seemed like a non-problem to Sam. He stuttered a little, she smoothed things out for him. Big deal—lots of politicians hired voice coaches. The voters wouldn't have cared, was her guess, until sex entered the picture.

Maybe she wouldn't have pushed the issue, if Tommy had been honest with her...if Tommy had asked her out. If that made her some kind of journalistic whore, so be it. She'd used every trick she could think of to get his attention. But except for one angry kiss, he treated her like Lois Lane—untouchable.

So she'd tried to beat him at his own game. And lost. Still, she had something to work with. If the engagement was a sham, it was bound to fall apart under the pressures of the campaign. She only had to be there when the breakdown happened. Shouldn't be too hard—all she had in her life these days was work, anyway. Tommy certainly wasn't asking to monopolize her nights.

But, just by doing her job, she could go a long, long way toward monopolizing his.

"MR. DEVRIES IS HERE."

Phoebe couldn't help smiling. "Thanks, Willa. I'll be right out."

She smoothed her hair, stood up and shook out her dress. This morning, she could almost believe she'd dreamed Adam's visit last night. Seeing him would be the proof, one way or the other. On a deep breath, she opened the office door and walked down the hallway.

As soon as she entered the waiting room, he looked up. And smiled.

No, last night hadn't been a dream.

"I saw your picture in the paper," Willa said, as she had when Phoebe first came in, and produced her copy as proof. "Y'all look so sweet, sittin' there and holdin' hands. But why the big secret about the engagement?"

She pretended to pout. "We could've had a party, Phoebe, dear, if you'd let us know."

"It was...sudden." Phoebe tried to think of a reason and drew a complete blank. "We're still getting used to the idea, ourselves."

"I understand that. Eddie and me were engaged for two years and five months. He was in the army and stationed in Georgia and we just weren't sure what was going to happen, so we kept quiet for all but the six months before the weddin'." She held out a hand to Adam as he walked by her desk. "Congratulations, Mr. DeVries. That's a wonderful girl you'll be gettin'."

He took her hand and smiled. "I'm s-sure of that, thanks."

In her office, Phoebe retreated to the desk and collapsed into her chair. "I hadn't even thought about the paper this morning until I got here. Have you seen the article?"

"Don't b-bother. J-just the usual hype."

The "usual hype" would definitely bother her. She took a deep breath. "Okay, then what do you want to work on? You must have other speeches to make. Shall we go over those?"

Adam pulled a paper out of his wallet. "We n-need to set some d-dates, f-first. D-do you have a c-calendar?"

"Set dates?" Her heart skidded, then started pounding. "What kind of dates?"

He unfolded two sheets and slid one across the desk to her. "These are the c-campaign events f-for the n-next week. C-can you j-join us?"

She blinked hard to focus on the words, trying to take a deep breath, hoping the room would stop spinning around her head. "The l-lunches won't work. I have appointments sc-scheduled until twelve-thirty and after one-thirty. How l-long do the meetings that s-s-start at 8:00 p.m. usually l-last?"

He winced. "Two hours, sometimes three."

"That would get me home really late."

"Right." He marked on his sheet, fully intent on business. "How about S-Saturday? There's a p-pancake b-breakfast at eight, a p-picnic at lunch, and then a d-dinner d-debate for the chamber of commerce."

Phoebe realized she had a headache. "If I d-do my chores early, I c-could c̄-come in for breakfast and stay f-for lunch. Or I c-could come for d-dinner, after my chores."

Adam looked up from his schedule. "Am I pushing too hard?"

"Um…"

He nodded. "Right." The folded sheet went back into his pocket. "D-don't let me pr-pressure you. If you c-can c-come to an event, we'll be glad to have you. J-just think about it and let us know, okay?"

She smiled. "Sounds g-good." Except for the "we" and "us" part. But she'd worry about that later. "You're debating the mayor? That could be tricky."

"I gu-guess we n-need to work on that, d-don't we?"

"We'll do free-speech exercises, get you used to thinking and answering quickly."

Thirty minutes later, they were both tense. "M-maybe I should c-cancel the debate," Adam said.

"You can do this. We'll need to work on relaxation techniques." Phoebe came back around the desk and bent to put her hand on that stiff right fist. "Starting here."

He turned his head, and his lips were within whisper of her cheek. "See, I n-need you to hold my hand through this c-campaign if I'm going to get through it."

The idea of Adam needing her was as exciting as the

brush of his breath over her cheek. "I..." She met his gaze, and their mouths touched. Clung.

"Phoebe?" Willa knocked loudly on the closed door. "Your next appointment is here."

She jerked herself upright like a mishandled marionette, and took a long step back. "I-I have to go."

"Right." At the door, Adam paused. "C-can we have lunch today?"

She couldn't resist. "Is one too late?"

His smile appeared. "P-perfect."

Watching him leave, Phoebe wondered if "perfect" was really the right word.

Or was "perilous" closer to the truth?

THE FALLOUT FROM HIS political rally was waiting for Adam when he walked into the office of DeVries Construction at noon.

"Your parents are in your office," his secretary told him, with a nervous glance in that direction. "Your mother is...um..."

"Right. Thanks, Jody." Since she was watching, Adam went directly to the door, turned the knob and stepped inside. He closed the panel behind him before speaking. "This is a s-surprise. I'm gl-gl...happy to s-see you both."

His dad came over to shake his hand. "Good to see you. Looks like you're a busy man these days."

"I don't l-lack w-work." Bending, he pressed a kiss to his mother's very cool cheek. "How are you?"

No one who knew Cynthia DeVries ever asked her a question unless he was prepared for an honest answer. "Shocked and appalled, of course. After everything I've said, you're going ahead with this ridiculous campaign."

Adam sat down behind his desk. "Each time you

b-brought the s-subject up, M-Mother, I told you I would.'' He could feel his right hand stiffening on his thigh and tried to think of Phoebe's soft touch.

"And, adding insult to injury, you announce your engagement to all of those people without informing your own family. We've never even met this girl, for heaven's sake. Who is she?"

With an inward groan, Adam accepted the necessity of yet another deception. No matter which way he turned, he seemed to sink deeper into the quicksand created by Tommy's initial lie. "Her n-name is Phoebe Moss.''

"I read the article, Adam. I know her name. Where is she from?"

"Atlanta." He held up a hand to forestall the next question. "Her d-dad is a pl-pl-plastic surgeon, her m-mother is a m-math p-professor at Georgia T-Tech. She was in the d-department when I was there, though I d-didn't take her classes."

Cynthia sat back, somewhat calmer. "You knew this Phoebe Moss when you were in school?"

Adam started to tell the truth, but remembered Tommy's story at the last instant. "We were there at the s-same time."

"And I understand she is a professional? A therapist?"

"A s-speech therapist."

"She's been helping you?"

"S-some."

"Well, at least she seems presentable. Are we permitted to know the date for the wedding? And will it be in Atlanta?"

"We...haven't s-set a d-date. This is all v-very s-sudden and we hadn't meant to tell anybody y-yet. We haven't made any d-d-decisions."

"Certainly a reasonable approach, since you have to

get through this campaign first. I'm sure the mayor is laughing up his sleeve at the prospect of debating someone with your…difficulty.''

"He who l-laughs l-last, l-l-l—" Adam swore under his breath. "We'll s-see how things go."

"Yes, we will." She got to her feet and crossed to the door, with his dad following. "We'll have dinner on Sunday. Be sure to bring Phoebe Moss."

"We'll b-be there. Thanks."

Cynthia left her son's office in a state of agitation so unusual that Preston suggested they have lunch together before he went back to work. He drove to her favorite tearoom, the Trellis, and secured for them a table by the garden window that had been reserved for some other party. Under the influence of a glass of wine and her husband's soothing care, she managed to recover her poise, if not her peace of mind.

"How can he pursue this disaster without regard for his family?" Cynthia spoke quietly, looking out the window. The tables sat close together in the dining room of what used to be one of New Skye's grand old homes.

"He has your strong will, my dear."

"I suppose so. But surely strong will should be tempered with good sense."

"Adam shows more good sense than some his age. He's built a thriving business."

Cynthia waited to reply until the server had set down Preston's chicken salad sandwich and her own salad plate. "One expects a few wild hares from students. Tim was certainly a handful before he went to medical school. And Theresa gave me some concern in high school and college. But they've both settled down nicely. No crazy stunts to worry about, even if they aren't married yet."

"Each one's an individual, with their own path to follow."

"Nevertheless, I don't believe we can sit by while Adam makes a fool of himself, and of our family."

Preston finished his sandwich and then his wine before leaning closer, his elbows braced on the edge of the table. "Will he make a fool of himself, my dear? Simply because of his speech difficulties?"

Tears stung her eyes, but she kept her voice as low as his. "How many times have we waited, Preston, and agonized, struggling not to interfere as he fought for words? The press, the people of the city will not be so patient. Curtis Tate will not be so patient, and L. T. LaRue, standing behind him, will note every mistake. That man has no honor, no sense of obligation to anyone but himself, and he will use every opportunity Adam gives him to capitalize on this misfortune. Should Adam win, which I grant is highly improbable, we'll endure three years of mockery as he attempts to run this city."

"He's an effective manager. His business makes money."

"He's hired friends who put up with his impediment as foremen, you know that as well as I do. The city council will not be so kind, especially since they are all Curtis Tate's cronies to begin with."

Her husband sat back. "So what do you intend to do?"

"Talk to him again, Sunday. It's possible that Phoebe Moss is no more enthusiastic about the campaign than we are. Perhaps she can be drawn to our side to convince him to drop this foolish effort."

"My dear, I have to say I doubt that will happen."

"I don't want Adam hurt any more than is necessary. I just want to protect him, and us."

Preston put his hand at her waist as they left the restaurant. "Whatever you think is best." He opened the car door for her and kissed her cheek before she sat down. "I'm a lucky man to have you, and I'll be behind you every step of the way."

Finally, Cynthia could relax. She touched his cheek with her fingertips. "Thank you, Preston. Now I know I can face what must be done."

CHAPTER SEVEN

PHOEBE REFUSED TO ALLOW Adam to drive out to pick her up before the debate on Saturday night. "You need to be relaxed and ready," she told him during lunch on Friday, "not rushing around at the last minute on the highway. You've got three other appearances scheduled that day." She finished writing the last of the upcoming week's campaign activities in her daybook and closed the cover.

"Focus, DeVries." Tommy had joined them at the diner. "You need to focus."

Adam looked from Phoebe to Tommy and back again, his brows lowered, his mouth set in a straight line. "Why wouldn't I escort my fiancée to a c-campaign event? I thought this election was about honor and decent behavior."

"Phoebe can meet you ahead of time and y'all can arrive together," Tommy said. "I'll drive. It'll look okay."

"Looks are n-not the issue, Crawford. That's the whole damn point of the campaign."

She put her hand over his. "I'm a big girl. I can get into town on my own."

"I know you c-can take c-care of yourself. It's a matter of respect."

"Thank you." She smiled at him. "But I'll meet you

at your house at six and we'll go from there. That way I get to see where you live, too.''

His face relaxed into a grin. ''Guess I'll have to d-do some cleaning b-before tomorrow n-night.''

Tommy snorted. ''Don't let him fool you. He's the only guy on the planet who organizes his socks by color.''

Abby arrived with drink refills. ''I don't know about you, Phoebe, but as far as I'm concerned a guy who organizes his socks sounds like the answer to every woman's dream.''

Nodding, Phoebe lifted her glass in a toast. ''Amen to that.''

ADAM LIVED IN A SMALL cluster of cedar-sided, contemporary town homes built on a heavily wooded lot near Phoebe's office. Walking up to his door, she viewed the interesting angles and tall narrow windows with approval. The setting seemed to fit the man—unusual, complex, intriguing.

He opened the door before she could knock. ''You found me.'' Taking her hand, he drew her inside. ''And you look wonderful.''

''I'm glad you approve.'' She'd taken some extra time with her hair and was wearing a new dress in her favorite purple, so she welcomed the compliment. Just as she welcomed the smile in his eyes as he looked at her. ''Your fiancée should do you justice.''

''We've definitely got that covered.'' He paused, and for a second she thought he might rekindle that kiss from her office on Tuesday. The kiss she'd been thinking about all week long.

Then Tommy came through a doorway to the back of

the house. "See? Mr. Neat. Makes the rest of us slobs look even worse."

Adam rolled his eyes. "Doesn't take much effort."

"Yeah, yeah." Tommy settled into an armchair and took a sip of the drink he'd brought with him. "So now that Phoebe's here, we can go over your opening statement again, get you warmed up. And we need to leave in—" he checked his watch "—about forty-five minutes."

"I want a tour, first." Determined not to let Tommy control the situation, Phoebe stepped farther into the living room. "Adam, this really is great."

Late-afternoon light streamed through the long windows, glinting on the rich tones of cherry, walnut and mahogany furniture. The mission-style couch and chairs offered cushions for comfort, but most of their beauty lay in the exposed wood. Above the fieldstone fireplace, the stained mantel shelf held an arrangement of primitive wooden figures.

Phoebe picked up a rearing horse. "Yours?" she asked as Adam came up behind her.

"Some of my earlier attempts."

She examined each piece in turn. "Where did you learn to carve?"

"We spent summers on my grandparents' plantation, d-down in South C-Carolina. An old b-black man lived on the place, k-k-kind of a c-caretaker, I guess. Chet Harris. He taught me about wood, encouraged me to try my hand."

At the end of the shelf she found a dog, the most carefully detailed of all the animals, painted black with a gold muzzle and feet and rich brown eyes. "Someone you knew?"

"We had a dog until I was eight. Pixie was her name."

"A sweet dog, I think."

"Yeah." The tone of the one word warned her not to go any further. Not that she got the chance. As she put Pixie back in place, Tommy began firing questions on local issues at his candidate. The more Adam hesitated, the less patience the campaign manager showed.

"Okay," he said finally, striding quickly to the door as if he wanted to get away from the whole affair. "Let's roll."

Adam stood for a long moment in the center of the room, and Phoebe wondered if he was tempted to call the campaign off, right then and there. She waited, speechless, afraid to move until he made up his mind.

Finally, he drew a deep breath and straightened his shoulders. With a set line to his mouth, he grabbed his coat and tie and ushered Phoebe out the door. Left hand at her waist, clenching and unclenching his right hand, he guided her to Tommy's silver car and the challenge of the night ahead.

SAM AND HER PHOTOGRAPHER waited outside the door to the Highlander Hotel after the chamber of commerce debate. When Tommy Crawford's Lexus pulled up to the curb, Sam nodded at Rory and stepped around to the driver's window to tap on the glass. The dark tint kept her from seeing Tommy until the pane finally slid down.

"If it isn't the Brash Girl Reporter." He didn't smile at her.

"Your candidate handled himself pretty well in there."

"What else did you expect? He's a smart man and he knows what this town needs."

"He should make some friends with his answer to the mayor's accusation that he's only running out of sour grapes because he didn't get that contract." She glanced at her notes. "Quote—'I would have liked the contract for my company. But I'm more concerned that my kids grow up in a town free of cronyism and good ol' boy kickbacks.' That's strong language."

"Mr. DeVries means what he says and says what he means."

"He and his fiancée looked very much together. No problems there?"

"Why should there be?"

"Campaigns are tough on even the most solid relationships."

"Could that be because reporters like you examine them under the microscope, looking for the tiniest crack?"

The truth stung, but she managed to stay in the fight. "Or because campaign managers like you try to create an image that'll hide the truth about your candidate?"

"You wouldn't know the truth if it bit you on—" his eyes slid to her hips, then away "—the ankle."

"Go ahead, Mr. Crawford. Feast your eyes. That's as close as you'll get." Shaking inside, hard enough that her teeth chattered, Sam turned and sashayed around the hood of the Lexus. Her skirt stretched to mid-calf, but she'd bought it because of the slit in the back—cut up to *there*—and the fact that it shaped her rear end like a second skin. *Yeah, Tommy. Look all you want.*

Rory glanced at her as she joined him by the hotel door. "What'd he say? You seem a little shell-shocked."

"Crawford rubs me the wrong way, is all." She blew out a deep breath. "Got a cigarette?"

"I don't smoke, Pettit. Neither do you."

"Oh, yeah. Suppose they'll be out soon? How long can these people make chitchat, anyway?"

Longer than she cared to think about, standing there

on the side of the street with Tommy Crawford sitting in a car not ten feet away, with her permission to stare at her all he wanted. Sam couldn't turn to face him, but she felt his eyes on her like hot fingertips stroking her spine. And, worse, the backs of her legs, from her ankles to the hem of her skirt and along that stupid slit…all the way up to *there*.

Boy, did she need a shower. Ice cold, preferably.

The big brass doors eventually creaked open and the crowd streamed through, Mayor Tate and his wife at the forefront, as befitted their status, Sam supposed. She pushed the obligatory ''How do you think it went?'' at him, got the standard confident smile and total BS in reply. L. T. LaRue walked at the mayor's right shoulder, his smile not quite so confident. Kinda brittle, in fact.

Sam could understand his anxiety. If the mayor lost the election, LaRue would lose access to the bureacracy that set aside zoning rules, modified inspection reports and deflected lawsuits over substandard building, not to mention the influence that gave bankers an excuse to risk money on his company long after a reasonable lender would have balked. Having dumped his debutante wife and made enemies among the real aristocrats of New Skye society, LaRue retained very few options. The mayor's defeat might well mean the end of LaRue Construction. And Sam doubted anyone in town would step in to save it.

As the crush thinned, Adam DeVries and Phoebe Moss stepped outside. Their entourage was smaller but impressive—Dixon Bell and his fiancée, Kate, plus Dixon's grandmother, Daisy Crawford, a feisty old lady if ever there was one. Kate's father, John Bowdrey, a respected attorney and city council member, walked out with Judge Taylor and the judge's sister, LuAnn, who were about as formidable as the town got. Charlie and Abby Brannon from the Carolina Diner followed alongside Rob Warren, who ran a locksmith business with his dad, the current president of the chamber of commerce. Not a shabby display of power. Not at all.

But Adam's family was conspicuous by its absence. Now that she thought about it, Sam realized she'd missed some faces in the crowd at Monday's kickoff rally. Theresa DeVries had spoken on her brother's behalf, and Sam herself had parried Dr. Tim's verbal thrusts all afternoon. Adam's parents had yet to put in an appearance.

Antennae at full staff, she pushed her way to the edge of the sidewalk. "Mr. DeVries? Mr. DeVries?"

He looked over as he opened the door of the Lexus for Phoebe. "What c-can I do for you?" His smile said he felt pretty good about the evening, maybe anticipated an easy question he could answer.

"Your family isn't here tonight?"

The smile dimmed. "They aren't members of the chamber."

"But they certainly could have attended the dinner and debate, to show their support for you."

His hand clenched the edge of the door. "I think my brother is on c-call at the hospital today. My s-sister has a big c-case to prepare for trial."

"And your parents? Surely Dr. and Mrs. DeVries would want to see their son shine."

Adam glanced into the car, where Phoebe Moss leaned forward anxiously. Then he looked back to Sam. "My p-parents don't support my c-candidacy. I wouldn't expect them to attend." He bent his head and dropped down on the seat.

Sam caught the door before he could close it. "Why don't they support you, Mr. DeVries?"

Tommy Crawford gunned the engine. The Lexus screeched away from the curb with the door still open. A block away, at the red light, DeVries slammed the panel shut.

"He could've fallen out on that handsome face," Rory commented. "Guess you hit a nerve." The crowd of people around them had dispersed as if there was a disease in the air they might catch. Sam would have liked to question Adam's friends about the situation.

But the real story would be with his parents. Why not just go to the source?

TOMMY SWORE ALL THE WAY back to Adam's town house. Adam sat with his head against the back of the seat and his eyes closed, his hands limp on his thighs. Phoebe wondered how triumph could have turned to tragedy so fast.

Adam sat up when Tommy stopped the car in the space between the white DeVries Construction truck and Phoebe's Beetle. "I'll skip the p-postmortem tonight. We c-can talk t-tomorrow."

His campaign manager—friend—lifted a hand off the steering wheel, let it fall back. "Sure."

Once out of the car, Adam turned to give Phoebe a hand in sliding across the seat and standing up. Before they'd reached the door to the town house, Tommy's car was just a pair of taillights in the dark.

"Why is he so mad?"

Adam unlocked his door and ushered her in ahead of him. "Tommy's a p-p-perf-f...he wants things to g-go j-just right."

"You did a terrific job with the debate." Phoebe sat down on the couch. "You were clear and persuasive.

You hardly stumbled. Certainly no more than the mayor did.''

"B-but what will b-be in the paper is that last qu-question. Why d-don't my p-parents s-s-support my c-campaign?'' He sat beside her, close enough to brush his fingertips lightly through the hair at her temples as he propped his elbow on the back of the sofa.

Phoebe smiled at the touch. "It's hardly likely you could have kept that a secret. Somebody was bound to notice your parents weren't there.''

"We c-could've c-controlled the information, though. N-not had it thrown at us like that.'' He sighed, leaned close enough to kiss her cheek. "T-tonight's over. Let's forget it.''

"Gladly.'' She started to get up, then dropped back with a groan at the effort. "I'm too comfortable to move. Just wake me up in the morning.''

She felt his chuckle. "That's what got us into trouble to begin with.''

"True.'' Turning her head, she met his gaze with her own.

His hand came up, his fingers stroked her cheek, her chin. He took her mouth slowly, thoroughly, with such devastating tenderness that Phoebe squeezed her eyes shut against tears. His fingers were gentle on her shoulder, her throat, and she thought she felt him tremble.

Small wonder. Her whole world was shaking. "Oh, Adam.''

"Mmm.'' He kissed her eyelids, her forehead, the tip of her nose. His lips brushed over hers again, but then he lifted his head. "It's late. Are you sure I can't drive you home? I could pick you up tomorrow for dinner at my folks' house, and then you could get your car at a more reasonable hour.''

"N-no, I'm okay." She wasn't ready to leave, wasn't ready to end this lovely moment. But for a reason she didn't understand, Adam had decided that he was. Most guys would have pushed for all they could get, under the guise of this situation. Maybe that was the issue—because the engagement wasn't real, Adam didn't intend to take advantage. That proved him to be a kind, decent man. Phoebe knew she should feel grateful, rather than…bereft.

He walked her to the door, even bent to kiss her cheek again, but she kept her eyes on the keys in her fingers. "'Night."

"Drive safe."

"Of course." Trying not to feel hurt, she settled for not feeling anything at all.

The party tunes of a country music station distracted her from thoughts about Adam on the drive home. She reached her dark little lane sometime after midnight, unlocked the gate and locked it again behind her, then drove through the warm black night with the loud music still blasting from her open windows.

Even before she stopped the car, she realized the horses were upset. Marian and Cristal paced the fence line, ears twitching, tails high, eyes wide and staring. Rob and Brady trotted back and forth across the pasture between the mares and the near side of the barn, clearly uneasy. At first she thought the noise of the radio bothered them. But long after she'd turned the car off, long after her eyes adjusted to the darkness, the horses registered disturbance. Phoebe sensed it as well. Something in the air felt wrong.

Her night vision finally showed her what the car lights had not. Every window in her house had been shattered.

Someone had thrown rocks or bricks—or even fired a gun—at every sheet of glass.

And they might still be here.

DINNER DRINKS WERE scheduled for five o'clock. "Is this Phoebe Moss usually tardy?" Cynthia asked at ten after. "That's a rather annoying habit."

"No, she's always on time." Adam stood by the window in the living room, watching the street. "Something must have happened."

"Traffic might be bad," his dad suggested.

"On a Sunday?" Cynthia's skeptical frown torpedoed the idea.

"She's got animals, right?" Tim clapped Adam on the shoulder as he went to the bar to make himself another drink. "There might have been an emergency she needed to deal with."

Adam didn't want to think about a problem with the animals. "Maybe her car wouldn't start."

At five-forty-five, the phone rang. Cynthia answered. "DeVries residence. Yes, Miss Moss? I see. Of course, we'll be waiting for you. Oh, no. No trouble at all. Certainly, I'll tell him." She turned to Adam. "Miss Moss will be here in thirty minutes or so. She's dreadfully sorry and begs we go on without her. We won't, of course. But I am afraid the roast will be ruined." With an expressive sigh, she crossed the hall into the dining room and went into the kitchen.

The mantel clock had chimed six-thirty before Phoebe arrived. Adam answered the doorbell and found her on the porch step, looking harried and less tidy than he'd ever seen her. "Hey, c-come in." He took her hand and pulled her into the entry hall. "Is everything all right?"

She smoothed her wind-blown hair with her hands and

tried to neaten the scarf at her throat, without much success. "I am so sorry," she said, her eyes round and beseeching. "I c-can't believe this happened. I had everything planned and I set the clock for four—I was just going to close my eyes for an hour. And the next thing I knew, it was five-thirty."

A step in the hallway behind him sounded to Adam like the approach of doom. "Miss Moss," Cynthia said in a voice of pure astonishment. "Are you telling us you overslept? That's why you are late for dinner?"

Tim, Theresa and their dad had come to stand in the entrance to the living room. All eyes were on Phoebe. She looked from one to the other, her face flaming with a blush as she registered their amusement and surprise and indignation.

"It's j-just that I was working on my windows all m-morning and afternoon—"

"You don't attend services?" Cynthia, again.

Phoebe nodded. "I usually do. But I n-needed to get the windows b-boarded up because there's rain headed this way. And so I worked all m-morning and until three this afternoon. That's when I set the clock. But s-s-since I didn't get b-but an hour's sleep, between eight and nine this morning, I guess I couldn't wake up...." Her voice dwindled, died as she stared at Adam.

"What happened?" he asked tersely.

Her gaze fell to her twisting hands. "S-some kids came b-by last night and b-broke my windows."

"How?"

"Bricks."

"How many windows?"

She swallowed hard. "All of them."

"Your house was vandalized?" Tim whistled long and low. "I'm sorry to hear that. You called the police?"

"The sheriff's d-deputies came out."

Theresa stepped forward and put an arm around Phoebe's shoulders. "Do they think there's a chance of catching the idiots?"

Phoebe shook her head. "Just a couple of d-drunk k-kids playing tricks, probably."

"That's always the way. If they find out anything, let me know. I'm in the D.A.'s office and I'll do whatever I can to help nail the brats."

"Thanks."

"Well." Cynthia stepped up beside Adam. "I am certainly sorry for your misfortune. Since we've already waited a considerable time, let's sit down for dinner."

"Y'all go ahead." Adam caught Phoebe by the hand and opened the front door. "We'll be with you in just a couple of minutes."

"I beg your pardon," his mother said, "but we are ready to eat."

"In a minute, Mother." He shut the door between them, then put his hands on Phoebe's shoulders and backed her firmly, inexorably, up against the front door.

"Now," he said, from between clenched teeth, "I want you to tell me exactly what happened. More important, I want to know why the hell you didn't call me this afternoon to drive you into town. Or this morning to help you with the windows.

"And, for God's sake, tell me why you didn't call me last night when you had to be scared out of your mind!"

CHAPTER EIGHT

IN PHOEBE'S GRAY EYES, Adam read regret, fear, pride, wistfulness. And, finally, obstinate anger.

"I appreciate what I t-t-take to be your c-concern," she said. "B-but you wouldn't have gotten there any faster than the d-d-deputies did. I think I handled the situation quite adequately, thank you very much."

He gentled his hold on her shoulders. "S-sure, you did. I just mean…I hate to think of you f-facing s-something like that b-by yourself."

She closed her eyes for a second. "I told you, Adam. I'm a b-big girl. I choose to live by myself out in the country. I'm prepared to face the risks and d-deal with the consequences of that choice. Including situations just like this."

"Has it happened b-before? Have you b-been v-vandalized in the past?"

"No. This is a first."

"Are the horses okay? The d-dogs weren't hurt?"

Her eyebrows lifted in surprise. "The dogs hid under the bed. They're fine."

"I'm s-sorry I got worked up. I just d-don't like thinking of you out there d-defenseless." He blew out a breath of relief and remorse. "And you're not s-such a b-big g-girl, really. B-barely five-three in your shoes."

The comment got a smile. "I'm just a little taller than my pal Remington."

"Rem—" He remembered the shotgun. "Oh, yeah." Then he thought further. "If somebody had b-been in the house, and f-found the g-gun…" His gut twisted as he considered the possibility.

"But they weren't." She put her hands on his chest and pushed him back a step. "Everything's all right. I ordered new windows, and they'll be here next week. It was a scary hour, waiting for the sheriff, but that was last night. Let's move on to today's problem."

Since she seemed to need the space, he dropped his arms to his sides and kept his distance. He didn't, after all, have any real rights as far as she was concerned. "Which is?"

"Repairing some of the damage I've done by showing up so late. I figure I've still got a slim chance at proving myself the perfect Southern fiancée. I even wore heels and stockings, though the temperature has to be over ninety degrees."

"That's true sacrifice." They shared a smile. Then, because the door had locked automatically, they had to ring the bell and wait to be admitted, which pretty much set the tone for the rest of the evening.

Adam expected his mother to grill Phoebe on her background, her education and her family, and Cynthia didn't disappoint him.

"My mother grew up in Atlanta," Phoebe said calmly, in response to the first question. "She went to Wellesley for her undergraduate degree and then to Princeton for her graduate work. She and my father were glad to get back to the South when she was appointed to the staff at Georgia Tech."

"Ah, yes. I stayed nearer home for my education— Mary Baldwin and Vanderbilt." Cynthia's tone conveyed the superiority of a Southern education. "I taught English literature at Duke University for several years while Preston completed his residency in surgery. Then we returned to New Skye, his home, to set up practice. I come from the Low Country, of course, where my family has held property since the Revolutionary War. Minton Hall is on the register of historic homes, you know."

Phoebe managed to look suitably impressed and pass the platter of roast beef at the same time. "Adam mentioned that he spent summers there with his grandparents."

"The children and I would go down for a couple of months when school was out. When I was younger, we had a home in Charleston, as well. Winters in town for the social season and summers in the country—I do miss those exciting days. Tell me, Miss Moss, did you make your debut in Atlanta? Theresa had quite a nice presentation here with her friends in New Skye."

Adam glanced at his sister just in time to see her roll her eyes. The year-long agony of Theresa's debutante experience had satisfied no one but his mother.

Phoebe's reply surprised him. "Yes, ma'am, I did."

Obviously, his mother had expected a different answer, as well. "That's…that's lovely." Outmaneuvered, the general initiated a flanking movement. "Do you have brothers and sisters?"

"Two brothers, a lawyer and a doctor, and a sister who's an attorney, as well."

"Impressive." Cynthia paused for a dramatic moment. "And you chose speech therapy? Quite a different direction from the professionals in your family."

At the barely veiled insult, Adam let his fork and knife clatter onto his plate. "M-Mother…"

She gazed at him, her dark eyes wide. "I'm simply

curious. Why did you choose speech therapy, Miss Moss?''

''Please, Mrs. DeVries, call me Phoebe.'' Cynthia tilted her head in agreement. ''I chose my field in gratitude to the therapist who helped me deal with my own stutter.''

''You stuttered?''

''I still do, upon occasion.''

''Amazing,'' Preston said. ''I never would have guessed.''

Adam judged the depth of his mother's disapproval by her lowered brows. ''You appear to be quite successful in controlling your…disability.''

Phoebe smiled serenely. ''We all have flaws, weaknesses or, at the least, aspects of ourselves we would like to change. I decided a long time ago that stuttering was not as disagreeable as some other faults I might be burdened with.'' She glanced around the table, where the rest of the family sat openmouthed at the sight of someone putting Cynthia DeVries in her place. ''Could I have some more of this delicious squash casserole, please?''

Wordlessly, Adam's mother passed the dish. The conversation drifted for a few minutes, from Theresa's latest trial to Tim's upcoming vacation in the Caribbean.

''I'm looking forward to getting in a lot of time on the reefs,'' Tim said. ''Have you done any scuba diving, Phoebe?''

She nodded as she took a sip of tea. ''In high school and college.''

Cynthia had marshaled her forces. ''That's when Adam took several diving trips, as I recall. Did you go together?''

Phoebe cast him a panicked glance. Adam cleared his

throat. "N-no, Mother. We d-didn't know each other well at school."

Theresa unintentionally joined in the attack. "When did you get better acquainted?"

After too long a silence, Phoebe answered, "I've been in New Skye for over a year now."

"How exactly did the two of you find each other again?" This time, his father led the charge.

Adam realized with a silent curse that they should have considered their story beforehand. "J-just an accidental m-meeting…"

"At the bookstore," Phoebe added. "We were standing in line for coffee and recognized each other."

"We sat d-d-down to talk…"

"And only realized how much time had passed when the staff asked us to leave because the store was closing."

Phoebe looked at him in triumph and Adam grinned back at her. They'd come up with a good explanation, if he did say so himself. Only as the silence around the table stretched uncomfortably, and he glanced at the puzzled faces of his family, did he wonder if they'd actually believed the story.

Well, they would have to pretend they did. Just like he and Phoebe were pretending to be engaged.

"Very interesting." Cynthia got to her feet. "Let's clear the table for dessert." Phoebe stood up but was waved back into her chair. "You are a guest, Miss Moss. Please stay seated. We won't be but a moment."

"You c-could have let her help," Adam told his mother when they were alone in the kitchen. "You've m-made her feel like an intruder."

"I don't allow guests to do kitchen work." His mother continued rinsing the dishes without betraying any regret. "This is her first visit to our house. There's plenty of

time for your fiancée to become part of the family.''
Something about her tone of voice persuaded Adam that
Cynthia would delay that moment just as long as she
possibly could.

"I d-don't appreciate your attitude," he said. "You
interrogate her, then refuse to accept her help. What's
next? Genetic t-testing?" Theresa brought plates and
glasses to the counter, gave him a sympathetic glance,
but left without adding to the discussion.

"Hardly. Carry the cake into the dining room, please."

He picked up the cut-glass stand that had belonged to
his grandmother and that now held a German chocolate
cake. "M-Mother, I—"

Still with her back to him, she slapped her hands down
on the counter. "If you are not prepared to listen to me
when I object to your foolish foray into the political
arena, I don't believe I am willing to listen to your demands in regards to a young woman you obviously
scarcely know, whether you are engaged to her or not."
Her shoulders lifted on a deep breath. "Now, please, take
the cake into the dining room. I will follow with coffee
in just a moment."

Adam didn't argue. He hadn't realized how big a gulf
had opened between his parents and himself—a distance
he wasn't at all sure could ever be successfully bridged.

LEFT IN THE DINING ROOM with Dr. DeVries for company,
Phoebe thought she could relax a little. His eyes seemed
kind, and he conveyed an impression of the perfect
Southern gentleman—tall and lean, with a slight slouch,
wavy light brown hair and a close-clipped mustache over
his smile.

"So how do you like our fair city, Phoebe?" He sat

back in his chair with his hands tented under his chin. "Quite a change from Atlanta."

"I love living in a small town. I was so tired of being just a face in a car on the Atlanta expressways."

"People do tend to get to know one another better here. That's true even if your face doesn't appear on the front page of the Sunday morning paper."

That didn't sound quite so kind. "I suppose I should get used to a certain amount of publicity, at least until the campaign ends." And then she would be totally out of the picture. Which was what she wanted, right?

Theresa and Tim came back from the kitchen, picked up more dishes and left again.

Preston DeVries shifted in his chair. "I'm sure you know by now that Adam's mother isn't happy with his decision to run for mayor. I support her in that."

"I think his reasons are good. He wants to make a difference in his town."

"He's more likely to make a fool of himself."

She sat up straight. "Because he stutters?"

"Surely you of all people recognize how folks feel about waiting for someone like Adam to finish what they're trying to say. How is that going to work in a political campaign?"

"What he says matters much more than how he says it."

"Not to most voters." He held out his hands and smiled a charming, Southern gentleman smile. "I agree we need a change at city hall. But I'm doubtful Adam is the man to bring that change about."

"I'm sorry to be rude, Dr. DeVries, but I completely disagree with you. I think Adam can do anything he sets his mind to, which includes winning this election."

Adam came through the door as she spoke, and smiled

as he heard her declaration. He set the cake he carried on the table in front of his mother's place, then stepped behind Phoebe and put his hands on her shoulders. "Thanks," he said, leaning close to kiss her cheek. "I knew I could count on you."

The simple touch sent a shiver down her spine. She wondered if Adam was acting the part of the loving fiancé, or if he was simply grateful for her defense. And did he think she, too, was pretending? Phoebe knew she meant every word. She already had far too much of her heart invested in Adam's campaign.

Cynthia DeVries entered the dining room, sat down and began serving large portions of German chocolate cake. "Well, Miss Moss...er, Phoebe, since you've experienced the social whirl in Atlanta, I'm sure you will feel right at home in our quieter gatherings here in New Skye."

Phoebe trotted out yet another platitude from the etiquette classes her mother had insisted upon. "Everyone I've met has been very kind and made me welcome."

"Of course. I was just thinking that you might want to participate in a project I'm working on for this fall—the Stargazer Fundraiser."

After the first bite of cake, Phoebe took a sip of tea and said, with complete honesty, "This is absolutely delicious. Too rich to resist." And then, with more caution, she added, "The Stargazer Fundraiser?"

"A dinner dance to raise money for the New Skye Botanical Gardens, held in the gardens themselves."

"What a great idea. I've never visited the park, but I've heard it's lovely."

"Yes, but always in need of more operating funds. Hence this effort of mine. I expect quite a turnout, if preliminary interest is any indication."

"I'm sure." The conversation sounded nice, normal...but underneath the surface was the sensation of walking on razor blades.

"As the fiancée of a mayoral candidate, you might find having your name attached to this event quite... profitable."

Phoebe glanced at Adam, who said, "M-Mother, I don't think Phoebe has time for any more c-commitments. The c-campaign sc-schedule is really tight."

His mother looked at him with raised brows. "But surely the benefits outweigh the extra effort required. The mayor's wife is working with us. How will it look to the voters if Phoebe declines?"

"Like she's got her own life and responsibilities to take care of." He'd clenched his fist on his thigh.

Cynthia gave that some patient thought. "Do you mean that your future wife is more concerned with her own personal interests than working with you for this campaign and the future of the city?"

"I mean—"

Phoebe put a hand on Adam's wrist. "I would be delighted to participate in the fundraiser, Mrs. DeVries. I haven't been as involved as I would like this past year, because setting up my practice and getting settled in my home has taken most of my time. But now I can start. When is the next meeting of the committee?"

The older woman smiled serenely. "I thought you would see my point. The next meeting is tomorrow night, here, at seven. We'll look forward to having your input."

"I c-can't b-believe you l-let her talk you into that m-meeting," Adam said, once they'd escaped after dessert for a walk through the neighborhood. "You didn't have to."

"But she's right. This is a way to get involved in the

community. And I'm glad to do that, whether your campaign is an issue or not.''

"I see you as the k-kind to be working with Habitat for Humanity, or serving meals in a s-soup k-kitchen. V-volunteering for story hour at the library. N-not p-planning a d-d-dance for p-people who have too m-much time on their hands.''

Phoebe smiled at his insight. ''Well, I can't say this would be my first choice. These are also people with money to donate, though, and the Botanical Gardens benefit the whole community. That's a good cause.''

"I g-guess." He pulled a sprig of leaves off a boxwood shrub as they passed. ''We g-grew up with her charity work, and we're all p-pretty b-burned out on the idea of fundraisers. There's more to be d-done for dis-dis-disadvantaged families than just g-give m-money. I'd like to see folks p-personally involved.''

"Which is what your campaign is about, isn't it? Being personally involved? You wanted a different government, so you put yourself on the line to implement that change.''

His eyes were warm as he glanced at her. ''I'm c-consistent, anyway.''

Phoebe linked her hands through his elbow. ''A good thing, in a mayor. So this is where you grew up. Did you have friends in all these houses?''

"There were a lot of k-kids in the n-neighborhood. I was a loner, though, even b-before the s-stutter. Tim and Theresa were always hanging out with a c-crowd.''

"Did Tommy live nearby?''

"B-biking d-distance, in the d-days when p-parents let you ride around without helmets and without s-so m-much worry.''

"And Dixon?" Maybe she was prying, but he didn't volunteer much information.

"He g-grew up in M-Miss D-Daisy's house, out on the edge of town. I s-saw more of him in high school, when we all s-started d-driving. That's when we g-g-got in the habit of p-playing b-ball on Saturday mornings. D-Dixon was kinda strange, though." Adam shook his head. "Always wrapped around his g-g-guitar, making up tunes."

"A preoccupation that seems to have paid off nicely for him, since he's writing hit songs these days, getting awards and making friends in high places. I hear Evan Carter, the country music star, is coming to sing at their wedding next weekend. Are you going?"

"Wouldn't m-miss it."

"Me, neither. Kate will be a beautiful bride."

"That's her p-parents' house, across the street." He pointed to an elegant brick home on immaculate grounds. "And Kate lives a few bl-blocks away with her kids. L.T. b-bought one of the run-down old houses and sh-she turned it into a sh-showplace for him. Then he walked out on her."

"But now she has Dixon. Pretty much a fairy-tale ending, if you ask me."

"Except that the dr-dragon—L.T.—is still hanging around, b-breathing fire and s-s-smoke."

"But you're about to hose him down, right?"

Adam put his head back and laughed aloud, something she'd never seen him do before. "I hope so," he said, still chuckling. "I really hope so."

After she said goodbye to his parents and Tim and Theresa, Adam walked her to her car in the almost-dark. "The days are definitely shorter," Phoebe said, out of nervousness as much as anything else. "In June, when we've got the whole summer ahead, it's always hard to remember that the longest day is that month, and then the balance starts shifting back.''

He took the keys she was fumbling with, punched the button to unlock the car, then opened the door. ''You p-pay a lot of attention to the…what?…the n-natural world.''

''I'm a throwback, I think. A farm dweller in a family of urbanites. My parents never understood my fondness for dirt and mud and sunlight.'' She couldn't help a sigh as she remembered. ''And they never let me keep the animals I brought home.''

''Their m-mistake.'' His fingertips under her chin tipped her face up to his. ''Th-thanks for c-coming today, Phoebe. I know how much effort this was. P-pretending to be my fiancée in front of my family really is above and beyond the call of duty.''

Was he reminding her, in case she'd forgotten? ''I told you, I'm glad to help.'' She couldn't seem to escape from his hold, gentle as it was. But she didn't have to look at him.

''And I'm glad for everything you have to give.'' His voice was low, husky. The kiss began as a light brush of his mouth over hers, back and forth until she nearly whimpered with her need for more. He closed his teeth on her lower lip and played for a moment, before soothing the tiny bite with his tongue. Helplessly, Phoebe curled her fingers in his shirt and let him take whatever he wanted.

Full darkness fell before he lifted his head. They were both breathing hard, stiff with unsatisfied desire. Adam smoothed his shaking hands over Phoebe's hair and managed a step back. ''I d-didn't intend to g-get so c-carried away.''

She sighed and opened her eyes. ''I know.'' With a

look around, as if to get her bearings, she stepped to the side and dropped into the seat of her car. "Good night, Adam."

"D-drive safely. C-call me when you get home so I'll know everything's okay at your p-place."

She stared up at him for a few seconds, but he couldn't tell what she was thinking. "Sure," she said finally. He stepped back, and in another minute she was putt-putting away into the night.

He said a brisk goodbye to his family, refusing even to come inside the front door. If he had, the same old arguments would have been trotted out, and he didn't have the patience tonight. Maybe he never would again. His mother stood back from the doorway, very regal, very unreachable in her isolation. Adam didn't consider stepping in for a kiss.

At his house, he checked the answering machine while waiting for Phoebe to call. Tommy had left six separate messages, all of which essentially amounted to "Call me." Adam decided that Tommy could wait until the morning.

He stared at the clock, trying to imagine where on the road she would be at any given minute, until the phone rang. "I'm here," Phoebe said. She sounded tired. "No problems—horses are fine, dogs and cats are asleep, windows still boarded up."

"G-good." He sat on the side of the bed. "I was b-beginning to worry."

There was a silence. "I stopped for gas so I wouldn't have to bother about it on the way into work tomorrow morning."

"M-makes sense." He hated to let her go. But he knew how lousy he was to talk to on the phone. "Sl-sleep w-w-well."

"You, too." Another pause. "'Night, Adam."

"'N-night." And still they couldn't seem to hang up. "I'll s-see you T-Tuesday for my appointment."

"Right." With a gentle click, the phone on her end disconnected. Adam did the same and dropped back on the bed to stare at the ceiling.

Phoebe. His speech therapist. His counterfeit fiancée. His friend. A woman who lived in the country with horses and cats. And, worst of all, dogs. The situation couldn't get much more complicated. Unless he fell in love with her.

But Adam had the feeling that worrying about that now was—in a phrase Phoebe would appreciate—like closing the barn door after the horse has gone.

PHOEBE MET HER FRIEND and farrier Jacquie Archer for breakfast at the diner Monday morning. "I hate to ask you for another favor...."

Her friend grinned. "But..."

"Can you feed the horses for me tonight? By the time I finish at the office, I won't have time to run out, get all hot and sweaty, then clean up and come back into town."

"No problem. Erin and I love to visit with your bunch, don't we, sweetie?"

"Yep." At thirteen, Jacquie's daughter Erin was still an elf of a girl, with dark hair and eyes and a pixie face. She loved to ride and stuck like a burr to the back of the flightiest horse. Even Cristal couldn't dislodge Erin Archer.

"Thanks so much. Be sure to let me return the favor."

"I will." Jacquie flipped her long blond braid behind her shoulder and took a sip of coffee. "So, is this a date you've got scheduled? You and your fiancé slipping off for a romantic evening together?"

"Oh, of course." Phoebe had trusted Jacquie with the truth about her engagement to Adam, knowing it would go no further. "I only wish. I'm going to his mother's house tonight for a meeting of the Stargazer Fundraiser committee."

"Say again?"

She explained about the dinner dance. "Mrs. DeVries didn't leave me much room to say no. And I really don't mind, except that I have a feeling it's going to be an opportunity to put me in my place."

"A woman's place is on a horse," Erin commented.

Phoebe sighed. "I wish that's where I could be tonight."

Instead, she spent quite a lot of time in the bathroom after work, twisting her hair into a smooth chignon, cleaning her face and reapplying all her makeup. She wore one of her favorite dresses, a high-waisted black floral print in soft cotton, with long sleeves and a hem that nearly reached the floor. A silver and black crystal necklace filled in above the neckline, and she wore dangling earrings to match. The ensemble gave her confidence.

Until, that is, Cynthia DeVries opened the door to her home and Phoebe got a glimpse of the women inside. There appeared to be a uniform dress code—khaki slacks or skirt, oxford-cloth shirt or a knit sweater set, and some kind of leather slide shoe on feet obviously tanned at the beach. Gold jewelry and diamonds glinted in ears, on fingers, at the base of the throat. Hair was shoulder length at the longest, shiny and dark or expertly tinted in shades of honey, gold and silver. Phoebe suddenly felt like a country mouse—completely out of her element, a sensation she hadn't experienced since she left Atlanta.

She took a deep breath as she crossed the threshold. What a long evening this would be.

Fortunately, there were friendly faces in the crowd. Across the living room, Kate Bowdrey stood with her sister Mary Rose Mitchell and Kate's soon-to-be grandmother-in-law, Miss Daisy Crawford. Grateful that someone else had claimed Cynthia DeVries's attention, Phoebe made her way to her friends.

"I'm so glad to see you." She hugged Kate and gave the other two women a smile. "But don't you have a million things to do before the wedding?"

"A million and one," Mary Rose confirmed. "But Dixon mentioned you would be here, and so we thought we'd make sure you had moral support."

"Dixon?" Which meant Adam had asked him to send in reinforcements. Thoughtful, but…a bit managerial. "Well, I'm glad to see you all. How are you, Miss Daisy?"

"Never better. I'm so thrilled about this wedding I can hardly sleep." She put an arm around Kate's waist and squeezed. "I lost my daughter so many years ago, and now I've finally got another one. And grandchildren, to boot."

They were chatting about the wedding details, enjoying the punch and cookies in the dining room, when one of the uniformed women joined them. "Well, hello there, Kate. Mary Rose. And Miss Daisy—what a pleasure to see you." She leaned down to place a kiss on both of the older woman's smooth cheeks. Then she turned to Phoebe. "I don't believe we've met. I'm Jessica Hyde. My husband is the district attorney."

Phoebe shook the perfectly manicured hand offered her. "I'm Phoebe Moss."

"Adam DeVries's fiancée?"

Strange as it seemed. "Yes, that's right."

Jessica gave her a long look up and down. "How nice. Miss Cynthia dragged you into her fundraising frenzy, did she?"

"I thought a dance under the stars sounded like fun. And it's a good cause."

"Of course." Jessica turned her head as if she'd accomplished her business and had no reason to stay. "Thanks to all of you for coming." Turning on one stacked, Brazilian leather heel, she drifted across the room and joined another group of similarly groomed women.

Mary Rose muttered an unkind word under her breath. "That woman should be taken down a peg or two."

"When Adam wins, she will be," Kate said optimistically. "I imagine Jimmy Hyde will have a hard time getting his way with Adam as mayor."

"Next election, we'll get somebody honest to run against Jimmy for D.A." Miss Daisy's blue eyes narrowed in concentration.

"Who would take on Jimmy Hyde?" Mary Rose asked. "He'll be tough to beat."

"Well, Adam can't be the last honest man in New Skye," Dixon's grandmother insisted. "So we'll just have to find someone else. Maybe I'll talk Dixon into running for office."

"Oh, my stars." Kate gasped with laughter. "I can see his reaction now!"

"He's not a lawyer," Mary Rose reminded them. "You need a lawyer for D.A."

"Ladies, ladies, take your seats, please." Cynthia DeVries stood in front of the marble-faced fireplace. "We must begin our business meeting."

The committees for the fundraiser had already been

established, and each chairperson stood to make a report. Jessica Hyde headed up the decoration committee. Kate and Mary Rose were working on invitations, while Miss Daisy solicited sponsorships from area businesses. Entertainment, Parking, CleanUp and a number of other divisions of labor discussed plans and progress. Once they'd all finished, Cynthia glanced in Phoebe's direction.

"We have someone new joining us tonight. As most of you are probably aware, my son Adam has recently become engaged to a nice young woman, Phoebe Moss. Phoebe is a speech therapist who has only lived in New Skye for a year, but she says she is willing and able to participate with us in this worthy cause. Stand up, Phoebe."

In the midst of a sea of casual sophistication, Phoebe got to her feet, certain she looked like a drab milkmaid.

"I know there are several committees who could use another member to get their work accomplished. Phoebe, do you have a preference? Is there one committee you would be particularly interested in helping?"

How kind, to make her choose in front of everyone concerned. She would have loved to play it safe, stay with Kate and Mary Rose, whom she knew. But that wasn't the point here. Getting to know people, serving the community, meant branching out and trying new things.

"I don't have a preference," she said honestly. "I'll be glad to help wherever I'm needed."

"Aha." Cynthia looked down at the agenda in her hand, which listed each committee in the order their reports were made. "In that case, perhaps you'd like to work on the committee responsible for running the raffle that will take place during the dance."

"That's just fine," Phoebe said. A raffle wouldn't demand too much attention except on the night of the event.

"And the head of that committee is…" Cynthia checked her list, looked up and smiled. "Why, Kellie Tate, of course. Our illustrious mayor's wife."

CHAPTER NINE

KELLIE TATE, ONE OF THE honey blondes seated across the room, lifted her chin and met Phoebe's stare. "Welcome to the Raffle Committee. Give me your phone number and I'll let you know when we have our next meeting."

"Thanks." Knees shaking, Phoebe sank back into her chair. She couldn't imagine what Cynthia hoped to gain from forcing her to work with the mayor's wife. But her only recourse was a pleasant smile and a stiff upper lip, though Phoebe wasn't sure she could manage both at the same time.

The meeting ended with Cynthia's invitation to enjoy refreshments and "socialize." Phoebe started calculating how soon she could sneak out.

"That's a dirty hit, if ever I saw one." Mary Rose hitched her chair closer to Phoebe's. "Working with you isn't going to make Kellie happy. What's the point?"

Kate put her hands on Phoebe's shoulders. "Maybe she knows Phoebe doesn't have a lot of free time, and the Raffle Committee has the least to do before the actual night of the dance."

Mary Rose lifted an eyebrow. "Do you have a bitchy bone in your body, sister dear?"

Miss Daisy laughed. "No, she doesn't. I'd say Cynthia saw the Raffle Committee as a chance to…oh, what do they call it in politics?…marginalize Phoebe. Keep her out of the way.''

And that was the most insulting possibility of all. Phoebe got to her feet. "I refuse to be marginalized. I'm going in there and make my mark on this soiree.''

"We're right behind you.'' Mary Rose pumped her fist in the air. "You go, girl.''

Surrounded by clusters of chattering women, the dining room table offered a bounty of finger foods, savory and sweet. Phoebe selected a plate of goodies she didn't intend to eat and looked around to determine which group she would conquer first.

She chose the nearest and stepped close, positioning herself between and just behind two women. "Lisa sold the shop on the Hill and moved down to Main Street,'' the woman to her left said. "I still go to her because she does color better than anybody else in town. But I can tell you I'm not happy sitting in that big picture window with my hair spiked in foil and all of Main Street looking on.''

The group laughed and nodded. "Have you suggested a curtain? Or blinds?''

"Of course, but Lisa insists it's good for business to have people see her at work. I told her, 'It might be good for your business, honey, but it's hell on my marriage. You think I want my husband to know this color isn't real?'''

When Phoebe chuckled along with the group, the speaker looked back over her shoulder. "Are we in your way?'' Before Phoebe could answer, the huddle broke apart and reformed farther along the room, leaving her standing quite awkwardly by herself.

The second group she approached represented a slightly older population. A woman across from Phoebe was relaying the latest news. "He started up an affair with the church organist. She had a husband and three children of her own, but here she is, meeting the pastor late at night in a restaurant out of town."

"And now he's left the church without a preacher or an organist," said another, "and his children without a daddy and it's just the biggest mess."

Phoebe listened for a while as the saga was expanded and commented on, but none of the group acknowledged her presence and she didn't have any fascinating gossip with which to break into the story...unless she told them about the mayoral candidate's counterfeit fiancé. That would probably draw a great deal of attention.

She looked around the room, assessing other possibilities. Kellie Tate stood in the center of a small circle, and the glances cast Phoebe's way over the last few minutes suggested that she was more important to them as a topic than as a participant. Kate and Mary Rose had been cornered by Adam's mother. Miss Daisy sat by herself in the living room with a cup of punch for company. Sometimes, the best way was the easy way out.

Sinking down into the chair by the older woman, Phoebe sighed. "You have the right idea, Miss Daisy."

"Of course. I've been to so many of these over the years, I could probably tell you what they're all talking about."

"Besides me, you mean?"

Daisy put her hand over Phoebe's. "Have they been cruel?"

"Oh...no. Just exclusive."

"These younger women are so ill-behaved." She clucked her tongue. "I tell you what—I'm having a tea for Kate and a few of my friends Thursday afternoon. I want you to come. I'm staying with LuAnn Taylor while my house is being renovated, so we'll be holding our little celebration there."

"That sounds lovely, Miss Daisy, but you don't have to feel sorry for me."

"I don't. I feel sorry for these young hussies who are going to regret snubbing you when you're the wife of our mayor. And I'm going to introduce you to some people who have a lot more courage and courtesy, and a lot more leverage when it comes to affairs in this town. You'll get the last laugh. I promise."

Phoebe couldn't help being enticed by the prospect of winning in the end. But she was only pretending to be Adam's fiancée, deceiving Miss Daisy as well as her friends and the voting public. The whole situation was becoming too complicated to sustain without a slip-up. Could they really expect to keep the masquerade going for the eight weeks between now and the election?

And after all that time spent in Adam's company, could she once again be satisfied without him in her life?

SAM LET THE DUST FROM the Sunday engagement article settle for a week before she called Adam DeVries's mother to arrange an interview. Cynthia DeVries met her at the front door on Wednesday morning and invited her into the living room.

"Please, sit down. Would you like coffee?" A silver service on a silver tray occupied the table in front of the gold brocade sofa.

"No, thank you." The elegant room looked like a photograph from a museum catalog. Sam had toned downed the vamp look, but she still felt out of place. "Thank you for agreeing to meet with me, Mrs. DeVries."

"Of course. I'm glad to get the opportunity to publicize our Stargazer Fundraiser."

As Sam tried to remember what the hell her hostess was talking about, footsteps descended the stairway out in the hall. Shrugging into his coat, Preston DeVries came into the room. "I'm out of here." He bent and gave his wife a sweet kiss on the mouth. "Have a good day."

She touched his cheek. "Thanks, darling. Before you go, Preston, this is Samantha Pettit from the *New Skye News*. She's doing an article on the Stargazer Fund-raiser."

Dr. DeVries gave her a smile. "That's great. Should be a fun evening." With quick strides, he crossed to the front door and left the house.

"I've prepared an information sheet about the fund-raiser." Cynthia offered a folder that Sam had no choice but to take. "I hope that will help you with your article."

"Um…sure. But, Mrs. DeVries, the real purpose of the interview—"

"Is to talk about my son Adam and his campaign for mayor." She nodded. "Of course. But I thought that you would also be able to run a feature on the gardens and the dinner dance. Not at the same time, of course, but in the near future. We certainly can use all the publicity we can get."

"I understand." And she did. If Sam agreed to write up the fundraiser, Mrs. DeVries would agree to be candid about the candidate. If not… "I'm sure an article on the Stargazer Fundraiser will be a great addition to the paper. I'll talk to my editor about scheduling when I go back to the office this morning."

"That's lovely." Cynthia stirred her coffee and took a delicate sip. "Now, what did you want to ask me about Adam?"

An hour later, Sam had almost more facts than she knew what to do with—his grades, "average," his dating history, "minimal," his college years, "uneventful." She had the family perspective on his run for mayor, "quixotic, at best" and "foolishly unnecessary." As for Phoebe Moss...

"I'm not certain about their relationship," Cynthia confessed. "We had never heard of her until your article in the paper. She came to dinner on Sunday and she seemed like a nice-enough young woman." Her shrug expressed doubt. "I didn't feel quite comfortable about her, if you know what I mean. She says she's from Atlanta, but who knows, really? I'm concerned that Adam may have gotten involved with someone he doesn't really know, and shouldn't trust, but will he listen? I'm afraid I don't have the influence with him I once did. And the suddenness of it all...what does that mean? Is there something disreputable going on?"

Cynthia DeVries looked the picture of bewildered motherhood. Sam took down the quotes, shoving to the back of her mind her distaste for the woman across the table. She had the feeling she was being used as a weapon against Cynthia's son. And while she wanted the facts, she didn't intend to be anybody's tool.

She folded her notebook. "Well, that covers all my questions. I really appreciate your time and your candor."

Cynthia stood as Sam did. "I regret being at such odds with my son's purpose, of course. I did my best to talk him out of this doomed effort. But if he's being honest, then I must be as well."

"I'm sure." Sam escaped from the elegant, immaculate house, feeling as if she wanted to rush home and jump into the shower. Though she'd committed herself to the investigation of Adam DeVries, she'd never expected his mother to be such a...a rat.

The questions about Phoebe Moss were interesting, though. And Sam knew one sure way to answer them. Instead of a shower, she went straight to the office and knocked on her editor's door. "I need to take a trip out of town. This week or next, at the latest."

Laura Custer stared at her over the tops of her glasses. "Just like that?"

"Yeah."

"What story?"

"DeVries."

"DeVries lives, works and runs for office here."

"But his fiancée came from Hot 'Lanta. And I've got a gut feeling there's more to her than meets the eye. The only way I'm gonna find out is to dig on-site."

"Reporters and their gut feelings. Give me just one who operates on logic and reasoned argument—a breath of fresh air." Laura drew a deep breath and let it out again. "Why do you need to investigate Phoebe Moss? She's peripheral to the campaign. DeVries is the one running for mayor."

"You assigned me a piece on Kellie Tate, and a companion on Ms. Moss."

"Yeah, the usual fluff stuff. Can't you just interview the subject?"

"Will she tell me the truth?"

"Why would she lie?"

"Because the truth would hurt the campaign."

"You're making assumptions."

"So let me go to Atlanta for the facts."

Laura sighed. "Two days. After that, expenses are on you."

"Thanks."

Sam went to her desk and flipped through the Stargazer information with her mind already halfway to Atlanta.

Two days and an expense account. What couldn't she find out about Phoebe Moss in two whole days?

IN THE MIDST OF THE campaign madness, Adam looked forward to his therapy appointments with Phoebe, since that was the only time these days they could be together without a crowd of people looking on. She kept the sessions focused on work, but that work included the chance to talk with her, to catch her sweet smile, to enjoy the relaxation being with her created inside of him.

The third week of September, he canceled his Tuesday appointment because of a campaign event Tommy scheduled without consulting him. Thursday started out with a problem at one of his construction sites and went downhill from there. By one o'clock, when he was due at Phoebe's, he was several hours behind on his schedule for the day with no hope of catching up.

He stopped at her office to apologize. "I c-can't b-believe the way this week has g-gone. Every time I turn around, s-s-some new d-disas-ster cr-crops up."

"Do you have minute to sit down, have a cup of coffee?"

"I really d-don't." He allowed himself the pleasure of stroking her cheek with his fingertips. "How's your week b-been?"

"Okay. I'm going to a tea this afternoon for Kate. At Miss LuAnn Taylor's house. That's pretty exciting."

"It's a terrific old house, always taken c-c-care of. The Taylors are p-powerful in this town. I'm glad to have them as supporters."

Her brows drew together and she turned her gaze away from his. "I can imagine."

He had the feeling he'd said something wrong. "What is it?"

"Nothing." She slipped away from him, barricaded herself behind her desk. "Do you want to reschedule an appointment for next week?"

"I don't think I can...seems like Tommy's got every minute booked, even the ones I don't have to spare."

"Well, then." She fiddled with a pencil for a few seconds, then looked at him. "I guess I'll see you at the wedding on Saturday?"

"You're going to let me pick you up this time, right?"

Again she hesitated, but finally nodded. "Sure. That would be fine."

With the distance she'd put between them, Adam didn't try for a kiss. On his way out, he remembered he'd meant to ask her about the fundraiser meeting. He turned back to Phoebe. "How was the meeting Monday night at my mother's?"

She didn't smile, as he'd thought she would. "Enlightening."

"What does that mean?" He took a couple of steps back into the room, toward her desk.

But someone knocked at the door. "Phoebe? Can I interrupt?"

"Come in, Jenna." The relief in her eyes made plain the fact that she didn't want to deal with the issue. Considering Phoebe's direct approach, that gave him an idea of just how bad things had been.

"We'll talk about this," Adam promised her as Jenna came in behind him. "I want to know what happened."

If his mother had been anything but kind to Phoebe, he was going to raise hell. She would not be allowed to sabotage their engagement. The success of the campaign depended on his relationship with this intelligent, compassionate woman.

Almost as much as he did, himself.

THE MAYOR OF NEW SKYE waited on Cynthia DeVries, not the other way around. Curtis Tate hadn't become a successful businessman and politician without understanding exactly how important the support of the community could be. Especially the wealthy members of the community.

"Mr. Tate, please come in."

"Be glad to, Mrs. DeVries. Do you suppose this weather is ever going to break? We're about due for cooler temperatures, I'm thinking."

"Yes, indeed." She showed him into the living room. "Have a seat."

"Yes, ma'am." He chose an armchair, and she faced him from the mat across the fireplace. "You had something you wanted to talk to me about?"

"Your wife mentioned the possibility that the city could provide matching funds for the money we raise at the Stargazer Fundraiser."

"Yes, ma'am, she talked over the idea with me. And I told her I thought that might be a possibility."

"You don't sound very sure."

He shrugged his thin shoulders. "Something like that will take a little juggling, a little smooth talking, you know what I mean. There's never a guarantee when you have to deal with the bureaucracy."

"I would like a guarantee."

"Ma'am?"

She slipped a folded piece of paper out of her skirt pocket and smoothed it into the shape of a check. "I thought this might…secure…me that guarantee." Holding the check between two fingers, she offered it to Curtis Tate.

The mayor looked at the sum, and then at Cynthia. "That's…that's very generous of you, Mrs. DeVries."

"And do I have my matching funds?"

"Oh, yes, ma'am. I can definitely promise that the city will match you dollar for dollar. Your Stargazer Fundraiser is guaranteed to be a huge success!"

FRIDAY BROUGHT RAIN showers and a weather front that blew through quickly, cutting the humidity and settling the dust on the roads. Saturday dawned with a soft blue sky and high white clouds, gentle autumn sunshine and a playful breeze. Kate and Dixon's wedding day would be perfect.

Phoebe's replacement windows had been delivered late Friday afternoon and sat stacked against the house, waiting to be installed. She'd thought she could handle the job herself—a little slower than a team of men, maybe, but she looked forward to the sense of accomplishment she would gain from putting in her own windows.

Then she actually tackled the job. Even the smaller windows were almost more than she could lift. The downside, she supposed, of choosing quality. Hoisting, balancing, shimming, hammering...the cool day turned hot and sweaty as Phoebe struggled with the work.

At noon she gave up and, with one window installed, went inside to clean up. Just as Phoebe was putting on her earrings, she heard Adam's truck rumble up the drive. Her heart started beating harder, faster, and she gave herself a stern look in the mirror. She couldn't afford to get excited about seeing Adam. He didn't like dogs. And he was running for mayor—two big reasons this engagement of theirs would remain strictly in the "let's pretend" category.

As he got out of the truck, she locked Lance, Gawain and Gally in the kitchen. Armed with her new purse to go with her new suit and shoes, she met Adam at the door to the porch.

Proving himself a typical male, he noticed the new windows first. "When will they be installed?"

"I got one in today," she said with pride, and walked him around to the bathroom window. "Looks good, if I do say so myself."

Hands in the pockets of his suit slacks, he surveyed her work, so intensely that she began to wonder what he was thinking. "Is something wrong?"

"You did this by yourself."

"Yes."

"And you're planning on doing all the others."

"Um, yes."

"Phoebe, what am I going to do with you?" He stared at her with exasperation in his face. "Are you crazy?"

She straightened her back. "I don't understand your point."

"You can't do this job by yourself. I couldn't do this job by myself. It takes two guys to put in one window with any kind of efficiency. You're not going to be able to lift half of those units you've ordered, and I'm willing to bet you'd end up with half of the frames you take out falling before you get them to the ground. You'd be lucky not to get hurt in the process." He shook his head. "Why didn't you have them installed?"

"Because the installation time was eight weeks."

"Then why didn't you ask for help?"

"Ask who?"

"Me, for God's sake. How do you think I make my living?"

She turned away from him and walked toward the truck. "I'm not used to asking for help. I handle my life by myself."

He caught up with her and put a hand on her shoulder, bringing her around to face him again. "But sometimes you have to get somebody to lend a hand. Why not me?"

"Because…" She didn't have an answer she could verbalize. Telling Adam she didn't want to impose on him would not, she was sure, go over well.

But it seemed she didn't need to say the words. "I came to you for help, and you've made a big difference in my life. Now we're engaged, and it seems like you should be able to ask me for some assistance now and then."

"We are not engaged." To her horror, she practically shouted at him. "We are pretending to be engaged. There's a big, big difference, Adam. And it's a difference that means I can't just run to you with every little problem on my plate."

"Is that so?" He looked shocked and angry at her protest. Then he glanced at his watch. "I guess we can argue about this on the way to town, or be late for the wedding. It's up to you."

Without a word, Phoebe went to climb into the truck— a tricky accomplishment, since the skirt of her suit was narrow and short and didn't allow much freedom of movement. She made it, though, and sat quietly as Adam headed down the drive. When they reached the gate, she felt for the door handle.

"I'll get it," he said quietly. And this time she didn't argue with him.

They didn't argue on the way into town; they didn't talk at all. At the church, Adam came around and opened her door and helped her step down to the pavement. He'd put on his jacket, and she couldn't help admiring the elegant picture he made in a dark gray suit and white shirt with a deep purple tie. Her raw-silk suit was a shade similar to his tie, with a short jacket over a camisole in dull gold. She wore a gold choker necklace and big gold ball earrings, and could only hope she did him justice. Appearances seemed to matter more and more these days.

During the wedding, though, she realized that appearances mattered not at all when two people loved each other as much as Kate and Dixon did. They had invited only close friends and family to the ceremony, but the church was still quite full. Kate's daughter, Kelsey, joined Mary Rose as a bridal attendant, and Dixon had asked Trace, Kate's son, to stand beside him, along with Kelsey's boyfriend, Sal Torres. When the bride and groom kissed, there was a moment of breathless silence and a sense of blessing in the air...broken by several heartfelt sniffs and someone's sob of joy.

The reception afterward took place in Miss LuAnn Taylor's garden, famous in several states for the beauty of its design. Today, gold and white chrysanthemums decked the flower beds, graced the white-draped tables, edged the terrace and the dance floor. All the trees and shrubs were still in full leaf, creating a bower of shifting sunlight and shadow for guests to enjoy as they waited to greet the bride and groom.

Tommy cornered Adam and Phoebe as soon as they came through the gate. "Hey, man," he said, with a nod and a grin for Phoebe. "Just wanted to warn you that the paper is here. You two need to look like a pair of lovebirds contemplating their own blissful future. And any contacts you can make with the high and mighty will be a bonus. I'd say most of the New Skye elite is here this afternoon. Even the mayor and his wife. Minus LaRue, of course."

Adam shook his head. "This isn't the campaign, Crawford. We're celebrating a friend's marriage."

"Yeah, yeah, but you gotta make good use of your time." He hurried off, presumably to do just that.

Phoebe sighed. "Does he ever stop calculating?"

"Not s-since I've known him. Tommy's family has a tendency to lose m-money f-f-faster than they earn it. The C-Crawfords go back a long ways in New Skye, but they're always on the edge of d-d-disaster. His dad came up with one g-great scheme after another for making a mi-million while we were g-growing up and all of them f-fell through, while his m-mom worked as a sc-school-teacher, keeping the three of them f-fed. Tommy's decided on a different approach—a s-s-solid insurance business and as much p-political cl-clout as he can pull in. I'm just the hook for the big fish."

A wave of applause moved across the crowd as Dixon and Kate appeared on the terrace. "They're so terribly happy," Phoebe said, almost to herself.

"It's enough to make you b-b-believe in true l-love and f-forever after," Adam replied quietly.

She looked up at him, searching his eyes. "Is it?"

In the next instant, light exploded all around them. "Good shot," the redheaded photographer commented. "Thanks, Mr. DeVries, Ms. Moss."

So much for the moment. Adam offered her his arm. "Would you like something to drink?"

The band struck up, and the party got under way. Guests clustered around the food tables, lavishly stocked by New Skye's premier caterer, Sugar and Spice, Inc. The owner and chief cook, Cass Baker, handed Phoebe and Adam bite-size crab quiches to sample. "I don't tell Ian what's in them," she confided, referring to her husband, a heart surgeon. "He'd have them slapped with a warning label—Dangerous to Your Health."

Ian appeared at her side. "Not at all, beautiful. I'm a

walking advertisement for just how healthy your cooking really is.'' He leaned in to give his wife a kiss.

"Not to mention delicious," Phoebe added. "I understand you'll be doing the food for the Stargazer Fundraiser."

Cass nodded. "Should be lots of fun. I'm working on pastries and cakes with star shapes and star decorations, plus flowers. Will you be there?"

Adam put his hand on Phoebe's elbow. "We b-both will. Which means we'd b-b-etter get in some pr-practice on the d-dance f-floor. Phoebe?"

She really hadn't expected to dance with him. But she couldn't say no. "See you later, Cass."

Stepping into Adam's arms on the dance floor was like stepping off a high dive, terrifying, exhilarating and totally insane. He held her in the old-fashioned way, right hand to left, his arm around her waist, but not formally. Not at all formally. Their bodies touched from breast to knee, far more intimately than ever before. The band played a jazzy version of "It Had to Be You," and each move they made, every step they took, generated friction. Heat. When she glanced up, Adam's firm chin was inches above her, his subtly scented skin all too tempting to her lips. Then he looked down, and their mouths connected without a second's pause.

No camera flash stopped the kiss, but a simple realization that the desire they were generating could not be fulfilled on the dance floor. Adam lifted his head, eased a little space between his body and Phoebe's and worked on getting control of his breath. "You p-pack quite a p-punch," he murmured against the top of her head.

"It's the atmosphere." He could feel her hand trembling in his. "An overload of romance."

The song came to an end and he slowed their dance

to a stop, but didn't let her go right away. "D-d-don't think so."

Before she could respond, they were jostled apart by the movement of the crowd. Then Dixon and Kate cut the wedding cake and handed out the pieces. The reception took on a livelier tone, and the dances were faster, more upbeat. Every few seconds, a hand slapped Adam on the back and someone stepped up to quiz him about the campaign. Phoebe drifted away—he caught glimpses of her talking to Mary Rose and Pete Mitchell, to Abby and Charlie Brannon, to Trace LaRue and Erin Archer. And then, with a sinking stomach, he saw her standing with Samantha Pettit.

He couldn't get over there to monitor the conversation. Tommy, he saw, was deep in discussion with the principal of the high school, Harrison Floyd, who had been a Tate supporter in the past but, just lately, was indicating a possible switch to Adam's side.

So Phoebe was on her own with the shark reporter. He regretted leaving her open to attack, hoped she could handle the pressure. What disaster awaited them, after this development, he could only wait and see.

Meanwhile, he turned from the latest backslapper and came face-to-face with his own disaster. "Hello, M-Mother." He kissed her cheek, shook his dad's hand. "G-good to see you. N-nice wedding, isn't it?"

Cynthia looked around with approval. "Very. The Bowdreys have always known how to do things properly. Where is your fiancée?"

Adam unclenched his jaw. "We agreed to m-mingle some. I'm n-not sure exactly where she got to."

"Ah…over there, talking to the young woman with no sense of decorum, at least when it comes to dress."

He pretended to look, though the description couldn't

have identified the reporter any more clearly. Samantha Pettit's spiked hair, red nails and black leather suit did stand out in the conservative crowd.

"Phoebe, on the other hand, l-looks g-great, as usual. Speaking of which..." He turned back to his mother. "What happened at your m-meeting M-Monday n-night?"

"Nothing out of the ordinary. Why?"

"I think things d-didn't g-go well for Phoebe."

"She said that?"

"N-no. 'Enlightening' was the word she used."

"That sounds like a good thing, to me."

"Unless it m-means that you and your f-friends took it upon themselves to d-demonstrate to Phoebe just how much of an outsider she is and how you d-don't intend to let her into your t-tight little circle."

His dad took a step forward. "I think you do your mother a great disservice, son."

But Cynthia was gazing at him with narrowed eyes. "I beg your pardon?"

"You should." He ignored her gasp. "I'm warning you, M-Mother, you're p-pushing me. H-hard. If you d-don't treat Phoebe with the respect she d-deserves as my fiancée, I'll have to choose sides. And the side I choose will be hers. Are you ready to br-break up the f-family over this?"

His mother stared at him for a long silent moment. "As far as I'm concerned," she said stiffly, "you already have."

CHAPTER TEN

KATÉ AND DIXON SLIPPED out of their wedding reception and were on their way before most of the crowd missed them. The cry went up as the limousine left the curb in front of Miss Taylor's house, but Phoebe decided against running in high heels to catch a last glimpse. Samantha Pettit, wearing boots that matched her leather suit, dashed off with the rest of the party, leaving Phoebe, mercifully, alone.

For a moment. Jessica Hyde joined her in watching the hunt. "I think they should have at least let us see them off. It's not very polite to just run away."

"They've waited a long time to be together. I imagine they're anxious to start their new life."

Jessica's mouth tilted up in a smile, but her eyes stayed cold. "And are you and Adam anxious to start your new life?"

Phoebe had been prepared for this question. "Of course. But the campaign has to come first."

"Will you be getting married right away, regardless of whether he wins or loses?"

"Um…I'm not sure." She wasn't so prepared for that question. "Everything's happened so fast, we haven't made any decisions."

"I can imagine. No one even knew Adam was dating, and the next thing we hear, he's running for mayor and engaged to be married. Quite a surprise."

"Well, I knew." Abby Brannon joined them, putting an arm around Phoebe's waist. "They've been in the diner often enough this summer. I always figured when Adam met the woman for him, he wouldn't waste any time."

Jessica surveyed them both with suspicion. "Funny, I never had that impression. And you don't have a ring yet?"

Until that moment, the thought hadn't occurred to Phoebe. "We—"

"Adam told me he wanted to go to New York for a ring," Abby volunteered. "And that'll have to wait until after the election, too. But you just can't find great jewelry in New Skye, he said."

"Oh, really?" Jessica's mouth pursed as if she'd eaten a rotten lemon. "If you'll excuse me, I think I'll go get a refill on champagne."

Abby chuckled as the willowy blonde left them behind. "Snake in the grass."

Phoebe gave her a hug. "Thanks for the rescue."

"Just call me the Lone Ranger. And my reward," she said as Adam came up, "is a dance with your fiancé. No protests allowed."

"N-not a p-peep." He grinned at Phoebe over his shoulder. "I'll b-be b-back."

She toasted him with her wineglass, then watched as he and Abby came together with the beat of the music. Was she imagining the distance between their bodies, the casual nature of their embrace? Was it really different for Adam, holding *her?* What did that difference mean?

The guests continued to mingle for quite some time after the bride and groom had left. As the twilight deepened, fairy lights came on in the trees of the garden and candles appeared on the tables, along with more food and champagne. Phoebe danced with Adam several times, though without the intensity of that first encounter. She also danced with Pete Mitchell, Mary Rose's husband, and Judge Taylor, Miss LuAnn's brother. Even Tommy gave her a waltz, though she thought his mind was on Samantha Pettit, dancing with Tim DeVries. His eyes certainly were.

But at last the band played a final number and people began to leave. Phoebe had given up on dancing and joined Theresa on the terrace, where both of them put their sore feet up on a chair.

Adam came up from the lawn. "Why women d-don't wear c-comfortable shoes is b-beyond me."

"Why do men wear ties?" Theresa sat up and slipped into her heels with a groan.

"B-because women f-force them to, of c-course."

Phoebe smiled. "There you go."

"You're saying men f-force women to wear high heels?"

"Exactly." She, too, got to her feet, wincing. "If men didn't prefer women in high heels, the whole industry would collapse in a matter of days."

"We can only hope." Theresa drifted toward the garden gate, limping a little. "'Night, Phoebe. 'Night, brother of mine."

In the truck on the way out to her house, Adam didn't have much to say. Phoebe allowed the silence to lengthen undisturbed for a time, but she could feel his frustration growing with every mile.

"Did something happen during the reception?" she said at last. "Are you okay?"

His right fist bounced off the steering wheel. "I g-guess I'm not too g-good at c-camouflaging m-my m-m-moods. With you, anyway."

"You don't have to."

He blew out a long breath. "As you m-might imagine, I had a run-in with m-my p-parents."

"About the campaign?"

"N-not exactly. I asked about that m-meeting last M-Monday."

"You didn't fight with them over me, did you?"

"I told m-my m-mother she had to show the respect you d-deserved or else she would force m-me into a choice that c-could break up the family. And she said I already had. End of argument."

"Adam, you shouldn't have chosen me over them. You know this isn't a real engagement. But they don't."

"I'm not sure I do, either." With that statement, he stopped the truck at the gate, took her key and released the lock, then got back in to drive down the lane. At the house, he stopped the engine and made a motion for her to stay where she was. "Let me look around, first."

In a few minutes, he opened her door. "Everything's okay."

During those minutes, her mind had tried and failed to grapple with what he'd said. Without speaking, she went through the screened porch and opened the door to the house, with Adam following. When she turned on the light, the dogs came bounding in from the bedroom. Their screeching halt, at the sight of Adam in the kitchen, was almost comical.

Almost.

"Come on, guys, outside." She led them out, and they slipped by the man at the counter as if they were pretending to be shadows, hoping to remain unnoticed. Once in the yard, they resumed their usual frolicsome behavior.

Phoebe went back to the kitchen. "Would you like some coffee for the drive back?"

"No, thanks. I'm fine." He stroked his finger down the edge of the plaque he'd been examining, a folk-art angel in red and green with the legend Friends Are Our Guardian Angels.

"Jacquie Archer gave me that as a housewarming present."

Adam nodded, smiling slightly. "She's a g-good friend, herself." He jammed his fists into his pockets. "So, if it's okay with you, I'll show up with a couple of guys tomorrow morning, and we'll get these windows put in for you."

She whirled to face him. "What?"

"I know two or three men on my c-c-crew who c-could use the extra work." He spoke slowly, as if she hadn't understood him the first time. "We'll b-be out about nine and g-get s-started on the windows."

Phoebe wanted to argue. But the project was beyond her, and she really did need the windows for safety. So she conceded quickly. "If you come at eight-thirty, I'll have breakfast ready."

That grin of his really was special. "D-deal. S-see you then." Without so much as a peck on the cheek, he was out the door and down the drive. She knew he would lock the gate, without her having to ask.

What she didn't know was what he'd meant when he'd said, "I'm not sure I do, either."

And she didn't know how long she could wait to find out.

TOMMY HUNG AROUND at the end of the wedding reception, lending a hand when needed, keeping an eye on Tim DeVries and Sam Pettit as they sat on Miss Taylor's terrace. Seemed like they'd been talking for hours, and would be there when the sun came up, still talking. What could they have to say that kept them absorbed in each other like a couple of teenagers?

He decided he didn't want the answer to that question. And he decided that if he didn't leave soon, Miss Taylor would be asking him in for hot milk and cookies before bed. Damn Sam Pettit, anyway. She was more annoyance than she was worth.

Dixon and Kate had provided valet parking, but Tommy just asked the kid for his keys and a general idea of where the Lexus had gone, then set out on foot to find his car. The night was cool, the moon full, the neighborhood about as safe as they came these days. Who needed a valet?

When he heard footsteps on the asphalt behind him, he began to wonder about that judgment. A glance over his shoulder, however, showed him that being mugged by a stranger might have been the better choice.

He did an about-face, now walking backward. "Following me, Ms. Pettit?"

"Just going to my car."

"The good doctor wouldn't take you home?"

"I didn't need a ride." She caught up with him and would have passed by, but he pivoted and picked up his pace.

"How's the news business?"

"Busy, like always. How's the campaign business?"

"Looking better all the time. Especially since you haven't torpedoed my candidate's reputation or lifestyle for almost a whole week now. Should I be expecting a nasty surprise in tomorrow's paper?"

She glanced at him. "No. Not a thing."

Her lack of humor worried him. "Monday?"

"Give me a break. I'm not going to let you in on all my upcoming articles."

"Why don't you give *me* a break? Or, better yet, Adam DeVries? The least you could do is warn us in advance when something's about to hit the fan." Coming to a stop, he caught her arm and turned her to face him. "What d'you say, Sam? A day or two's notice before you drop another bombshell?"

Moonlight poured over her face, turning her skin white, her hair and eyes and reddened lips black. She looked tired, he thought.

Not too tired for sass. "So you can censor me? Forgetting about freedom of the press?"

"Life, liberty and the pursuit of happiness. The good doctor makes you happy, does he?"

"Jealous, Tommy?"

The truth slipped out. "Yeah."

Those big dark eyes closed for a long moment. "Turns out my college roommate went to medical school at Duke with Tim. They lived together for a couple of years, and then broke up. He's not over her, whatever he thinks. So I listened to him rant and rave and..." She shrugged. "Not exactly a torrid romance."

Relief washed through him. "You're looking for torrid romance?" Somehow, both of his hands were on her, holding her shoulders, his thumbs stroking leather-covered collarbones.

Her mouth curved in a half smile. "Torrid's nice, occasionally." Then she opened her eyes and looked at him again. "At this point, I'd settle for solid friendship."

"Sorry," Tommy said, stroking his hands down her back to her waist, pulling her closer. "We're way beyond friendship."

He bent his head—she really was short—and kissed her the way he'd wanted to. Like he would never, ever have to stop.

This, *this,* was what she wanted. Sam leaned into Tommy and let him have everything she could give. Not the angry kiss they'd shared before, but a deep, searching fusion of mouths that blended bodies and souls. She tried to tell him, with her sighs, with her lips, with her hands, all the yearning she'd never been able to share with words.

A car screeched to a halt beside them. Jeering, mocking teenagers hung out of every window. Tommy jerked Sam to stand behind him, just as a couple of beer cans, already shaken, launched in their direction and exploded at his feet. Leaving a trail of raucous laughter, the vehicle then roared farther down the street.

"Jeez." He stamped the flow of beer off his suit pants. "Boy Scouts, they aren't. Are you okay?"

"I think so. Leather's hard to hurt." But she was quivering with reaction, her teeth chattering in a completely unsophisticated way. What girl got the shakes just because she'd been kissed, and then rudely interrupted?

"Hey, it's okay." Tommy put his arm around her, pressed her head against his shoulder. "Just relax. Where's your car?"

"On down the street." He kept her close to his side as they walked, and the trembling subsided, though she still felt shell-shocked. Was this the beginning of what she'd dreamed about for more than a year?

With the door to the Mustang open, Tommy turned her so she stood within the car's protective shell. "You need to get home, get warm, get some sleep." He laid his hand along her jawline. "I'll give you a call late tomorrow."

"Sounds good." They shared a kiss—a promise, a temporary goodbye. As Tommy stepped back, Sam dropped into the driver's seat and fitted the key in the ignition.

"And, Sam..." He gave her a wink and a grin. "I'll be expecting a little advance notice from now on when it comes to political news, right?"

She sprang out of the car like a jack-in-the-box. "Is that what you're doing? You think you can seduce me into covering up for your candidate?"

"What the hell are you talking about?"

"Sweet talk and kisses and this protective macho stuff, and you think you've got the right to dictate what I report in the news? Well, let me tell you, jerk, I don't compromise my work for anybody."

"Sam, you're crazy."

"And I'll tell you something else—I'm headed for Atlanta Monday morning and I'm gonna be looking real hard into your future Mrs. Mayor's background. If there's something to find, I'll find it. And you can be damn sure I'll report it." She dropped back into the car, shoved the engine into gear and swerved out from between the two cars on either end. Ready to sprint, she rolled down her window. "Don't call me tomorrow. Or at all."

She heard his profane response as she took off down the street.

WHEN PHOEBE HEARD THE rumble of wheels on her drive at seven Sunday morning, she thought Adam had arrived extra early. Peering out the window, though, she recognized Jacquie Archer's truck, towing a horse trailer. Dragging on shorts and a T-shirt, Phoebe hurried outside, the dogs dancing in delight ahead of her.

Jacquie had her windows down in the cool morning. "Hey, Phoebe. Sorry to show up so early, but it's kinda an emergency."

"What's wrong?" A shrill neigh and the thud of

hooves against metal came from the trailer. "Who's back there?"

"Didn't you get my message?" The farrier, whose small size belied her great strength, dropped to the ground and led the way to the trailer door, where Erin joined them.

"I didn't even look at the machine last night. I'm sorry. What's going on?"

"I had a call on my machine when I got home from the wedding, an owner in a real panic. She returned from Europe last week after six months away, went to see her horse yesterday, and this is what she found." Jacquie and Erin pulled back the double doors on the trailer.

Phoebe stared at the wild-eyed stallion tied to the front of the trailer. His hipbones poked up under his coat, which was dull, dirty and scarred. Each individual rib was sharply visible, his overgrown hooves split and broken.

She blinked back tears. "Oh, my God. Where has this horse been?" Even as she spoke, the stallion kicked out at the wall again. He might be half starved, but he wasn't giving up.

"High-Tailin' It Farm."

"Ah." High-Tailin' It Farm had a bad reputation among responsible horse owners in the area. Burt Treble, the owner, spent more time at the local bars than at the barn. His training methods were harsh, sometimes violent—rumor said he'd ridden or beaten a couple of horses to death. Troublesome animals always got the bad end of Burt's deal. Unless the owner kept a close eye on their horse, chances were good the animal would end up like this one, a victim of neglect.

"We woke up ol' Burt last night and made him give us the horse," Jacquie said. "I took him to my place and put him in a stall, where he proceeded to bounce off the walls for the rest of the night. But I've got pregnant mares in one pasture and a stallion in the other. So I'm hoping you can take this guy and rehabilitate him. The owner does care, but she's stationed in Germany with the army, so what's she going to do?''

''Of course I'll take him. No question. What's his name?''

''Samson.''

''Fits a big black son of a gun like him, doesn't it?'' To prove his worth, Samson took another shot at the trailer wall. ''Guess we'd better get him out of there.''

Samson wasn't interested in cooperating, and a half hour had passed before they coaxed him to set foot on solid ground again. His first instinct was to bolt, but Phoebe hung on to the lead rope with all her weight and managed to keep him more or less in one place. Staring up at a thousand pounds of angry, frightened horse was enough to set her life flashing before her eyes. But she kept her cool and, gradually, Samson regained a little of his, enough to walk sanely to the gate for the lower pasture. Erin released the chain lock and Phoebe led the horse through. Her knees were knocking—he could strike her down at any instant, and especially at the moment when she released the halter. She wished she'd put on a helmet. Too late now.

The stallion danced around her, surveying the field from every angle, eyes wide and wary, poor bedraggled tail thrashing from side to side. In the sunlight she could see his wounds, some horse-inflicted, some very definitely man-made. What she wouldn't give for the chance to treat Burt Treble the way he treated horses.

''Whoa, Samson. Whoa, boy.'' She spoke quietly, low

in her throat, trying for eye contact. "Nobody's gonna hurt you. It's okay. Whoa, boy. You're safe now."

With some more coaxing, Samson seemed to relax a bit. He slowed his feverish pacing, stood still for seconds at a time. Phoebe continued to croon, to hold his attention. If he trusted her, he might not try to kill her. This time, anyway.

Finally, he lowered his head and sniffed at the grass, full and thick after the recent rains. "Good boy, good boy." She placed her hand lightly on his shoulder, stroked softly. "That's it. Have some breakfast." He took several mouthfuls of rich grass and tore them off, then looked up and around as he chewed. Moving slowly, Phoebe stroked her hand up his neck to the buckle of the halter. Fingers trembling, breath stuck in her throat, she slipped the tongue out and let the restraint fall into her other hand. Eyes always on the horse, she backed away.

Samson finished his grass and realized, suddenly, that he was free. With another clarion cry, he exploded into action. Phoebe ran for the gate, but the horse galloped in the opposite direction, down the length of the pasture at full speed. Even in his emaciated state, it was an impressive sight. He came back as she shut the gate between them, kicking and bucking and tossing his head like a mustang on the plains. Down and back, down and back again…he couldn't seem to get enough air and space and freedom.

"Has he been out of a stall in the last six months?" Phoebe asked, catching her breath.

"Doesn't look like it."

"Is there anything we can do to Burt Treble?"

"How about gelding?"

They laughed, but only out of desperation. The chances of prosecuting the man were slim to none.

As they stood watching Samson run, another truck came rumbling down the drive. It was Adam, followed by a couple of cars transporting his workers. When they all parked and got out, there were six strong-looking guys standing in her yard, ready to eat.

"I'd better get cooking." Phoebe grinned at Jacquie and Erin. "Want to stay for breakfast?"

Fortunately, she had muffins and bagels available, plus lots of juice and coffee, so the crowd didn't starve while she cooked. Because her kitchen table wouldn't accommodate that many, people ate sitting in lawn chairs outside, enjoying the morning and throwing bits of egg, bacon and toast to the dogs, who were very well mannered about the whole process.

But the surprise came when Phoebe glanced at Adam just as he took a small piece of bacon off his plate and let his hand dangle over the side of his chair. Gally crept up beside him in a crouch and Phoebe gazed in amazement to see the dog reach slowly forward with his nose. Adam moved his hand a little closer. Another adjustment by Gally, and the bacon was his.

With her heart pounding in her chest, Phoebe thought she'd never seen anything quite so wonderful.

"Adam's working on getting used to the dogs, isn't he?" Jacquie came in to help clean up the kitchen. "I saw him feed each of them a couple of times. You told me he wouldn't have anything to do with them."

"That's what I thought. I don't understand what's changed."

"Maybe he realizes there's a package deal, here."

"The deal isn't real, though."

Jacquie winked at her. "Are you sure?"

"Not at all." Phoebe sighed and changed the subject to one she did understand. "I'll call the vet and get him to come out to check Samson over. I'm guessing from the way he moves that he's not unsound, but I'm sure the owner would like a professional opinion.''

''Definitely. I'll leave you her name and number. I know she'll take care of the charges—she's paid Burt Treble plenty over the last six months. And she'll pay boarding fees, too.''

''Sounds good.'' As Phoebe stood at the sink, a friendly face appeared at the window. In a much shorter time than she could have managed, the old window had vanished and the frame was prepped for a new one. ''Amazing what testosterone can do.''

''Yeah. I would never have tackled this job by myself. I'm glad you were smart enough to ask Adam for help.''

Phoebe felt her cheeks heat up. ''Intelligence is my middle name.''

Jacquie and Erin left around noon and the men continued their work. Phoebe observed but stayed out of the way, except for providing drinks, cookies and snacks. By six o'clock the guys were dirty and sweaty, and her house had new eyes.

''Thank you so much,'' she told them, handing over checks for twice the amount Adam had suggested. ''I can't tell you how much I appreciate what you've done.''

None of them had been very talkative, but they all grinned, and bowed their heads, then piled into the two cars and hit the road. Adam watched them go, wiping his face with the sleeve of his shirt. ''They're g-good g-guys. I trust them to d-do the j-j-job right.''

''And you, of course, were right when you said I should let them install the windows. I guess I carry my independence too far sometimes.''

''Could b-be.'' But his smile was kind and he stroked

a knuckle down her cheek. "Who's the b-big bl-black g-guy in the other pasture?"

She walked with him down to the fence to watch Samson graze and explained the story. "Stallions aren't easy, but I think what he needs most is some patience and space. I plan to make friends without making many demands on him."

"Why did Jacquie br-bring him to you? Aren't there p-people who do this k-kind of rescue?"

"I'm one of them." He was obviously surprised. "Maybe I never explained. Marian and Robin were both rescues from an auction truck, about to be shipped hours across country with twenty other horses to the slaughterhouse. All my dogs and cats were abused or abandoned. It's what I've wanted to do for as long as I can remember—live on a farm where I could give homes to animals who needed one."

"I wasn't paying attention." Adam shook his head. "But it m-makes sense, knowing you." He put his hands on his hips and arched his back. "It's been a long d-day. I'm used to other g-guys d-doing the work and m-me writing the paychecks."

"And so you deserve a good dinner. I've got fresh tomatoes and mozzarella cheese, pasta with pesto and garlic bread. Want to stay?"

He closed his eyes and groaned. "How c-could I not?"

This time they ate inside, at the table she'd set with candles and glasses for the bottle of chardonnay he opened, with Celtic music on the CD player. Both of them had a window view, and Adam spent a lot of the time watching the horses.

"Your four regulars are fascinated by the new arrival. They're congregated at the fence, watching him."

"They'll accommodate. Unless he charges through the

fence at them. Or goes over, God forbid. Samson is big enough to make that kind of jump, if it occurs to him.''

But the stallion stayed where he was during dinner, and while she and Adam cleaned up in a companionable silence.

"Having help with the chores is really nice," she told him as they finished. "I probably should have worked in a therapy session over the dishes, though. You're not making many appointments these days."

"Just being with you is therapy." He folded the last dish towel and came to lean against the counter where she stood. "I haven't s-seen the world the s-same way s-since I m-met you. You're a woman in a m-million, Phoebe M-Moss."

The wine had softened her. The tone of his voice melted her. Without thinking, she twined her arms around Adam's shoulders. His hands came to her waist, and the lightest pressure of her hold bent his head. Then she kissed him.

Nothing like it had ever happened to him before. The warmth, the generosity with which Phoebe gave herself was beyond any experience Adam could claim. He tightened his hold, let Phoebe's kisses take him deeper into a whirlpool he knew he could drown in. Wanted to drown in. Her breasts yielded against his chest as she moved closer, close enough that he could feel her heart pounding over his own. Her fingers played in his hair, slipped under his shirt collar to wander over the skin of his shoulders, the hollow of his throat, and he was dying with the need to feel her touch on every inch of his skin. *Every single inch.*

He moved his hands, all too aware of the curves, the hollows of her body. His palm shaped her waist, the arch of her back and the muscles in her arm, where he found warm, bare skin. He hadn't thought his heart could beat any faster...until he slipped the other hand underneath her shirt to encounter the beautiful flesh over her strong and supple spine. Shoulder blades, ribs, all sheathed with a velvety softness that was Phoebe's skin. His knuckles brushed the underside of her breast, and they both gasped.

"Adam." Her whisper was the wind rustling the leaves of the trees, mysterious, irresistible. "Don't leave tonight. Stay and make love to me."

An invitation to paradise. Who else but Phoebe could offer him heaven with such simple generosity? And what could he offer her?

His body aching to the bone, Adam drew back. Away. "I..." God, this was hard to say. "I think I'd b-b-better leave."

She closed the distance he'd opened, placed her hands on his chest and stared up at him. "Please, Adam. You won't be taking advantage. I know what I'm doing. I want this. With you."

He tried to smile. "I want it, too. B-but..." A deep breath didn't help. "B-b-but n-not to-n-night." Closing her hands inside his, he kissed her fingertips, then let go quickly and left before she could say anything else. Because another word might convince him to stay.

Fist pounding on the steering wheel, he made the drive home without thinking beyond the next traffic signal. He walked into the house and threw his keys on the kitchen counter, ignored the flashing light on the answering machine, and went directly to his bedroom, where thoughts of Phoebe pounced like a cat keeping watch outside the mouse's hole.

She had offered herself without reservation. And he'd turned her down without explanation. Maybe he should write a letter, set out the reasons he hadn't… couldn't?…accept what she wanted to give him. What he so desperately wanted, what he dreamed about night after night, woke up sweating over time and time again. At least he wouldn't stutter in writing.

Stripping off his shirt and jeans, he thought about that hypothetical letter. *Dear Phoebe,* it would say. *I'd like nothing better than to lay you down on cool, smooth sheets and drive my body into yours until neither of us could think. Or even breathe.*

Only one problem with that scenario, sweet Phoebe. I've never been with a woman before. And while I'm used to fumbling with words, I couldn't stand to fumble with you.

He threw himself down on the bed and buried his face in the pillow.

Love, Adam.

CHAPTER ELEVEN

PHOEBE ARRIVED LATE FOR the weekly planning breakfast with Adam and Tommy—understandable she thought, since she'd driven home from a campaign dinner at midnight last night and awakened with what was beginning to feel like the flu. Both men stood as she came around the corner of the booth, and Adam stepped out to let her slide in beside him. That was about as close as they got to each other these days.

"Did you see this?" Tommy waved a newspaper in front of her nose. "Did you see it?"

She squinted her eyes. "I'm not seeing much of anything this morning." Three sneezes and a cough later, she looked up out of her handkerchief. "What is it?"

Abby set a mug of hot tea in front of her. "This'll help. I put honey in it."

"Oh, thank you." Wrapping her hands around the mug, she breathed in the fragrance. "Wonderful."

Adam put a cool hand on her forehead. "You're sick. You should have stayed home."

"Work," she murmured, and sipped the tea. His shoulder brushed hers, his hip and thigh aligned with her leg. The contact made her breathless, and miserable. More miserable.

"This," Tommy exclaimed, "is an article on Kellie Tate. Her childhood, her education, her family. Her children, her charity work—did you know she volunteers at the hospital in the children's ward? And her hobbies—golf, tennis, horses.''

Phoebe took another sip to ease her throat. ''Sounds nice.'' She knew about Kellie Tate and her dubious concern for her horses. Samson still thundered around the lower pasture most of the day, still refused to trust a human hand. Getting him checked over by the vet had been a life-threatening experience for all of them.

''You know what comes next? An article on you, of course.''

''S-so?'' Adam took the paper and opened the sheet flat. ''That's not a b-bad thing. Phoebe has a lot of appeal for the v-voters.''

''Sam Pettit told me she was going to Atlanta to do research. Anything she found out could show up in that article. So I need to know the possibilities. What kind of dirt can she dig up on you, Phoebe?''

''I—''

Adam set his mug down with a clank. ''You're out of line, C-Crawford. The p-presumption that Phoebe has anything in her life to be ashamed of is s-s-stupid, not to m-mention insulting.''

''Everybody has something to be ashamed of, DeVries. You stole a dollar in the third grade.''

''Yeah, and I learned my lesson. We're talking about s-s-serious s-stuff. Just b-back off.''

''Oh, sure. And let your campaign go down the toilet.''

More and more, Phoebe felt like a tool, or a pawn, in this endeavor. She was tempted just to slip out and let them argue. But she owed Adam—and Tommy, she supposed—the truth.

''There is one thing,'' she said quietly.

Adam snapped his head around to stare at her. Tommy

dropped back against his seat. "I told you so. Let me have it."

"I was seeing a patient shortly before I left. A teenager who stuttered. Before I realized it, he'd developed a crush on me. His mother called to ask why he wasn't making progress, which was not my experience—I thought he did quite well in our sessions. Turned out he didn't want his parents to think he was better and make him quit coming."

"What happened?" Adam asked quietly.

"I talked to him and transferred him to another therapist. He wasn't happy, but I broke things off as cleanly as I could. I'd already made plans to leave Atlanta." She coughed, drank some tea. "That's all."

Abby came to the table with her order book. "Same as usual, everybody?"

The men nodded, but Phoebe knew she couldn't eat. "Just more tea."

"Nope, sorry. Not possible. How about a small bowl of oatmeal? Not too hot, not too thick, with milk and brown sugar. You need something to run on, sweetie."

Arguing with Abby was useless. "Sure. I'll try."

"Good girl."

Adam put his hand on the nape of her neck, and she nearly wept at the relief, the pleasure of his cool touch. "Why d-don't you let me d-drive you home? Your c-clients can re-sch-sch-sch-…c-come another day."

Tommy had been quiet too long. "So you think this teenager or his parents lodged a complaint about your treatment? And could Sam Pettit dig that up?"

"Enough." Adam's voice was harsh. "You're a j-jerk, Tommy. Whatever g-gets into the paper, we'll d-d-deal with it. Leave Phoebe alone."

The man across the table stared at Adam for a second,

glanced at Phoebe, then slid out of the booth. "Great. Terrific," Tommy said. "I don't need the hassle of trying to win, anyway. I'll send the bills to your office." The wild clamor of the bell on the door announced his departure.

"G-good riddance," Adam muttered, just as Abby arrived with their breakfast.

She looked at Tommy's empty place, set Phoebe's oatmeal and another mug of tea in front of her, then slid Adam's plate onto the table. "I haven't had a chance to eat, myself," she commented, and took the extra meal back to the kitchen.

Phoebe eyed the oatmeal without enthusiasm. "You shouldn't have done that."

"He f-forgets there are limits."

"Maybe you think too much about limits."

"M-maybe. Are you g-going to let me take you home?"

"No."

He shrugged. "Whatever you say."

After an uncomfortable silence, she roused herself enough to ask, "Things going better at work?"

"No."

The last three weeks had been hard ones, even without their personal complications. Adam's campaign appearances had taken over his regular schedule to such an extent that he'd missed a couple of bid deadlines. While most builders got the work done whenever it suited them, Adam cared about delivering quality building on time. But when he didn't get supplies ordered, or inspections arranged because he was out of the office, when something had to be done twice or three times because he didn't get there to supervise the special details, the jobs suffered. Throw in three instances of vandalism, and she could understand his irritation.

"Have the police found out anything about the vandalism? Any hint of who might have done it?"

"They're sure it's just drugged-out kids."

"You're not?"

He shrugged. "Given his track record, I'm more likely to suspect L. T. LaRue. But I don't have a shred of evidence to support the idea."

Phoebe let her jaw drop. "He has a track record?"

"When he wanted to take over M-Magnolia C-Cottage—D-Dixon's house, you know?—there were some incidents that were traced back to LaRue. I wouldn't put it past him to try to intimidate me."

"Then he doesn't know you very well, does he?"

Adam smiled. "N-not very. He d-didn't gr-grow up with the rest of us, but c-came to town after he married K-Kate. I g-guess he's always f-felt like an outsider. Buying off the city c-council and the m-mayor is his way of fitting in."

"Have you told the police what you think?"

"The chief goes f-fishing with the m-mayor and LaRue."

"Oh." She sniffled, then coughed. "Well, in six weeks, your life will go back to normal…except for the part about being mayor."

He didn't smile, didn't comment. She heard him blow out a long breath.

And in six weeks, her life could go back to normal. She wouldn't dress in the morning with consideration for which luncheon or dinner she might have to attend. She wouldn't plan her weekend around pancake breakfasts, ball games and pig pickin's. Sunday would be a day for cleaning the tack room and riding the horses, not walking mile after mile through the neighborhoods in town, knocking on doors and smiling while Adam met the constituents.

In six weeks, she could stop wondering why Adam walked out on her that Sunday night. She had tried every day since to forget, but seeing him, being with him, holding hands and smiling, posing for pictures with his arm around her, made forgetting impossible. With all the campaign frenzy, they'd had no chance to talk. The barrier he'd built was so solid now, Phoebe doubted they could knock it down with a sledgehammer.

Just as well, since six weeks would see the end. Of everything.

He glanced at her untouched cereal. "You're not g-going to eat?"

"No."

"Abby'll be m-mad."

"She can sue me."

He gave a ghost of a chuckle. "N-no, she'll just yell at me for making you s-sick to begin with. I'll take c-care of the b-b-bill. B-back in a m-minute."

Phoebe watched him walk away, admired his straight back and narrow hips, his easy stride. Even sick, tired, discouraged, she wanted him with an ache worse than any she'd ever known. But for a reason she didn't understand, he had said no.

The memory brought tears, and she was too weak today to stop them. Sliding clumsily across the seat, she struggled to her feet and, like Tommy, escaped from Adam DeVries. He came out of the diner as she braked the Beetle at the red light on the corner, but she didn't think about going back.

Instead, she called Willa to cancel all her appointments

for the day, drove herself home and hid with her misery under the covers of her bed.

ADAM CHECKED LATER IN the day and was relieved to hear from her receptionist that Phoebe had done as he suggested and gone home. "Poor girl sounded terrible," Willa told him. "No need for her to be drivin' all the way into town and back when she's so sick."

Guilt struck him, hard. "She c-can b-be stubborn about her work, though."

"That she can. I canceled her clients for tomorrow, too. We'll see how she's feelin' for Wednesday."

Adam didn't intend to wait two days to see how Phoebe was feeling. As soon as he could break away from work that evening, he headed out to Swallowtail Farm, thankful that this Monday, at least, he didn't have a campaign appearance scheduled.

The gate for the farm stood open, as if she hadn't had the energy to close it after her. In the lower pasture, the big black stallion raced Adam's truck along the fence until forced to turn at the corner. Robin and Marian greeted his arrival with pricked ears but didn't stop their grazing. Brady and Cristal stood at the far fence with their backs to him and didn't notice him at all.

The dogs made up for the horses' lack of enthusiasm. The three of them sat at the door to the porch, sharp-eared and panting, obviously anxious to get inside.

"What's wrong, guys?" He talked to them as he approached, whether for his own reassurance or theirs, he wasn't sure. "Have you been out all day? Where's Phoebe?" When he opened the door, the three animals waited patiently to be invited in, as Phoebe had no doubt trained them to do. "Come on. Let's find her."

Not a single lamp or light had been turned on in the

dark house. Adam wasn't surprised—he would have walked straight through and fallen into bed, himself. Phoebe, it appeared, had done the same. But that would have been twelve hours ago. Had she been asleep all this time?

He turned on the lamp nearest her bedroom and went to the doorway. In the darkness, a woman-sized lump was just barely visible underneath the bedspread. Leaving the room light off, he sat beside the lump, feeling gently for a shoulder or an arm.

"Phoebe? Phoebe, wake up." She stirred, but briefly. "C-c'mon, Phoebe, honey. Roll over." He pulled at her shoulder to turn her slightly.

"Go 'way." She sounded parched. Adam felt for her cheek and nearly jerked his fingers away from the heat.

"You're b-burning up." Abandoning caution, he switched on the lamp on the nearby table.

Red-faced and glassy-eyed, still wearing the dress she'd had on at breakfast, Phoebe glared at him from her rumpled bed. "What're you doing here?"

"Taking c-care of you. Where's your aspirin? When d-did you last d-drink something?"

"Go away." She huddled under the covers again.

"Like hell." Since she wouldn't tell him, he went on a foraging mission for medicine, along with clean sheets and blankets and a nightgown. With supplies at hand, he tackled the woman in the bed again.

Figuratively, anyway. "C'mon, honey, you've g-got to g-give me some help, here. Sit up, Phoebe."

"Don't make me."

"I have to. You n-need to d-drink. You n-need m-medicine. I've got you a c-clean n-nightgown," he wheedled, hoping that might be a bribe.

She peered at him over the edge of the blanket. "You are not undressing me."

"I will if I have to."

The word she used was so unlike her that Adam smiled. "I can change my own clothes." Pushing weakly at the covers, she dragged herself to the edge of the bed, sat up and felt for the floor with her feet. "I am capable of taking care of myself." She stood up...swayed, and would have fallen if Adam hadn't caught her.

"I can see that." He eased her to sit again on the bed. "Close your eyes and think of England, Phoebe. I'm going to undress you."

"Adam..." She closed her eyes, and tears streaked down her cheeks. "I hate you."

"I know." He lowered the zipper on her dress and lifted her enough to get the fabric free, then drew it over her head.

Immediately, her teeth chattered. "It's so cold."

"You've got a fever, honey. And goose bumps on your goose bumps." He took off her silky slip and her bra, forcing his eyes and his thoughts away from her small, rose-tipped breasts, her smooth and creamy skin. "This'll help." The nightgown he'd found was flannel, soft, worn, and she sighed as he slipped it over her arms.

"My favorite." She smiled. "You're a smart man."

"Sure. Lie back and let me get these hose off."

"I hate you," she said again.

"I know." Adam was hating himself pretty well, too. He should never have let her come home alone this morning. If their engagement had been real, he would have taken care of her properly. And he wouldn't have used the campaign as an excuse to avoid her these last three weeks.

"Okay. Wrap up in this b-blanket and come sit in the chair while I change the b-bed."

"I don't want you to make my bed." But she let him take her weight in his hands, let him move her to the armchair by the window.

"Here's some medicine, and water. Drink all the water, Phoebe. Every last drop in the glass."

"Please don't make my bed."

"You don't have enough energy to stop me, or even argue." She did fuss at him, sporadically, as he changed the sheets and blanket. "Now, back you go."

She lay under the patchwork quilt, staring at him with shadowed eyes. "You've done your duty. Now go home."

"I will," he lied. "Go to sleep."

"Let the dogs in here…oh, but I didn't feed them. Or the cats. The horses." Again, she started to get up and, again, fell back on the bed. More tears. "They haven't eaten. They'll think I forgot them."

"Shh. No, they won't." He smoothed the hair away from her face, and realized he should have braided it out of her way. That could wait until he woke her up in four hours for more pain reliever. "I'll feed the dogs and the cats. They'll be fine."

Whimpering, Phoebe closed her eyes. "But you don't like dogs."

He didn't bother to answer, just stayed there, bending over her, until she fell asleep.

TOMMY SPENT THE DAY alternately swearing at DeVries and at himself. About sundown, he vented the last of his spleen and went to the diner, figuring to get the apology over with and get on with the business of winning an election.

But DeVries had missed dinner. "Haven't seen him," Charlie Brannon said. "We've been pretty busy, but I would've noticed if he was here."

Moping over his own meal—the first food he'd seen all day—Tommy made some phone calls, trying to track Adam down. No luck at the office. An answering machine greeted him at Theresa's number, and Tim's. He wouldn't be at his parents' house. Which left one reasonable option.

Adam picked up the phone at Phoebe's on the first ring. "Hello?"

Tommy blew out a breath. "It's me."

"Something wrong?"

"Probably. Listen, I blew it this morning. I was pushing too hard. I'll apologize to Phoebe if you put her on."

"C-can't. She's in b-bed, s-seriously s-sick."

"Oh, man. That means I beat up on a sick woman."

"Yeah, you d-did."

"*Jerk* doesn't cover it."

"N-no."

"Okay, look, I'm sorry. I'll do better. I just want to see this election turn out in our favor."

"I know. B-but life will g-go on, Tommy, win or lose. You oughta k-keep that in m-mind."

"I'll try. So, you'll be at the dinner tomorrow night, right?" The change of subject was abrupt, and gave the lie to what he'd just said. But his job was details.

"M-maybe. I'm s-staying around here tonight, to k-keep watch on Phoebe. If she's d-doing okay tomorrow, I'll be there."

"What about work?"

"I c-can handle m-most of it on the phone." And that was a real giveaway, because DeVries hated doing work on the phone. He drove all over town to avoid phone calls.

"Well, okay. Let me know."

"S-sure."

"DeVries?"

"Yeah?"

"Are we...okay?"

Tommy heard the sigh, imagined the roll of the eyes that went with it. "We're okay, Crawford. I've p-put too m-many years into training you to g-give up n-now."

"Thanks, man. Tomorrow." Almost relieved enough to be in a good mood, Tommy shut off his cell phone and applied himself to the rest of his dinner. The bell on the door behind him jingled as folks came and went, but he didn't feel like socializing, let alone campaigning. For once, he was off duty.

So what was it that made him glance over his shoulder at one new arrival? A whiff of familiar scent? An extra sensitivity to this particular person?

Or a very good instinct for self-destruction? "Hey, Sam."

Sam debated about whether to answer Tommy's greeting or just walk past. Unfortunately, she'd stopped dead when she saw him sitting there, and now was blocking the door just as a family of six wanted to leave. "Sorry." She squeezed between the kids and Tommy's booth, which left her standing right there at his shoulder, facing him. "Hi." Brief, to the point. Now to turn and walk away...

"Would you like to sit down?" He glanced past her at the room. "Pretty crowded in here tonight."

No, thanks. The appropriate response. Sam sighed. "Sure."

Facing him across the booth was easier than she'd expected. He looked tired, kind of forlorn. "Eating alone? Where's your candidate?"

"Nursing a sick fiancée. But I'm not eating alone anymore, right?"

Abby appeared with coffee for Sam. "Menu?"

"Um, no." Was she really going to have dinner with Tommy? "I'll have the grilled chicken with salad and green beans."

"Saving room for dessert? I've got chocolate cake with caramel icing tonight."

Tommy raised his hand. "I'll take half."

Sam looked at him. "Half a piece?"

Chuckling, Abby shook her head. "He means half a cake. I baked a whole one for you, Tommy. It'll be ready when you leave."

"You really like chocolate cake with caramel icing that much?"

"Oh, yeah. My grandmother's specialty, which she made for me on my birthday every year. I gave the recipe to Abby so somebody would still be making the cake after Grandma passed away."

"That's…" She let the idea sink in, swirl inside her head a minute. "Tommy, is this your birthday?"

He shrugged a shoulder. "As it happens, yeah."

Comments crowded her brain. Why was he here all alone? Didn't he have a family to celebrate with? Surely Adam DeVries knew this was his friend's big day. Maybe they'd had the male version of a birthday party earlier?

"And before you go getting all sympathetic about it, I'll tell you that I stopped thinking about birthdays at the same time I stopped thinking of centerfolds as fine art."

"Last year?"

He grinned. "Today's the day I roll over another year on the personal odometer. End of story."

"If that's the way you want it."

"Thanks."

But as long as they were talking, she decided to ask some of the questions she'd wondered about for more than a year now. "So does your family cooperate with this 'Ignore the Day' dictate?"

"You're fishing, Sam."

"Are you biting?"

"You wish." Then he shrugged. "Okay, there's no family to speak of, except for my cousin Dixon and Great-aunt Daisy. No brothers or sisters. The parents drove down to Florida about five years ago to start their brand-new life on the beach. We're close enough for a phone call on Christmas that lasts us for about a year."

"Why'd they leave?"

"The old man had cheated or conned just about everybody in town and he couldn't drum up enough cash for his harebrained schemes anymore, so he moved to new pastures."

"You're bitter."

"Nah." When she gave a disbelieving snort, he shrugged. "Okay, maybe. But I'm glad they're gone. I was trying to get my own life started and I didn't have the wherewithal to keep bailing them out."

They sat silently as Abby removed their empty plates and then returned with coffee refills and two giant slices of cake served with ice cream. Just before leaving, she put a hand on Tommy's shoulder and leaned in close to his ear. "Happy birthday," she whispered, loud enough for Sam to hear. And then hopped away, laughing, before Tommy could connect the pretend punch he aimed at her chin.

"Prepare for the taste of your life," he warned as Sam picked up her fork.

And the cake was, indeed, rich, sweet, soul-satisfying. She forgot to ask questions, she got so involved in enjoying her dessert.

"So now it's your turn," Tommy said as they took a breather halfway through. "Where's your family? What do they think of you coming down here to work?"

"Mom and Dad live outside Chicago, in Urbana. No brothers or sisters for me, either. They're thinking about Florida when he retires from the police force in a few years. Should I send them to live next door to your parents?"

"Not if they value their pension. Your dad's a cop?"

"Twenty years and counting."

"Didn't you want to follow in his footsteps?"

A question she didn't get asked very often. "Not really. I see too many shades of gray. My dad's strictly a black-and-white thinker."

Tommy nodded, as if he understood. "And the move south?"

"Tired of the cold, the snow. I worked on the Urbana rag for several years, but when I got passed over for a couple of juicy pieces, I decided to get a fresh start somewhere warm. The *New Skye News* had an advertisement floating around at the same time. Serendipity strikes again."

"That Serendipity dude throws a mean punch."

"You said it."

They shared a grin, then finished their cake. When Sam saw Abby coming back with the coffeepot and the check, she tensed in preparation and snatched the bill away before Tommy could touch it.

"Sam…"

"My treat." She used a tone that brooked no argument. "I won't say the words. But I'm buying your dinner. Deal."

He sat back against the seat. "Okay, I will. Thanks."

"You're welcome."

She brought his cake back with her from the register. "This thing weighs ten pounds. But," she said, looking him up and down as he stood up, "I bet you don't gain an ounce."

He held the door open for her as they left. "A few rounds with the punching bag works off the average piece."

"You have a punching bag? That's so cool. Do you use it every day?"

"Pretty much."

"I want one, but I can't 'deface' the walls in my apartment. And who has time to go to the gym?"

"Nobody who's running around trying to dig up dirt on mayoral candidates, that's for sure."

She refused to get mad at him on his birthday. "Right. Maybe sometime I could come over and try out the punching bag? Just for fun?"

Once again, Tommy had walked her to her car. She met his gaze in the chilly darkness, saw the conflict between caution and desire in his eyes. "Sure," he said slowly. "Sometime soon."

If she made the right move, he would kiss her again. This time wouldn't be angry, or crazy. This time would be vulnerable. They'd been more open tonight than she'd believed possible. They hadn't argued at all.

There were still six weeks of the campaign left to run, though. And her article on Phoebe Moss would appear in next Sunday's paper.

Sam called up a bright smile, then turned and unlocked

the Mustang. "So...have a good night. I'll see you around the ol' campaign circuit."

"Right. Thanks again for dinner." He backed away as she dropped into the driver's seat, gave her a wave when she lifted her hand.

She didn't look at him in the rearview mirror as she left the parking lot. Sometimes, you couldn't afford to think twice.

CHAPTER TWELVE

WAKING UP HURT, SO PHOEBE avoided the process as long as she could. The point arrived, however, where oblivion no longer hovered within reach. Like it or not, she would need to open her eyes.

Early morning light poured in her east-facing bedroom window. Tuesday morning, she decided, pushing herself up a little higher on the pillow. All she'd needed was a bit more rest.

That theory suffered when she tried to stand up to go to the bathroom and her knees gave her all the support of warm jelly. Lurching from table to dresser to doorway, she made the trip, but her muscles responded with shrieks of pain.

Passing the mirror, she stopped short at the sight of a pale woman in a wrinkled gown with her messy braid hanging over her shoulder. A closer look revealed the shadows under her eyes and the hollows in her normally plump cheeks.

"I would remember being run over by a truck, wouldn't I?" She did have memories of some encounter…a voice tormenting her, someone shoving her around. What was that all about?

Were the dogs okay? "Gawain? Galahad? Lance, boy, where are you?" Her throat didn't produce much sound. The dogs didn't respond.

Had she left them outside all night? Had she even fed

them? Possibly not. Boy, did she have some pouting to endure now.

When she stumbled into the living room, though, another sight stopped her dead. The dogs were not outside. Lance and Gawain slept on the rug by the fireplace, their favorite spot when she was in the room. Gally occupied one armchair and Arthur the other. All of them were still fast asleep.

Merlin, however, had awakened and watched her from his spot on the couch. Not *on* the couch, precisely, but on the chest of the man sleeping on the couch, with his ankles stretching beyond the edge of the cushion and one arm dangling to the floor because the seat wasn't wide enough for his shoulders.

"Adam?" The word squeaked, broke. She sagged against the wall. "What are you doing here?"

His long lashes fluttered against his cheeks, then lifted. He sent her a sleepy smile. "You should g-go b-back to b-bed."

"What is my cat doing on your chest?"

Man and cat looked at each other nose to nose for a moment. Then Adam glanced around the room. "I g-guess all other spots were taken." He pushed himself up to sit with his back against the arm of the couch, bending his leg and putting one foot on the floor to free up the other half. "At least s-sit d-down, if you won't g-go b-back to b-bed."

Phoebe took that suggestion with unspoken gratitude, and Merlin settled on the cushion between them. "You didn't answer my question. Why are you here?"

"I came to see how you were, and thought you were sick enough that I needed to stay."

"That's...I..." Her head had started to ache again, which must be why she couldn't seem to deal with the situation. Adam, here. All night. Taking care of her. "Well, thank you. But I think I just needed a good night's sleep."

"Now the fever's b-broken, maybe you c-can g-get one."

"Fever? I had a fever?"

"A hundred and two for the b-better part of two d-days. If it hadn't b-broken last n-night, or had g-gone up a s-single n-notch, I was taking you to the hospital."

"Two days? What day is this?"

"Wednesday."

Phoebe could only stare at him. She'd lost track of a whole day? The thought made her shiver.

"You're g-getting chilled." Adam was on his feet, helping her stand up, leading her back to the bedroom with an arm around her waist. "And it's time for more medicine." Leaving her standing for a minute, he worked magic on the bed, smoothing the sheets, shaking the pillows, folding back the blanket and quilt. "Climb in."

She had to admit that sliding under the covers felt wonderful. Her eyes were closing against her will. "Shouldn't you go to work?"

"S-sure. D-don't fall asleep on m-me till you get your medicine."

"Or else you'll beat me up?" The voice she'd heard would have been Adam's. He'd come to find her... undressed her and put her in a nightgown...given her medicine. For two days.

"S-something like that. S-swallow."

Phoebe swallowed, then cuddled deep into the pillow. "I love you," she said conversationally, and drifted off to sleep.

AFTER GETTING PHOEBE BACK into bed, Adam had just poured himself a cup of coffee when he noticed Jacquie Archer's truck coming down the drive.

"How's Phoebe?" Bright-eyed and energetic, the farrier and her daughter looked as if they'd been awake for hours. He'd called Jacquie on Monday night to let her know about Phoebe's illness, and she'd come by with her daughter yesterday to help out with the horses.

"B-better. The fever broke last n-night about 3:00 a.m. She got up this m-morning, staggered around a little bit and went b-back to b-bed."

"Looks like you should, too." A blush colored her cheeks, and Jacquie gave a self-conscious laugh. "You know what I mean."

He grinned at her and nodded. Not that the thought of crawling in beside Phoebe hadn't occurred to him, especially after the first few hours on her couch. But he'd been afraid she wouldn't rest if he was there. And, selfishly, he'd known he wouldn't relax with her so close, so vulnerable.

Especially once he'd heard her say "I love you." Illness talking, on par with the "I hate you" he heard so often during the fever? Or had she revealed what lived in her heart?

"We'll see to the horses," the farrier said. "Since Phoebe's a bit better, are you going back to town today?"

"I—" He'd handled work yesterday by phone. Tommy had covered the VFW appearance last night. But the job and the election could not stay on hold indefinitely.

"Because I've got to stay near home, once I get Erin to school," Jacquie continued. "The vet is coming out, and I made an appointment with my farrier to get my own horses' hooves done." Adam caught on after a second and joined Jacquie in a laugh. "Otherwise, I never get to it. So I can check on Phoebe every couple of hours, make sure she's okay.''

He looked around him, at the horses standing by the fence, noses pointed to the barn as they waited for their breakfast, at Galahad and Gawain and Lancelot, chasing one another, play fighting, rolling around in the dew-slick grass like puppies. At the sun coming up over the tips of the pines and the bird perched on the peak of the house roof, singing its heart out. A deep breath drew in the scents he'd come to associate with comfort. With freedom. With Phoebe.

God, he hated to leave. "I g-guess I will g-go b-back to work. I c-can take Erin with m-me and d-drop her at s-school, if that's the only r-reason you're g-going in.''

Jacquie slapped her hands together. ''Sounds like a plan.''

Within thirty minutes he and Erin were in the truck, headed to New Skye. He asked a couple of questions about what he knew to be her passion—three-day eventing, where, Phoebe had explained, horses competed in cross-country races, stadium jumping and dressage events—and Erin steered the conversation from then on, sharing her aspirations for Olympic gold with the unbounded confidence of a teenager with the whole world in front of her. And a mother who supported her every dream. Lucky kid.

Having dropped Erin off at the same New Skye High School entrance he'd used thirteen years ago, Adam went home to change. He intended to walk by the answering machine without checking messages, but responsibility had once again settled on his shoulders like a vulture.

Less than two days, eighteen messages—seven from Tommy, who had known where he was the whole time, a couple from Theresa and Tim, the rest from work.

Adam stood under the shower and thought again about Phoebe's farm, about the peace and contentment he found there. About the sustenance Phoebe herself drew from the animals and the land.

Then he thought about where and how he lived, the work he'd chosen for himself and the new venture he'd taken on when he decided to run for mayor. What kind of compromises would he need to make to blend his life with Phoebe's? How much would each of them give up in order to be together?

By the time the water ran cold, he knew the only truly important question was…what *wouldn't* he do to make and to keep Phoebe a part of his life, as long as they both should live?

WHEN PHOEBE WOKE UP AGAIN and wandered through the house, she found Jacquie sitting at her kitchen table with a cup of coffee and a book.

"Oh." She staggered a little, from weakness and surprise. "I didn't expect to see you." And she was too weak not to ask, "Where's Adam?"

"He had to go to work." Jacquie got up and pulled out the other chair. "Sit down before you fall down. I'm sure you would rather him still be here, but that's okay. Want some juice? Hot tea?"

"Tea, please." They were good-enough friends to make tact unnecessary. "I was hoping to see him again, though I couldn't believe he stayed to begin with. I can't even begin to think about him changing my clothes. Giving me medicine, putting up with the dogs…"

"Pretty heroic." Jacquie set down a steaming mug and took her own seat. "That's not a man you want to let get away. Most of them run the other direction when a woman gets sick and needs attention.'' Her usually cheer-ful, matter-of-fact voice wore an edge of bitterness.

Instead of protesting, Phoebe allowed herself to follow that line of thought. ''I don't know if Adam and I could make things work. There are so many differences, and that's before you stop to consider that he may be the next mayor.''

''You wouldn't move into town for him?''

''And leave the horses?''

''No, I guess not.'' The farrier studied her coffee cup. ''He couldn't live out here?''

''Why should he want to? I mean, the house is nice, but it's not special, like his place. He appreciates fine workmanship, and this is just a standard seventies ranch house.''

''Phoebe, you're hopeless. He would want to live out here because you are here. What other reason does he need?''

''I—'' The argument made sense, and Phoebe couldn't explain why she didn't accept the logic. Adam choosing to leave his life in town and move out to the country just because of her seemed too big a sacrifice for a man like him to make. ''I think I'll take my tea and go back to bed for a while.''

''Good idea. The vet is coming to my place in about an hour, so I'll take off and come back when he's fin-ished. I'll bring some soup with me—you need to eat something.''

''Thanks, Jacquie. What would I do without you?''

''If you were smart, you'd call Adam. And he'd come, you lucky woman, you.''

Phoebe shook her head. ''Give it up, why don't you?''

On the other hand, she thought, crawling back into the

bed Adam had made for her, why should she expect her friend to accomplish something she herself couldn't do?

BURIED UNDER OVERDUE paperwork, Adam snarled when the intercom buzzed late Wednesday afternoon. "What?"

Fortunately, the only person who scared his secretary was his mother. "Phoebe Moss would like to speak with you."

Though he hated phone calls, his mood improved on the instant. "Thanks. J-Jody?"

"Yes, sir?"

"S-sorry."

"You've still got my vote."

Grinning, he picked up the phone. "How are you?"

"Much, much better." She did sound stronger, though far from well. "That's why I called." A pause, then an audible breath. "You really don't have to come back out here tonight," she said in a rush. "I mean, you might not have been planning to, but I wanted to catch you before you left, if you did, so that you didn't make the trip. Because I'm better, really, and the fever hasn't come back at all, I've eaten the soup Jacquie brought and some toast, spent the day drinking juice and tea, and I've fed the dogs already and Jacquie will do the horses. So…"

"S-so you don't n-need m-me anymore?" He meant to tease her a little.

But she took him seriously. "Oh, Adam, no. Don't think that." Her voice thickened. With tears? "I am so grateful for what you did and I can't believe I wasn't even conscious enough to know you were here. I just want to spare you more trouble, and I know you have campaign events, and Tommy's going to have a fit—"

"Phoebe. Phoebe, s-stop." He held on to the phone

with both hands, since he couldn't hold on to her. "I was teasing, honey. It's okay." Listening intently, he tried to decide if she was crying. "I'm g-glad you're b-better. That's all that m-matters. You're not c-crying, are you? Please say n-no."

She sniffed, and sniffed again. "N-no."

The little joke reassured him, even though she was lying. "I'll stay in town, if it'll m-make you feel b-better. Promise me you'll c-call Jacquie if your fever c-comes b-back. Will you d-do that?"

"I promise. I'll be okay."

"I know you will." He wouldn't, though. Hanging up was going to feel like cutting off a hand.

"So," she said, after a few seconds of silence, "do you have an event tonight?"

"N-not official. There's a h-homecoming rally at the high school. Tommy wants me to show up and shake hands."

"Are you very behind at work?"

He looked at his stacked desk, his littered floor. "Only a little."

"You're lying."

"A little."

"I'll let you go back to what you were doing."

"I wish you wouldn't."

"No, you don't. Take care, Adam. And thank you so much."

"You're very welcome. You g-get well." He glanced at his calendar. "Don't worry about any of the c-campaign stuff. I'm hoping you'll be well enough to c-come with me to that s-speech for the League of Women V-voters n-next week. Pretty important."

"I'll take some extra vitamins to get ready."

"That's a plan. S-sleep well, Phoebe."

"Bye."

Phoebe hung up the phone and blotted her wet cheeks with the sleeves of her gown. She'd done the right thing, and sometimes doing the right thing hurt. Adults knew and accepted that fact of life.

So who wanted to be an adult, anyway?

Willa had canceled her appointments for the rest of the week, and both she and Jenna insisted they would change the door locks if Phoebe tried to come to work. So she stayed home. Jacquie brought over more soup, a chicken-and-rice casserole and a pumpkin pie. "Lots of iron," she insisted. "Good for you." Erin gave Brady and Cristal some exercise in Dixon's honeymoon absence, and they all walked down to watch Samson dominating his empty pasture. By Sunday morning, Phoebe felt like herself completely, and was only deterred from a full day's work outside by the chilly rain pouring down when she woke up.

So she would work inside, after church. She dressed, went to the service at the little chapel she'd found not far from her farm, and then, for a treat, decided to drive into New Skye for lunch at the Carolina Diner. Good food and Abby's friendly smile would complete her cure.

And maybe Adam would be there, too. They'd talked several times over the last few days, but she'd insisted he get back to his regularly scheduled life and not come out to see her. He'd complied, though whether with relief or regret, she couldn't tell. He didn't like using the telephone, so she tried not to keep him talking long.

The first thing she noticed, when she stepped inside the diner, was that his regular booth was occupied by someone else. After the surge of disappointment, she then noticed that the entire room had gone quiet. Phoebe looked around and realized that all eyes were on her.

In an instant, the noise picked up again, even louder than before. But she still felt the prick of observation as she found an empty table for two up near the counter.

"What's up?" Abby brought her a cup of hot tea. "Feeling better?"

"Much, thanks. And you tell me what's up. Why are they staring?"

For once, this frank, honest woman avoided her gaze. "I...um..." Abby glanced around the diner, and at all the customers, who now stared at something else. "Oh, hell. You're in the paper today, Phoebe."

Her recovered appetite vanished. "Is the picture that bad?"

"The picture's good." Abby went behind the counter and came back with a folded newspaper section. "You might as well see. And you should order before you read it."

"No, thanks. I don't think I'll be staying." If Abby was this upset, the article must be devastating.

Abby put a hand on Phoebe's shoulder and squeezed. "You'll be okay. I know you will. Your tea is on the house."

Great. Free tea meant really bad news. Phoebe took a sustaining gulp, opened up the folded paper, and prepared to meet her doom in front of the Sunday lunch crowd at the Carolina Diner.

THE POUNDING ON HIS FRONT door pulled Adam away from his account books in the dining room, where he'd been buried since about 7:00 a.m. "C-coming. D-dammit, Tommy, keep your pants on."

But when he flung open the door, Phoebe was the one standing there, breathing as if she'd run a marathon. "I'm s-s-sorry," she said. "S-so s-sorry."

"What are you talking about?" Hands on her shoulders, he pulled her into the house and shut the door. "You're wet. Where's your c-coat?"

"Did you read this?" She held up a soggy newspaper. "Did you read it?"

"N-no. Sit." He set her on the couch and went for a blanket and towels. "Take off your shoes. D-did you walk here?"

"I c-can't believe it." Her teeth chattered, but more worrisome was the wildness in her eyes. "She p-put the w-w-worst p-possible interpretation on anything anybody told her. I talked to my family last weekend. They didn't even m-mention they'd s-s-seen her. D-damn them. Oh, d-damn them." With the newspaper still clenched in her fist, Phoebe put her head on her knees and sobbed.

"Don't. Shh." Adam tried to put his arms around her, but she fought him.

"Read it." She shoved the paper at his chest. "J-j-just read it."

With the sound of her crying as a background, he did as she said.

This was the companion piece to the earlier article on Kellie Tate. Samantha Pettit had gone to Atlanta, had interviewed Phoebe's family, friends and co-workers, her professors at college and some of the women in her dormitory. The picture drawn from those interviews showed an aloof woman who didn't talk much, didn't mix well with other people, a woman who shunned her family and eventually abandoned them.

Even worse, the article created the image of a trusted therapist who encouraged a young boy's crush, then rejected and dismissed him for personal convenience.

Cynthia DeVries's comments went further, questioning

Phoebe's honor, her motives in becoming engaged to him, her honesty and personal values.

The fact that the woman in the article bore no resemblance at all to the real Phoebe Moss was small consolation.

Adam let the paper drop to the floor. "Phoebe, honey—"

The phone rang. There wasn't much doubt about who would be calling. "Hey, Tommy." The ensuing diatribe didn't require answers, so he simply listened until Tommy took a breath. "Phoebe is here. We'll talk later." Then he unplugged the phone from the wall.

When he turned back to her, she was on her feet, slipping into her wet shoes. "You're n-not going anywhere."

She pushed her hair back from her face. "I'm g-going h-home. But..." Swiping the heels of her hands over her cheeks, she took a breath that shook. "I w-w-want you to announce that I broke up w-with you. As soon as p-possible."

"Phoebe—"

"You and-and T-Tommy can f-f-figure out the best way to h-h-handle it. Nobody's going to blame you, or even ask qu-questions. I won't comment to anybody about anything." The smile she tried failed miserably. "And you'll still h-h-have my v-vote."

"No. No way."

"You h-have to, Adam. You deserve to w-win this election, because you care about the city and its people. I know what T-Tommy said just now, and I know that he's right. As long as I'm on board, the voters will run like lemmings over a cliff, away from you."

Unfortunately, that was pretty much exactly what Tommy had said. "S-so, in the interest of my election, I should d-dump my fiancée over a little n-negative publicity?''

''A m-massive amount of negative publicity. Y-y-yes.''

''What kind of man would do that to the woman he loves?''

''A smart one. Especially when...when it's all pretend, anyway.'' She stood with her fists clenched at her sides. ''But if you w-won't do it, I will. I don't w-want to see you anymore, Adam. Our engagement is officially over.'' A quick turn on her heel, and she headed for the door.

''The hell it is.'' Adam got there before she could touch the knob, put his arms around her and pulled her back against him. ''You don't really think I'm going to let you go, do you?'' He bent his head, breathed in the sweet scent of her hair. ''You're what I've looked for all my life. I'm not giving you up now.''

''Adam.'' Phoebe struggled, but he had too strong a hold on her body, on her heart. With a moan of protest at her own need, she turned in his arms and dragged his head down so their lips could meet.

Mind, logic, reason...gone. Yesterday, tomorrow... irrelevant. Only *now* mattered, only the desire arcing between them in the safe, solid fortress of Adam's home.

She wasn't sure how they got to his bedroom, didn't know if she'd led or followed. The light was dim, the walls dark blue, the bed firm as she lay beside the man she loved, staring into eyes that seemed to take on the darkness surrounding them. His hands moved over her, a quest for knowledge, for experience, in an adventure she was only too glad to share. Phoebe touched in return, learning the planes of his chest, the angles of collarbone and shoulder blade, the beautiful symmetry of his legs.

Their mouths clung, teased, wandered to taste and test, then met again in a frenzy of deep, drowning kisses.

"Phoebe." He whispered her name as the delirium built, as control started to shred. "Phoebe, tell me when. I want this to be perfect, but I'm not sure…" He broke off with a groan as she touched him.

Like the sudden flare of a match, she understood what he meant. That she was the first woman to know him so completely filled her with surprise, with awe, with an incredible gladness. Shaken and more aroused than she had ever been, Phoebe drew Adam deeply into her embrace, then brought him home.

ADAM ONLY REALIZED HE'D fallen asleep when he woke up. An apology came instantly to his lips, but then he realized that Phoebe was asleep, too. Smiling, he closed his eyes and relaxed. He was glad to be awake—this was too good to miss a single minute.

She lay curled against him, her head pillowed on his shoulder, her palm weighting the beat of his heart. Small, soft, and yet she had such incredible strength: she'd pulled his soul from his body, sent him crashing and sliding through ecstasy, and then put him back together in an entirely new way. Nothing, *nothing,* would ever be the same again.

"Mmm." She stirred, smiled, snuggled closer.

"That covers it," he agreed.

"Speaking of covers…" They managed to get underneath the sheets and the quilt without letting go of each other.

"Better?" He loved smoothing her hair over her shoulder, every so often touching the velvet skin underneath.

"Better than perfect? Nope. Just…good." She was

quiet so long, he thought she'd gone back to sleep. "Adam? I'm really honored."

He felt his cheeks heat up. "I d-don't know what to say to that."

"You don't have to say anything." She turned around so they could look at each other. "But you trusted me in a way you haven't trusted another woman. That's the most wonderful thing that's ever happened to me."

Setting his hand along the line of her jaw, Adam stroked his thumb over her pink, kiss-swollen mouth. "I should've d-done it sooner."

She returned the pressure with her lips...on the pad of his thumb, and at the base, and then in the center of his palm and at the pulse of his wrist. "I thought so at the time. Maybe I was wrong."

He drew a deep breath. "It's getting a little warm under all these blankets."

Phoebe flung off the covers, then returned to her kisses. "Better now?"

"Ah...no." Fire licked its way through his veins. "What's that saying? Abstinence makes the heart grow fonder?"

She fell away from him, laughing. "Idiot."

"Well, then, what does make the heart grow fonder?" He leaned over her, fitting his body along hers, welcoming the melting of her muscles, the hardening of his own.

"Practice," Phoebe said with a wicked smile.

And so they did.

CHAPTER THIRTEEN

TOMMY KNEW BETTER THAN to charge out to find Sam Pettit right after he'd read the article. What was left of Adam's election run would not be aided by the arrest of his friend and campaign manager for the murder of a Brash Girl Reporter.

So he waited until Monday morning. He was sitting in her desk chair in the newsroom when she came to work.

She gave him the satisfaction of halting dead in her tracks when she saw him. Her jaw dropped and her eyes went round.

"Hey, Sam." He waved. "Come on over. I brought doughnuts and coffee." Opening the box, he took out a jelly-filled specimen and offered it with a napkin. "These are your favorites, as I recall."

"Look, Tommy—"

"Sorry, I'm in your chair. Have a seat." He got to his feet, and gave her no real choice but to sit down. "Here's your coffee."

"I know you're mad—"

"No, I'm not." Her brows rose in question. "I am as far beyond mad as you are beyond shame."

"That's—"

"Bad enough that you stab my candidate in the back, don't give me any advance notice of the nuclear weapon you're about to launch on the campaign. All's fair in love, war and politics. Fine. I can deal. Adam can deal.

But, for God's sake, why did you do this to a nice person like Phoebe Moss? She didn't deserve this treatment, and I can't begin to figure out what kind of person you have to be if you can do something like this and still sleep at night. Or keep food in your stomach.''

She hadn't, in fact, taken a bite of the doughnut or a sip of coffee. ''I can explain. If you'll shut up.''

He crossed his arms and sat on the corner of her desk. ''Be my guest.''

Sam dragged a key chain from her purse, unlocked the bottom drawer of her desk and pulled out a fat blue file labeled Moss. Shoving the doughnut box aside, she slapped the file down and flipped it open.

''When I got to Atlanta and started nosing around, I discovered that somebody else had beat me to it. Everywhere I went, I was asking the same questions somebody else had asked. A private investigator, it turned out, named Dean Martin.''

''You're kidding.''

Her grin was brief. ''Wish I were. He, of course, would not tell me who he was working for. But he shared some of his results with me. Some, Tommy. Not all.''

She started pushing papers in his direction. ''Interview with a client who said she'd considered a lawsuit because her speech impediment didn't improve. Interview with a client's mother who tried to file charges with the licensing board over a kid who fell for Phoebe Moss during therapy. The board told her to take a hike, but it looks bad. This Martin guy obtained work evaluations that suggested Phoebe was ineffectual, inefficient. Of course, these were turned in by the therapist who took over her clients when she left Atlanta and, incidentally, is now married to a man Phoebe was dating at the time of the evals.''

Tommy looked at the papers. "Shit."

"Exactly. Phoebe's mother is a bitch, plain and simple—I talked with her for an hour and was never so glad to get away from anybody, including Cynthia DeVries. Her dad is a pompous bastard, and her brothers and sister carry the family genes." She shook her head. "I think Phoebe was adopted."

"So what's this all add up to?"

"There's more, but we don't have to go through it all. Somebody in New Skye—and there are only three suspects, as far as I'm concerned—had Phoebe investigated. Martin's really good at his job and totally without principles. He may have been authorized to pay people to make things sound as bad as possible. I'm sure all of this information, plus more he didn't show me, belongs to somebody here in town now."

"And so," Tommy concluded slowly, "you wrote the article trying to defuse the bomb, so to speak. You think that by walking the edge like this, you can take the thunder out of Martin's revelations?"

She shrugged. "I didn't know what else to do. If I'd withdrawn the article entirely, that left them a free field. I didn't want to write a 'they say this but it's not true' piece, 'cause what people remember is the accusation, not the defense. A fluffy, do-gooder write-up like Kellie Tate's would have set Phoebe up for a bigger fall. What's left?"

"Only this." He braced one hand on the arm of her chair, grabbed her chin with his free fingers and kissed her. Slowly, thoroughly. "Thanks, Sam. I owe you more than doughnuts."

She stared up at him with those big, dark eyes. "I'll remember that." Then she shook her head. "What are you going to do?"

Tommy was halfway to the newsroom door. "First, damage control. And second…attack."

THE REPERCUSSIONS OF Samantha Pettit's article hit about midmorning on Monday and, like a boulder heaved into a lake, set up waves of ever-expanding disaster.

Willa came to Phoebe's office after a spate of phone calls. "That's four appointments canceled so far this mornin', and two of them askin' for referrals to another practice. What's goin' on?"

"You read the article, right?"

"Well, yes. It wasn't so bad."

"But was there anything to inspire confidence in me as a therapist? Or even as a person you wanted to know?"

Willa couldn't answer and went back to the front desk shaking her head. Jenna knocked on the door shortly afterward. "Are you okay?"

"I am hanging by a thread between heaven and hell."

"Excuse me?"

"Too dramatic? Okay, then. I don't know whether to be deliriously happy or desperately depressed."

"Assuming I know the reasons for being depressed, would you like to share the good news?"

"Adam."

"Adam? Oh…Adam." Jenna smiled. "You do look a little tired this morning. I was assuming you'd lost sleep over the article."

"Yes, and no."

"Good for both of you. And listen, just hold tight and we'll get through all the rest of this mess. People will forget soon enough."

"I hope so." Terrible as the situation might be, however, Phoebe couldn't keep from smiling. Being with

Adam was so miraculous, so much *more* than she'd ever experienced with anyone....

The intercom buzzed. "Phoebe, Samantha Pettit would like to speak with you." The crisp, angry voice was barely recognizable as Willa's.

And Phoebe had the same gut reaction. "Does she need a speech therapist?"

"She says not."

"Then tell her she has nothing to say that I want to hear."

Standing at the desk with the receptionist, Sam got the message. She glanced over her shoulder at the waiting room, where reporters from two smaller newspapers in the county lurked, hoping to catch Phoebe Moss for a statement or a story. To her right, the hallway obviously led to the therapists' offices. One of those doors would be Phoebe's.

The nice, grandmotherly receptionist glared at Sam. "I am sorry, Ms. Pettit, but Ms. Moss is unavailable."

"Thanks." She stepped directly back, forcing the person behind her to sidestep. The brief confusion created all the distraction she needed. Before anyone could stop her, she was striding down that hallway in search of a door with the name Moss on it.

Having arrived, she knocked briskly and entered without being invited, then leaned back against the panel. "Sorry. But I really do have to talk to you."

At the desk across the room, Phoebe Moss got slowly to her feet, the shocked look giving way to indignant rage. "I imagine my receptionist will have the police here in a matter of minutes. You'd better talk fast."

"I've already explained to Tommy what's happened. I wanted to be sure you knew, too, as early as possible. The article was lousy...but it could have been so much

worse.'' Quickly, she recounted what had happened in
Atlanta, except for the part about hating Phoebe's family.
Maybe she didn't know how truly awful they were.
''Somebody in this town intended to bury Adam's campaign with twisted information about you. I don't know
if it would have worked. But I tried to head them off
with the article. I really am sorry you're hurt.''

Phoebe sank into her desk chair, still staring at Sam.
''Who would do something like that?''

Sam sat on the sofa nearby. ''I would bet on L. T.
LaRue. This is his style, for sure. Or it could have been
the mayor, though he usually lets LaRue do his dirty
work. The other possibility that occurs to me…Cynthia
DeVries.''

''Just because I'm engaged to Adam?''

''Just because Adam's running for mayor, and she really doesn't want him to. Maybe she planned to use the
information to force him to withdraw. Assuming she's
the one who paid for it. I don't know.''

''How awful for Adam.''

''And for you. I slanted the piece as best I could—
negative but innocuous. As opposed to deadly.''

''Right.'' She rubbed her eyes and straightened her
back. ''Well, then, I should thank you. Though it's
hard.''

''I know.'' Sam stood up to leave. ''You didn't bar-
gain for any of this, back when they sprang that engagement on you at the rally.'' Before Phoebe could confirm
or deny, she was on her way out the door. ''Keep a stiff
upper lip. And carry a big stick.''

In the waiting room, she nodded to the two reporters.
''I got the scoop while you were twiddling your thumbs,
guys. Better go look up the crop forecast for your big
news of the week.''

They came after her, protesting, and bought her lunch in an effort to mine a story out of her. Sam fed them old news and sent them on their way to do no harm. She'd warned and protected Phoebe as well as she could.

Tommy Crawford and Adam DeVries would have to do the rest.

SACRIFICE, PHOEBE DECIDED after just a few days, was the synonym for political campaigning.

Her days started at dawn, taking care of the horses and the cats and the dogs, with barely any time for a few throws of a stick or ball. Then she made the drive into town for breakfast—a sausage biscuit eaten standing in a drafty warehouse, talking and smiling with the workers, or a stale doughnut and bad coffee during a radio broadcast from the parking lot of the tool-and-die plant. Tommy had written scripts for her with a variety of possible questions and the best answers for any situation.

Today the radio announcer hit her with the most obvious right away. "What did you think of the article about you in the *New Skye News* last Sunday?"

"I thought it sounded like someone I've never met." She laughed, and the announcer joined her. "Unlike the article's suggestion, I enjoy meeting people and getting together with friends. And now, with the campaign in full swing, I'm really excited about Adam's chances, and his ideas for making New Skye an even better place to live." Launching into a campaign spiel, she gave the woman no chance to refer back to the negative publicity. When she glanced at Tommy, she got a double thumbs-up.

Given the drop-off in her client base, she had plenty of time at lunch to visit the mall and shake hands, to meet with the women in Miss Daisy Crawford's book club, the Woman's Club of New Skye, and the Women in Business Club. Late afternoons saw her racing back to the farm to feed the animals, let the dogs out, change clothes for whatever dinner meeting was on the agenda, then lock the dogs up again, jump in the Beetle and high-tail it back to town. With the short days of autumn, and then the change from Daylight Saving to Standard Time, she only saw her house and her animals in the dark. She hated that.

She hated, too, the fact that there was no time anymore to be with Adam, except in front of the voters. Their kisses were public, all their conversations for other ears. She'd come to depend on him for his strength and integrity, but what she missed most in these harried days was his generous, caring companionship. Phoebe had thought she was happy alone with her animals, until Adam showed her how much her solitary life lacked. Now she wanted him back.

The polls showed Adam closing the gap between himself and Curtis Tate. And the madness would stop on the first Tuesday in November. Two weeks. Phoebe assured herself she could do anything for two weeks, especially for Adam.

She could even put up with Kellie Tate. The Raffle Committee met at the mayor's house for a final meeting on the Friday before the Stargazer dinner dance at the Botanical Gardens. Phoebe arrived exactly on time, dressed in the uniform—she'd already made two campaign appearances by ten o'clock—with a smile on her face and a determination to remain unaffected by any and all insults.

"Do come in." Kellie stepped back to let her in the house. "Not everyone is here yet, so have some coffee cake and cider." The words were warm, the delivery as cold as the blustery day outside.

"Thanks so much."

Conversation around the dining room table stopped completely as Phoebe entered, and only gradually resumed. One brave woman to whom she'd never been introduced finally sidled over to speak with her. "I loved your article in the paper."

"You did?"

"Well, I mean, any publicity is good, right?"

Phoebe pretended to consider. "I suppose so. Unless it's your obituary."

After a shocked moment, the women around the table began to giggle, and then to laugh. Obituary jokes and horror stories followed, with Phoebe included as a member of the group. She actually found herself having fun, enjoying the chance to talk about something besides the damn campaign.

With a sharp click of her high heels, Kellie came into the dining room. "Everyone's arrived. Let's get started." The little cluster of friendly faces immediately broke apart to scurry across the hall under the baleful gaze of their hostess.

Another basilisk waited in the living room. Cynthia DeVries had come to the meeting. "I attend all the final committee sessions," she told Phoebe, who'd had no choice but to greet her future mother-in-law with a kiss on each smooth cheek. "How are you holding up, after such a dreadful article?"

Thinking of Sam Pettit's theories, Phoebe studied the cold, beautiful face. Could this woman be responsible for such misery? And then be bold enough to bring up the subject as if she knew nothing?

Phoebe decided she wouldn't bet against the possibility. "I'll be sure not to believe everything I read in the paper from now on, since I've seen firsthand how the truth can be distorted.''

Before Cynthia could comment, Kellie called the meeting to order. Settling all the details seemed to take more time than really necessary, but Phoebe waited patiently to be assigned her final task. She would have to leave by noon, regardless. The Association of Women Realtors expected her for lunch at twelve-thirty.

''That's all, then.'' Kellie looked over the paper she held, apparently double-checking the agenda. ''We're set. I'll expect to see each of you tomorrow night at six o'clock. We want everything in place before the guests begin to arrive. Cynthia, did you have anything to add?''

Adam's mother rose to her full, impressive height. ''Not a thing, Kellie dear, except to add my thanks for a marvelous effort. This event could not have come to pass without the assistance of every one of you. Future generations in New Skye will be grateful for your work and dedication.''

A smattering of applause broke up the meeting. Most of the women gathered to pay court to Cynthia. Phoebe headed toward her hostess.

''Kellie?'' The mayor's wife turned, the lingering remnants of a frown on her face. ''I'm sorry, but I missed my name when you went through the assignments. Could you let me know what you'd like me to do?''

One long, rose-painted fingernail ran down the list of names on Kellie's clipboard. Again. Finally, Kellie looked up in surprise. ''Why, I don't find your name on the list at all. You must have been left off. Inadvertently, of course.''

''Of course.'' Phoebe loosened her jaw. ''Just write me in wherever I'll be useful.''

''Well, you know I would. But the task list is really

quite complete. I believe we have everything covered just as is. So I suggest you just not worry about the raffle at all. You dance and drink and eat and have a good time. We'll be fine without you."

"I-I will. Th-thanks."

Phoebe left with her chin high, if trembling. She didn't have to work the raffle at the fundraiser. She could enjoy the whole evening in Adam's company—much more fun than counting tickets or reading out numbers or double-checking results. Most women would be grateful for the reprieve.

Unless, as she did, they understood the insult behind the "oversight." How better to say she wasn't wanted than to say, simply, "We can't use you"?

She couldn't arrive at the Realtors' luncheon with tears on her cheeks. Pulling into the parking lot of First Methodist Church, she dragged out her makeup bag—something she'd never carried before the campaign—and tried to repair the damage. Just as she put the mascara wand to her right eye, her cell phone rang.

With her eye now streaming tears from the jab and the smear of black goo under her lid, she answered the phone. "'Lo?" She couldn't find the tissues she'd put in her purse, couldn't stop crying. Both eyes were weeping now.

"Phoebe, it's Jacquie. You okay?"

"Um, not really. What's up?"

"I stopped at your place just to check on things. I know you're busy these days, so I've been looking in occasionally."

Her nose was running, too. Time to admit that mascara wasn't the real problem. "And you know how much I appreciate it."

"Yeah. Today, when I got here, Marian was on the ground, rolling."

A cold fist clamped down on Phoebe's stomach. "You don't mean for fun."

"She's in pain, Phoebe. I got her up and walking around. But she looks bad. I think you've got a case of colic on your hands."

CHAPTER FOURTEEN

AS A MEMBER OF THE LEAGUE of Women Voters, Cynthia encouraged political interest, discussion, even disagreement. But tonight, she did not look forward to the traditional candidate's dinner. This was the moment she had dreaded since Adam first took leave of his senses—the moment she would have to sit and listen to him fumble his way through a public statement.

"I don't think I can do this," she told Preston as they dressed. "How ever will I sit there calmly, watching him expose himself and us to ridicule and pity?"

Preston came to where she sat at the dressing table and put his hands on her shoulders. "I don't believe this evening will be as bad as you anticipate, darling. I've been present at a couple of events where Adam spoke. I thought he did well."

"Was his...disability...evident?"

"He stuttered now and then. But overall, I thought he came across as a clear thinker and a reasonable speaker."

"Perhaps in a forum where he doesn't suffer comparisons. But tonight, he'll be facing Curtis Tate, who speaks very well, indeed. And we will have to endure the smug sympathy of our friends and acquaintances."

Only traces of that condescending pity were available when she and Preston arrived at the country club for the dinner. The candidates in the upcoming election—including city council members, judges and the sheriff's office—had formed a receiving line, and Adam made as handsome a figure in his dinner jacket and bow tie as a mother could wish. Several friends stopped by Cynthia after meeting him to congratulate her.

"So impressive…he certainly looks the part of a mayor."

"That smile makes you forget his…problem."

"I wish my son wore his clothes so well. Too bad…"

Cynthia smiled and said all the right things, as she'd been taught to do. When she finally approached Adam, she felt tense enough to scream.

"Hello, son." She gave him her hand, and leaned in for a kiss on the cheek. "How are you?"

"J-just fine. You look b-beautiful, as always."

"Thank you." She glanced around them as if searching for someone, although she'd noticed the absence of his fiancée quite some time ago. "Where is Miss Moss? Couldn't she join us tonight?"

His brow furrowed in a way she'd seen in her mirror a thousand times over the years. "I expect her to arrive any m-minute. She was d-definitely planning to b-be here when we talked last."

That might have been before the Raffle Committee meeting. While Cynthia thought Kellie Tate had been rather heavy-handed in the way she made her point, she'd also been quite effective.

"I'll look forward to talking with her later." Cynthia turned on her heel and took only a few steps before running into Mayor Tate, and his wife.

"I'm looking forward to the Botanical Gardens dinner dance tomorrow night," he told Cynthia, and gave her a wink. "I'm bringing a blank check from the city to match your total."

"That will be fabulous. Kellie has certainly done her share to make this fundraiser a success."

Mayor Tate put his arm around his wife's waist. "She's a special girl, all right. Great organizer, terrific at analyzing a problem and coming up with the solution. I couldn't do my job without her."

Accepting the compliments, Kellie smiled sweetly and blushed prettily, though Cynthia knew from experience that behind the butter-wouldn't-melt smile sat a steel-trap mind. Curtis Tate owed fifty percent of his success to L. T. LaRue, and a good chunk of the rest to his wife.

And, in this campaign, to Cynthia DeVries.

Keeping an eye on Adam throughout dinner, she saw him leave the room several times, only to return to his seat next to an empty chair. Phoebe Moss had evidently decided to dismiss the League of Women Voters.

"Without even a phone call of regret," Lilah Semple, the current president, murmured in Cynthia's ear. "I'm sorry to say this to you, Cynthia honey, when the girl is your future daughter-in-law. But such manners! Certainly not what I'm used to in our young women."

The same had happened, Cynthia learned a few minutes later, at the Association of Women Realtors' luncheon. "Just didn't show." BeBe Holtz had stopped at her shoulder to say hello. "Left us all sitting there with nothing to do but talk about the lousy state of the market. I've never seen a group of women so depressed."

For a moment, Cynthia wondered if perhaps her reception at Kellie Tate's house this morning had been so demeaning that Phoebe Moss felt she couldn't face the rest of her engagements that day. The girl had done serious damage to her reputation, not to mention Adam's campaign, on top of that horrible article in the Sunday newspaper. Of course, in suggesting to the various women's organizations that they invite the candidates' wives and fiancées to speak, Cynthia had hoped for just this sort of debacle. But it did look tonight that perhaps she'd pushed the girl a bit too far.

Nonsense, she decided as the plates were cleared and the speeches began. If Phoebe Moss couldn't stand this kind of pressure, she certainly wouldn't be suitable as the mayor's wife. Or the wife of a DeVries, with a long and outstanding tradition of service to the community to uphold.

And the sooner everyone knew and recognized that fact, the better for all concerned. Including Phoebe Moss.

THE VETERINARIAN HAD COME, pumped mineral oil into Marian's stomach and examined her as far as he was able. She most likely had some sort of intestinal blockage. All they could do was make her more comfortable with painkillers, keep her on her feet and hope the block would dissolve or pass through with the oil. Sometimes, colic wasn't a major problem. Sometimes the horse didn't survive. And only time would tell which case they had on their hands tonight.

Phoebe had been standing beside her horse for most of eight hours, petting, talking, watching carefully for the smallest change in Marian's behavior. They must've walked ten miles in a circle around the house, hoping that motion would stimulate the action of the horse's bowels. Marian showed no interest in cropping grass, no interest in her favorite alfalfa hay, or even grain. When left to herself, she hung her head, breathing hard against the pain. Eventually, she dropped to her knees, then flipped onto her back, twisting and rolling in discomfort.

"No, Marian. No." With a crop and her voice and a few well-placed kicks to Marian's rear, Phoebe got the horse on her feet again. "A twisted intestine is the last thing we need, mare. Then you'd be going into surgery, for sure. Let's walk some more." Her feet ached, her back screamed. But she wouldn't stop walking until Marian was out of danger.

The vet returned, poured more mineral oil down the tube in Marian's throat, then left again with the promise to be available if needed. Jacquie and Erin came over and gave Phoebe the chance to go to the bathroom, feed the dogs and cats, and grab a peanut-butter-and-jelly sandwich. Together, they all walked another couple of miles around the house in the cold night air.

And still, Marian's beautiful white head drooped almost to her knees, her dark eyes dull and half closed against a pain Phoebe couldn't ease. For once, she'd come up against a situation completely out of her control.

ADAM SAT DOWN TO A HEARTY round of applause from the League of Women Voters and their guests. He didn't interpret the response as a promise of votes, but at least he'd done a decent job with tonight's address. His stutter sneaked in now and then, but he'd learned not to panic, which only made things worse. Thanks to Phoebe, he could relax and move on.

Where was she? They'd met for breakfast and managed a few private words before separating for the day. Tonight, she seemed to have disappeared off the face of the earth. Tommy, of course, was furious at the missed lunch with the women Realtors, and now the dinner. Adam simply worried.

His opponent finished up a hearty speech, acknowledging a warmer reception than Adam had received, and then the evening, thank God, was over. Adam worked his way through the crowd, no easy task when he got stopped every two feet by a handshake, a question, a pat on the back. He'd almost reached the door when he encountered the most formidable obstacle of them all.

"Mother."

She and his dad were waiting for him. No way he could hurry past with a smile. "Good job, son." Preston gave him a clap on the back and a handshake. "You're giving Tate a run for his money."

"I'm d-doing my b-best."

His mother cut to the heart of things. "Miss Moss had something better to do?"

"I d-don't know. I can't find her." He'd left so many messages on her machine, the tape was full.

"Strange behavior for a candidate's future wife."

"I'm sure there's an ex-explanation."

"Besides rank bad manners, you mean?"

"Yes." He kept the answer short, trying to hold on to his temper.

But his mother wasn't going to be satisfied with anything less than an all-out confrontation. "I must say, I feel I've been put in a very awkward position. My future daughter-in-law doesn't even have the grace to notify an organization to which I belong that she won't be accepting their generous invitation."

"You surely d-don't want to argue about this right here, right now. So I'll j-just say g-good-night." He attempted to step past, but she caught him by the arm.

"I will not be ignored."

Adam glanced around, saw that their encounter had been noted, was being observed with interest. Swearing under his breath, he put an arm around his mother's shoulders and walked her across the hall, into the small room where brides could change clothes at their wedding reception.

Standing in front of the shut door, he faced Cynthia again. "That's what this is all about, right? You gave an order—don't run for mayor. But I didn't follow orders this time, and you c-can't handle it."

"I have told you—"

"Oh, I know you think you have reasons. They never m-made any sense, but that's beside the point. You want c-control, Mother. You sent Tim to m-medical school, told him to be a c-cardiologist, told him to come home to start his practice. You sent Theresa to law school and brought her back again. Your expectations of me were a lot lower, but I got my education at a good engineering school and came back to start a construction company, as you decreed. God knows, if you hadn't liked the idea, Dad wouldn't have given me the start-up loan."

Preston had followed them into the room. "Now, son—"

Cynthia stood staring at him, her face as rigid as her spine. "Are you finished?"

"No. You've sabotaged my campaign with your friends, and your comments to Samantha Pettit about Phoebe were aimed at more destruction. I doubt that's all you've done." He saw her eyes flicker, and knew he'd hit the mark. "You've been cruel to Phoebe, organizing your minions against her. All because I wouldn't be a good boy and do as I was told."

He shrugged and put his hand on the doorknob. "That's too damn bad, Mother. I might win this election, or I might lose. Either way, I guarantee that you've already lost."

Stepping out into the hall, he closed the door behind him. The crowd had thinned considerably, and he made his escape with only a few delays. Once in his truck, he dragged off his bow tie, threw his jacket in the back and headed straight for Swallowtail Farm.

The locked gate he took as a good sign, and used the key Phoebe had given him just this week to get through. But when he got to the house, the picture changed. Lights were on in every room, but the door was locked and the only answer to his knock was the howling of the three dogs. He checked out the empty barn and turned off the lights left blazing there. In the darkness, he could see the horses in the pasture much better—Cristal, Brady and Robin. But no white ghost. Where was Marian?

Heedless of his dress shoes and pants, he climbed the fence and walked the pasture, in case she'd fallen and he couldn't see. The other horses moved uneasily around him, and Adam didn't think they were reacting to his presence alone. He didn't find Marian. Something had happened to the lovely white mare.

He called Jacquie Archer, but struck out there, too. The best he could do was a strongly worded message on her answering machine. "Somebody let me know what's going on. Please."

As he drove back to town, his mood swung between concern for Phoebe and her horse and an impotent rage. Once again, she'd faced a crisis without asking for his help. Damn her independence, anyway…. She trusted him enough to make love with him, but still intended to handle her problems without his help. Their future together couldn't possibly stand on such a shaky foundation. Might as well build a house out of cardboard boxes on the edge of the ocean.

His answering machine offered no message from Phoebe. He called Tommy. "Wake up. Have you heard from Phoebe?"

"No, dammit. And some notice that she wasn't going

to show would have saved me an earful from bitchy rich women. Where is she?"

"I don't know. One of her horses is gone—I suppose they took her to a vet, but I don't know which one."

"Too bad. She'll call you, though. Just hang tight."

"Sure."

"We've got breakfast with the insurance guys at nine."

"I'll b-be there."

The campaign would go on. He had a shot at winning, if no new disaster arrived to torpedo his chances. Of course, his mother would never forgive him for his defiance. And his dad always took her side. Preston DeVries had been so grateful to marry a woman who ran all aspects of his life outside his medical practice that he'd abdicated any kind of authority at home. He had opinions, but he rarely fought for them, and never against his wife. Tim would probably be the same. And Theresa would take after their mother. She was definitely the woman in charge.

Adam wanted control of his own life. The thought struck him hard, and he considered the idea as he might study a complex blueprint. Phoebe wanted the same for her own life. She'd escaped her family and come to New Skye for just that reason.

Two lives, two people determined to go their own road. Where, how did they merge? Did one of them have to give up the right of way?

Sick of metaphors, sick of thinking, Adam dropped his clothes where he stood, turned off the light and climbed into his cold bed. Sleep wouldn't come. But with his face buried in the pillow, he could pretend it might.

PHOEBE SPENT THE NIGHT at the vet's office, in a chair outside the stall where he was fighting to save her horse's life. She dozed off and on, her head back against the concrete blocks, but always woke in a few minutes to check on the mare. Despite repeated doses of oil, Marian remained blocked, bloated, miserable.

"If something doesn't change by noon," the vet warned, "I think surgery is our only hope. And even that's no guarantee of recovery."

Jacquie and Erin had driven Phoebe into town last night with Marian in their horse trailer. They came back about ten Saturday morning to see how things were going.

One glance told the farrier all she needed to know. "We fed and watered and let the dogs out at your place. I had a message on my machine from Adam, Phoebe. Do you want me to call him?"

She'd thought about him all night, and dreamed about him when she closed her eyes. The whole situation seemed completely hopeless at this point. Phoebe had no illusions about the damage she'd done yesterday, abandoning her obligations without so much as a phone call. She had tried, using her cell phone on the drive home, but her shaking hands, her teary eyes and the fear in her gut had made safe driving as much as she could handle. Once she'd seen poor Marian's agony, her mind had blanked on anything else.

So what happened now? She doubted that she alone could sink Adam's campaign. But there was little question in her mind that her life simply could not, would not, blend with his. She would lose herself, lose everything she'd worked so hard to build. To be. Perhaps if he lost the election…

She'd had that thought once before, but Phoebe wouldn't wish for him to lose, not even to be with her.

He'd taken on the campaign because the fate of his hometown mattered, because he wanted a part in improving the place where he lived. A woman who loved him would not take that dream away. And she did love him.

In the stall, Marian heaved a huge, groaning sigh. Erin, standing beside the mare, looked out the door. "Phoebe? Phoebe, something's happening."

"Come on out, Erin," Jacquie said. "She may try to roll…"

The girl slipped out of the stall. Before the door slid closed, Marian groaned again.

Then came a sound like the smack of a baseball against a wooden fence. And again. Phoebe gazed in through the barred window as the huge blockage that had made poor Marian so miserable was finally expelled, spattering the walls around her like well-aimed mud balls. Just like that, the nightmare ended.

"Sand and dirt" was the vet's assessment. "Happens sometimes, for no reason we can figure. She should be just fine now, ready to go home Monday morning."

Marian already looked a thousand percent better, having sipped at her water bucket and found the hay Phoebe put for her in the rack. Her eyes were calm again, her face placid. With a final hug, Phoebe left the stall and stepped back into real life.

She'd missed the appointment she'd made to get her hair done, so she was on her own as far as the dance tonight was concerned. Jacquie and Erin dropped her off at the farm and she walked up the drive, newly grateful for the beauty she lived with. Marian would come home Monday and everything would go back to normal. More or less, depending on whether you considered a mayoral campaign normal life.

Her first move, after feeding the dogs and cats, was a

call to Adam. She got his machine, of course, and left an apology, with an explanation of sorts. Who knew what his schedule was for today, and when he would check for messages? They'd decided she would drive into town and meet him at his place to go to the dinner dance. Would she show up to find him furious at being ignored? Worried out of his mind?

Or, most likely, just ready to give up?

SAM HAD VERY SPECIFIC goals for her evening at the Stargazer Fundraiser. She intended to glean as much information as she could on the political situation, eavesdrop on every conversation she could get within earshot of, and do her best to forecast the election based on the knowledge and insight of the power brokers in New Skye, all of whom would be there.

Equally important, she intended to dance with Tommy Crawford. Frequently. And she intended to lure him into a dark part of the gardens for at least ten minutes of wild and crazy kisses. Maybe a little more than mere kisses. She'd leave the guy some freedom of choice.

To that end, she had decided to alter her usual style. No cleavage tonight, no long length of leg left to view. Tonight was about imagination. And Tommy, she hoped, had a really good imagination.

Without mousse and spray, her hair was soft, touchable, its natural wave allowed free play around her face, with only a sequinned clip for control. Her makeup sparkled, designed to lure a man rather than demand that he notice her eyes, her mouth.

The dress was deceptive. Dark blue lace created the top layer, cut close to her throat, with long, narrow sleeves and a figure-skimming shape that fell into folds around her feet. Underneath, the lining matched her skin tone almost exactly. So a man would be forgiven, even encouraged, to believe that she wore lace…with nothing else at all.

To enhance the effect, she arrived just a little late, and took her time strolling through the Botanical Gardens, enjoying the atmosphere, both natural and decorative. Fairy lights studded the smaller trees, but since this weekend was the height of the fall color season, the leaves shone yellow, red and gold rather than green. White luminaries lined the paths, giving a glow to clusters of chrysanthemums and pansies planted in the flower beds. Beyond were the shadowed paths she intended to explore with Tommy, deep within the magnolia grove, or underneath the pines. She shivered in anticipation and turned back toward the lights.

Following the sound of a band, she arrived at the amphitheater, a slight bowl of grass at the center of the garden. Tall red-and-white amaryllis flowers, grown in glass containers sprinkled with gold, decorated the tables and stood banked against the stage where the band played. A wooden dance floor had been leveled in the center, with dining tables arranged around the edges. Already couples were dancing, champagne glasses in hand. The raffle table had been set up opposite the stage, flanked by the car some lucky person would win plus a display of the other prizes. Tall lanterns and heating elements gave light and warmth to the crowd—after last week's cool snap, the weather had warmed up nicely. Women should be able to show off their bare shoulders for a little while, at least.

While Sam invited one man to think she'd bared everything.

Heralded by a symphony of delicious aromas, Cass Baker's Sugar and Spice catering trucks were parked discreetly to the side. A small army of servers was unloading platters, bowls and mountains of food onto long serving tables, supervised by Cass herself in a black, sequin-spangled dress under a big white apron.

"What a bash." Rory Newman had come up beside Sam as she stood watching. "Only time I guess I'll ever see something this fancy is when I get assigned to the photo detail." He brought his camera to his eye. "Smile." Sam obliged, and he snapped the picture. "Reporter Samantha Pettit will do whatever's required to get her story, even doll herself up in a million-dollar dress and hobnob with the stiffs. You look hot, babe."

"Thanks. The sight of you in a tux leaves me nearly speechless."

"A lot of women I know say that. So what's happening?"

"Just scoping out the situation."

"Waiting for Tommy Crawford, you mean. He drove in as I walked up from the parking lot. You should get your shot any second now."

In fact, as she turned toward the entrance, Tommy stepped through the arch of gold, white and red balloons. His gaze met hers and he gave her the sidelong smile that was the first thing about him she'd come to love. Then he glanced at her dress. His jaw dropped, his eyes went round. He fidgeted with his tie, as if he suddenly couldn't breathe.

"Yes," she whispered, and sent him her most seductive smile.

The fun was about to begin.

ADAM GOT HOME LATE Saturday afternoon, after a full day of campaign events, with a headache pounding against his temples and absolutely no interest in spending

the night making small talk—*more* small talk—with potential voters. There was only one person he wanted to
talk to, but unless she'd left a message…

"Hi, Adam, it's Phoebe." He let his chin drop to his
chest in relief. Half the headache eased, just hearing her
voice. "I am s-so s-sorry to have disappeared on you.
Marian colicked yesterday and Jacquie luckily st-stopped
by and f-found her before she could get too sick. But I
couldn't leave her, and she didn't actually improve until
this morning, at the v-v-vet's office where we s-s-spent
the night. Anyway, she's much better now. I'm at home,
planning to get a little s-sleep, then dress for the f-fund-
raiser. I'll be at your house about s-seven o'clock. If you
don't open the door, I'll understand." A long pause followed. "S-see you later, I h-hope. Bye."

He dressed in record time, which included cleaning
pasture dirt from last night off of his dress shoes, then
stood at the window facing the parking lot, watching and
waiting for the lime-green Beetle to arrive. Before
Phoebe could get out of the car, he had opened the front
door and come down the walk to meet her.

She looked up in surprise when he arrived at her
bumper. "Oh." The uncertainty faded from her smile.
"Hi."

She got out of the car and came toward him, her dress
shimmering in the street lamps. He turned and walked
beside her toward the house.

"You're not completely forgiven, you know."

"No?" In the hallway, she turned to face him.

"No." He shut the door with his heel.

"What do I have to do to make amends?"

"Trust me."

She looked away from him, fidgeting with the catch

on her purse. "I don't know, Adam. I mean…I do know you're trustworthy. But—"

"Yes, 'but.'" He stepped close, took her face in his hands and kissed her gently on the forehead.

The doubt was there in her eyes as she gazed at him. And he couldn't change her mind in a manner of minutes.

"Tonight, though, is n-not the time to settle this. You're too beautiful, all silver sparkles from head to toe. I'm going to take you to the Botanical Gardens and show you off."

"Show me off?" She gave a disbelieving laugh, and shook her head. "You're crazy."

"Am n-not. See?" He turned her to face the big mirror hanging at the end of the hallway. The dark wood of the frame fashioned their portrait, a man in black behind a woman wearing a glittering dress that hinted subtly at the wonderful curves and planes underneath, her long, graceful throat revealed by a low neckline, her hair drawn up and sprinkled with stars. "N-not just good enough to be m-mayor," he teased, bending to kiss the creamy, jasmine-scented skin at the curve of her shoulder. "We look damn n-near presidential."

Now when she stared at him, the stars were in her eyes. "You've already created a beautiful evening." She put a finger to her lips, then placed it on his mouth. "Let's go and enjoy ourselves."

CHAPTER FIFTEEN

THE MAGIC LASTED FOR AN hour.

For that one shining hour, the glitterati of New Skye danced and drank and admired one another and themselves under a star-flecked sky, in a garden turned wonderland. A hundred perfumes scented the air like an exotic lily. Music danced on the breeze, hummed in the blood. This was a night to remember.

Cynthia approved. She stood with Preston at the lip of the amphitheater, near the balloon archway, and gazed over her creation, allowing herself a satisfied smile.

"Pleased, my dear?" Preston adjusted the set of her mink stole on her shoulders.

"I do believe I am. It's quite a scene, don't you think?"

"Without a doubt. The town owes you a tremendous debt of gratitude." He took her hand and brought her fingers to his lips. "As do I. You're a remarkable woman, Cynthia."

She squeezed his hand. "I didn't accomplish this by myself."

"But you could have, if you set your mind to it. Would you like to dance? Or shall we find our table?"

Before she could decide, a camera flash drew her attention to the latest arrivals. Framed by the gold, red and white arch of balloons, two couples stood side by side, frozen in place for the photographer's benefit. The mayoral candidates and their escorts had arrived.

"Shake hands, why don't you?" the redheaded photographer called. "No hard feelings and all that."

Curtis Tate grinned genially enough and extended his hand toward Adam, in front of his wife and Phoebe Moss as they stood side by side between the two men. Adam hesitated, and the mayor's grin began to falter. Finally, Adam took the offered hand and held it for the instant of the flash.

"Great shot." The photographer went in search of other prey. "Thanks."

The two couples separated immediately. Curtis and Kellie Tate came toward Cynthia. As she looked beyond them, Adam gave her a brief nod before leading his fiancée down the gentle slope toward the dance floor. They made a handsome couple: Adam was as polished as always, as precise as Cynthia had brought him up to be. The graceful design of Phoebe's dress, subtly glittering in shades of silver and plum when she moved, combined with the sleek braid wrapped around her head to create an elegant impression.

In contrast, Kellie Tate, wearing yellow taffeta and a gold-and-sapphire necklace, looked like an overblown rose.

The comparison suddenly seemed unbearable. "Let's dance," she told Preston, taking his arm with a tense grip. He managed to delay long enough to shake hands with the mayor, but Cynthia refused to dawdle and thus escaped before she had to acknowledge what a greedy, ambitious woman Kellie Tate really was. Because to admit that she'd chosen such a woman as a tool, an ally…

Brought her perilously close to recognizing the same qualities in herself.

SAM HAD ACCOMPLISHED PART of her agenda. She'd definitely blown Tommy away with the dress. He'd been barely verbal for the first ten minutes they danced.

Finally, he seemed to realize that more than lace covered her skin, and he started to relax. "I was thinking about yanking a cloth off one of the tables to wrap you in," he confessed.

"Could you do it without disturbing the dishes?"

"Oh, sure."

She stopped dancing. "Let me see."

He rolled his eyes and pulled her close...closer. "Forget it. You're more trouble than you're worth, as it is."

"Oh." She hadn't meant to sound so...sad. But she was tired of playing the game. "Well, thanks for the dance." Jerking free of his hold, she left the dance floor at a near run.

"Sam? Samantha." Tommy came after her, but she was good at dodging through crowds. He didn't catch up until she'd reached the edge of the grass bowl, the border between light and dark. "What are you doing? It was a joke, you know that. We always joke."

"Yeah, we always joke." She faced the dark, thankful for waterproof makeup. "Don't you ever get tired of being funny?"

"What's the alternative?"

"How about being real?"

She heard his sigh. "Real...hurts, Sam. Real scars."

"Real builds. And heals. If you let it."

He stood silently for a long, long time. Finally, he put his hand lightly on her elbow. "C'mon, let's get back. There's a party down there, and we're missing the food."

Her turn to sigh. "Sure. Why not? I've got a job to do." She turned and headed toward the tables, the crowd, the music. But she shook her arm free of Tommy's hold.

She wasn't surprised when he got snagged by someone who wanted to talk about the campaign. Despite his grab for her hand, she gave him a fake smile and slipped away, walking blindly in an effort to escape the disappointment being with Tommy always caused.

Being with Tommy but not *with* him.

The buffet line had shortened considerably, so she decided she might as well bandage her wounded pride with calories. Carrying her loaded plate and a glass of champagne, Sam bypassed the tables near the dance floor to sit on a bench tucked into the curve of a flower bed. A drift of cigar smoke teased her nose, coming from the other side of the trees behind her—not her favorite smell, especially with food, and she almost got up to leave. Then the conversation accompanying the fumes caught her attention.

"Come on, Curtis, stop worrying. The gap in the polls is closing, but not fast enough. He'll never catch up before election day." A man's voice, familiar but not immediately identifiable, especially while he chewed on a cigar.

Forgetting food, Sam tuned in. The mayor was worried about losing, was he?

"Yeah, well, the gap wasn't supposed to close at all. The guy can't spit out a straight sentence, for pity's sake."

"He played the vandalism low-key. If his girlfriend's house wasn't enough to warn him off, what can I say? I didn't want to get too creative, 'cause that would increase the chances of getting caught. But you've got the reports on Phoebe Moss from the investigator in Atlanta, right? All we have to do is decide how to release the information."

"That's what y'all keep saying. I'm still not seeing

what use it is to attack the fiancée. She isn't the one running for mayor.''

''We're attacking the package, Curtis. Planting doubt about DeVries's values, his priorities. When the voters go into the booth, we want them to see that name and think 'Oh, yeah, he's engaged to the therapist who mistreated that poor stuttering kid in Atlanta. What kind of man would take up with a woman like that? He probably kicks puppies and drowns kittens. I'm voting for the guy I know.' And they make their mark by your name.''

''They'd better. Kellie's in perpetual PMS, thinking she's not gonna be Mrs. Mayor anymore.''

The other man laughed. ''You have to admit, she's got the killer instinct you need in politics. Hiring that detective was a brilliant idea. Did you give her a suitable reward?''

''She wanted sapphires to wear tonight.'' Behind Sam, the dry grass rustled as the mayor and his friend left their smoking room. ''Smart lady, though—arranged the whole shebang before she told me the first thing about it. I've got my eye on a nice diamond necklace for election night.''

''You're a good man, Curtis.'' They walked away from Sam without noticing her, two ''gentlemen'' joining the festivities below.

The mayor put an arm around his friend's shoulders. ''Thanks, L.T. I do my best.''

LIKE CINDERELLA, PHOEBE gave herself over to the fantasy. For one night, fairy tales did come true, and the prince was hers to keep. Even the close encounter with Kellie Tate and her husband couldn't dim the brilliance of this evening.

"I didn't imagine all of this," she murmured as she and Adam swayed to the music.

He bent his head to hear her better. "All of what?"

She lifted her hand from his shoulder to indicate…well, everything. "The lights, the flowers, all of it. I sat in the meetings and heard the reports, but this is so much more."

"It's just a p-party."

"No, it's a mind-set. An organizational skill. Your mother may be…difficult…"

"That's one word for it."

"…but she has the same abilities as many CEOs. She can direct, delegate, inspire and create a good outcome with the force of her personality." She moved back a little, the better to see his face. "I'm sure those are the qualities you'll bring to the mayor's office."

"You're saying I take after my mother?" His brows lowered. "Thanks."

"Why else do you think you two have such trouble getting along?"

Adam stared down at the woman in his arms, struggling to reject her assessment. And failing, because the truth was easily recognized. "Just be sure to kick me before I start sabotaging our children's lives."

"Our children…" Phoebe's jaw dropped and her eyes went wide.

He gave her a wink, but before they could pursue the topic, a tap on his shoulder stopped their dance. Adam turned to see Samantha Pettit standing behind him. "Are you c-cutting in?"

"No." She grabbed his hand, and one of Phoebe's, and drew them off the dance floor. "You won't believe this." Excitement flashed in her eyes, practically sparked off her skin. Her hand shook as she led them through the tables to the edge of the amphitheater, just beyond the lights. "I don't. But I heard it from the horse's mouth, so to speak."

"Heard what?"

"There's good news, and there's good news. Which do you want first?"

"Sam..." Judging by her tone of voice, Phoebe shared his dislike of games.

She dragged in a deep breath. "Right. Guess who engineered the vandalism at your construction sites. And Phoebe's house?"

Adam had thought about this and come to only one conclusion. "LaRue?"

The reporter's face fell. "You knew?"

Phoebe gazed at him in horror. "My house, too?"

He shrugged. "S-seemed logical."

"But you didn't say anything?" Samantha rolled her eyes, then thumped the heel of her hand against her head. "Didn't try to investigate?"

"There was no p-proof. I thought the accusation would just c-confuse the c-campaign issues."

"You didn't even tell Tommy?"

The man in question joined their group. "Tell Tommy what?"

"That L. T. LaRue had Adam's work sites vandalized. And Phoebe's house."

Now Adam met his friend's laser stare. "That right, DeVries?"

"We'll talk about it later. Is this your big news, Samantha?"

"No, actually. The big news is who hired that P.I. in Atlanta."

"The mayor?"

"No. And—the really big news—not your mother, either."

A coil of tension in Adam's chest relaxed like a spring at rest. "So…who?"

Samantha shook her head.

"Well, tell us, why don't you?" Judging by his impatience, Tommy's mood had crashed, probably for the same reason that Sam had avoided looking at him since he walked up.

"Kellie Tate," Sam said quietly, her eyes on Adam's face.

Along with Phoebe and Tommy, Adam stood silent for a few seconds, staring at Samantha Pettit. "The m-mayor's wife," he said finally.

"That's right. Her idea, her plan, her execution."

"How do you know this?"

"I heard Curtis Tate talking to LaRue. No secrets between them."

Tommy muttered a string of words that should have gotten him kicked out of the party. Then he glared at Adam again. "You want to play fair. You think the ideas matter. And this is the kind of crap you're up against." His gaze moved to Sam. "And you…you've spent months tearing down a good man when you should've been moving heaven and earth to get the dirt on the scum who think elections are won with lies." Shaking his head, he shoved his hands in his pockets, turned on his heel and left them, his slouch more obvious than usual.

"Well," Phoebe said quietly, "what are we going to do about this information? Do we want to use it? Can we?"

Samantha looked at Adam, and he shrugged. "Hearsay d-doesn't m-make a great offense," he said. "I'm not ready to use gossip as a c-campaign tool."

"Think about it," Samantha advised. "If you wait until they attack, you might lose altogether."

When he was alone again with Phoebe, Adam met her gaze with his own. "What do you think?"

"I'm glad it wasn't your mother."

He laughed, in exasperation and in relief. "You're too generous." Then he dragged in a deep breath. "But I'm g-glad, too."

"As for the campaign…" She stood beside him, looking out over the vista of his mother's achievement, The Stargazer Fundraiser. "If you publish the news, you might win due to the voters' revulsion."

"*M-might* is the word. S-sometimes stuff like this doesn't affect the election one way or the other."

"Without a doubt, though, you'll reveal what kind of person Kellie Tate is, and her husband—the kind who would cheat to win. And while many of the people in town are aware of the Tates' true natures, life is easier if they ignore it."

"And so…?"

Phoebe turned to face him, her gray gaze serious, unflinching. "I would keep the information quiet. You're trying to improve the city, trying to benefit the community. I don't think exposing the personal shortcomings of the current mayor will accomplish your goal."

"That might mean I lose the election."

"Do you want to win at the expense of the town itself? And, even more important, do you want to win so badly that you'll become the person you're trying to defeat?"

Grinning, Adam took her hands and brought them to his lips, kissing each in turn. "That's the question. And the answer is…no." He pulled her close and set his arms around her, took the kisses she offered until they were both a little drunk with desire. "We could dance," he whispered over her ear. "Or we could leave and find a place to be alone."

"Both," she told him. "First we dance. Then we leave."

"And eat," Adam added. "I'm starved."

"Eat then dance," Phoebe agreed, and led him back into the crowd. She returned the wink he'd given earlier. "And then…"

CYNTHIA COULD FEEL HER heart pound in anticipation as the climax of the fundraiser approached. The raffle winners had been announced throughout the evening, and only the ticket claiming the car remained to be drawn.

The band played a fanfare, followed by a drumroll, and Kellie Tate reached into the bin for that last ticket. She held it high in the air and made her way through the tables and the crowd on the dance floor to the stage. Arriving at the microphone, she signaled for quiet and then smiled widely. "Here we have the last raffle prize of the evening, ladies and gentlemen, the grand-prize winner of that beautiful automobile donated by Dalrymple Cars of New Skye. Are you ready?" A round of applause answered the question. "Very well, then. The winner of the brand-new sports car is…" She looked at the ticket and gasped. "Oh, my God. I can't believe it. The name on the ticket is…Curtis Tate. Curtis, honey, you won the car!"

A dull silence smothered the crowd. No one moved, no one spoke; even the caterer's workers stood motionless. Cynthia felt a cold wave creep through her body. From all corners of the gathering, her committee members looked to her, their gazes begging her to salvage the situation.

She stepped onto the stage and went to stand beside

Kellie. "What a wonderful surprise," she said, forcing her voice to sound normal. "Luck favors the lucky, doesn't it? And our illustrious mayor is certainly among the fortunate tonight. Please, Mr. Mayor, do join us."

Red-faced, tugging at his bow tie, Curtis Tate stepped into place beside his wife at the microphone. "I'm flabbergasted," he admitted. "I had no expectation of winning—just wanted to help the cause by purchasing some tickets."

"Twenty of 'em," a voice from the back of the dance floor shouted. "That's one way to guarantee yourself a prize."

"Now, now." Cynthia took the microphone back. "There are more than twenty tickets left in the hopper. Let us all wish the Tates much pleasure from their new car." She clapped her hands, but the response from the audience was woefully apathetic.

The mayor pulled the microphone in his direction. "As long as we're talking about luck, I'd like to point out to the citizens of this town what great good fortune we have in calling Mrs. Cynthia DeVries a citizen." That round of applause was a bit stronger, thank God. "This fundraiser would never have happened without her efforts. It was her idea and she's spearheaded the effort from first to last. The New Skye Botanical Gardens will benefit tremendously from her dedication and her skills."

This time, the crowd applauded enthusiastically. "And so," Curtis Tate said, reaching into the breast pocket of his dinner jacket, "I would like to present a special gift to Mrs. DeVries and to the Botanical Gardens. I have here a check from the city, already signed by the treasurer. All I have to do is fill in the amount—an amount equal to the total sum of all the money raised here tonight. How's that? What do you think?"

The crowd cheered, and Cynthia smiled, savoring her triumph. Power didn't necessarily depend on elections or appointed office, on business acumen, or even on being a man. A woman could acquire power in her own sphere, given the aptitude and the drive.

Kellie edged her husband away from the microphone. "Curtis and I would like to express our gratitude to Mrs. DeVries for everything she's done for the gardens, for this city, for us personally. Her support of our reelection campaign means so much more than mere money...."

The mayor's hand tightened on his wife's arm. Her voice broke, stopped.

This wasn't just silence, this was a wave of shock that could be seen passing across the crowd. Unerringly, Cynthia found her gaze locked with her son's, though she hadn't until that moment known where he stood. Adam's face revealed nothing of his thoughts, unless you were his mother, unless you'd watched him grow from a baby to a little boy to a man, unless you'd seen that same recognition of betrayal over and over again in his blue eyes.

His father stood beside him. For the first time ever, Cynthia dreaded looking into Preston's face. She found everything she'd expected—outrage, confusion, disappointment. He never argued with her, never disputed her plans or questioned her motives. But she had never before so thoroughly betrayed one of their children. And this time, she doubted even the best of reasons would be good enough.

All she could do was end the travesty as quickly as possible. At the microphone once again, she said, simply, "Let's all go back to enjoying the evening," and then quickly slipped offstage.

She had no trouble penetrating the crush of people,

because a path opened in front of her as friends and acquaintances drew aside to let her through. None of them spoke, though once she'd passed she heard the conversations start up.

Sooner than she wished, she stood in front of her husband, her son and Phoebe Moss. No one said a word for a long moment. Cynthia finally made the effort. "You look lovely," she told the young woman. "That's a wonderful dress."

Her words broke the dam. "Am I to understand," Preston said, in a tone she had never heard from him before, "that you contributed money to the mayor's campaign?"

She met his gaze. "Yes."

"How much did you give him?"

This answer was much harder. "Ten thousand dollars."

Phoebe Moss gasped, and Adam winced.

Preston's face only hardened. "Without telling me, you donated a significant sum to the campaign of my son's opponent. Why?"

"For the same reasons I have opposed Adam's foolish effort all along. And because the mayor agreed to match the funds from this event with city funds. I wanted to ensure his cooperation and benefit the garden."

"Altruistic to the end." Adam spoke in a rough, unsteady voice. "I suppose you want me to thank you for your service to the city."

"The respect due your mother would be sufficient."

"What about the respect due your husband?" Preston stepped forward and took hold of her wrist. "Or your son? What about some kind of acknowledgment that other people and their ideas, their goals, matter?"

"This is not the time nor place—"

"You're damn right it's not. We're going home."

She resisted his pull. "I cannot leave until the evening is over. This entire celebration is my responsibility."

"I imagine the festivities will come to an end without your help." Preston faced Adam. "I'm sorry, son. I should've paid more attention. I regret the embarrassment your mother has caused you, and the rest of the family."

Cynthia desperately wanted to argue the point, wanted to defend herself against such an insult, and from her husband of all people. But his grip on her wrist would not be broken. All around them were curious onlookers, whispering to one another when they weren't actively observing the scene. She could not bear to give them more to talk about by actively protesting.

There would be hell to pay, though, when she got Preston DeVries home alone.

PHOEBE COULD ONLY GUESS at the emotions behind Adam's rigid face. She put a hand on his arm, like stone under her fingertips. "I'm sorry."

He jumped, as if he'd been asleep. "N-not really surprising, is it? She'd d-do anything to g-get her way. I've known that for years."

"At least the worst harm has already been done. And the Tates aren't going to be very popular, once the news gets out."

"And it will," Samantha Pettit assured them as she approached. "I couldn't keep this story quiet if I wanted to. Even Kellie Tate's dad can't squelch news that three hundred people have already heard. They've left the party, by the way."

Adam nodded. "I'm thinking that sounds like a g-great idea." Phoebe felt certain, however, that his mind was not on taking her home and making love all night.

Tommy stepped up beside Adam. "Oh, no, you don't. You're making hay while the sun shines, so to speak. The time to capitalize on everybody else's disaster is right now. Tonight. I want you talking to as many people as you can. You and Phoebe both."

"C-Crawford, maybe it escaped your n-notice, but I just found out in front of a c-crowd of social and p-political p-piranhas that my mother would p-pay to have me lose this election. That makes this my d-disaster, too."

"So you use your disaster. Build on it. You've got a chance to solidify yourself in the minds of these people as a noble figure, a man persevering in the face of intense opposition to accomplish something important for the community. JFK couldn't have asked for a better opportunity. Show them who you really are."

Phoebe pressed her fingers against her lips, tempted to protest, to sway Adam's decision with her own opinion. Tommy was such a manipulator that even honesty seemed sleazy in his grasp. He wanted Adam to behave with honor and generosity, not because those traits were a worthwhile goal in themselves, but as a means to an end. She hoped Adam would choose simply to walk away. With her.

Just for tonight, she pleaded silently. *Acknowledge your worth as a man because of who you are, not what you can do for someone else.*

But Adam nodded at Tommy, then turned to take her hand. "You d-don't have to stay," he said quietly, and bent to kiss her cheek. "If you want, you can take my truck and go back to my house. I'll get a ride with Tommy when we're done here."

Numb to the core, Phoebe shook her head. "I'll wait for you."

His smile lacked its usual brilliance. "Thanks." Following Tommy back into the crowd, he reminded her of a lone knight, heading off to fight the dragon with a broken lance as his only weapon.

"Stick with me." Sam Pettit linked an arm through hers. "I've got a lot of people to talk to, and I'll make sure they know the real story without you having to say a word."

The rest of the night passed in a kind of kaleidoscopic haze. Voices came at her out of the darkness and then receded without her being certain of who it was and what they'd actually said. Tired, with aching feet and head and a sore heart, Phoebe struggled to keep her wits, to say the right thing or, at the very least, to avoid saying something wrong. She spoke with so many different people, she wasn't sure whether or not she'd accomplished that goal.

Eventually, though, the crowd thinned. The music stopped; the band packed up and drove away. Adam and Tommy stayed to the bitter end, talking with the catering staff and the men who came to load tables and chairs on their truck. Samantha decided to do a story on the aftermath of such events, and went off with her photographer friend to interview the cleanup crew.

Phoebe sat on a bench by one of the flower beds, propped her elbows on her knees and put her chin on her hands. Tonight provided a glimpse of her future, she realized, if Adam won the election and they stayed together. Her life would resemble an unending carousel ride of public appearances, political successes and political catastrophes, with all of the seats on the ride occupied by people she didn't necessarily like, and more of them trying to climb on at the same time as others fell off. She would always be concerned about the right clothes to wear, the right words to say, the right way to say them. Neglecting her animals, her job, herself, she would constantly struggle to meet the standards of the job. And in her failure to be what he wanted and needed, Adam would come to see her as her parents always had.

Just the thought shut down her ability to think, to plan. Phoebe wanted to go home. Alone.

And figure out how to get on with the rest of her life. Alone.

WORKING THE CROWD, Tommy kept one eye on his candidate and one eye on Sam Pettit. Then, as the place cleared out, he watched Adam less and Sam more. That dress still stopped his heart, even though he knew the impression was deceptive. Just the thought of Sam Pettit's smooth, pale skin under dark blue lace was enough to send his engine racing into the danger zone.

As usual, though, they were at odds. She wanted him to be "real." Why couldn't she just settle for entertaining?

"You've got your candidate working hard," she commented, appearing suddenly beside him. "Are your chances better after tonight?"

He turned to face her. "Chances for what?"

She read him immediately, and her face lost its brittle smile. "I meant the election."

"There's more on the line than an election."

"What brought about this stunning revelation?"

"You. In that dress."

"It's all about sex?"

Tommy sighed. "For once, could we not argue? No, it's not about sex. But till we get the sex out of the way, I'm not gonna be able to think straight." He grabbed her hand. "Come on."

She laughed but didn't resist. "You're such a romantic. What girl could refuse a seductive invitation like that?"

"I'll show you seductive. When we get to my place."

Then she did stop dead, at a curve on the path. "No. Now." The kisses she showered on him were like fireworks falling on parched grass. Before he could pull back, they both swayed at the edge of insanity.

Panting, shivering with need, Tommy broke away. "I am not making love to you in the Botanical Gardens with the cleanup crew watching. Come on, Sam. We've put this off too long as it is."

As usual, she got the last word. "Race you to the car!" Then she picked up the skirt of that incredible dress and ran.

Grinning, Tommy followed.

ADAM WAS BEGINNING TO wonder if Phoebe had taken his advice and left the party when, at, last he spotted her sitting alone on a garden bench, up the slope from the dance floor. He climbed toward her, not sure she'd even noticed him. Her focus seemed to be inward and her face was somber, as if she confronted some terrible loss.

"Phoebe?" He sat beside her. "Earth to Phoebe."

She blinked and straightened up. "Hello, there. All finished?"

"Thank G-God. What are you p-pondering so d-deeply?"

"Oh…the campaign, I guess. These next two weeks will be the hardest."

"You're right, as usual." He put his arm around her, pulled her against him, and was surprised when she hesitated a moment before yielding. "B-but we d-don't have to think about that tonight."

She made a visible effort to brighten her mood. "What shall we think about?" Adam whispered a suggestion in her ear and Phoebe gasped. "That's quite a train of thought, Mr. DeVries. Would you care to elaborate?"

He glanced around the garden. "N-not right here, right n-now."

Once inside the warmth of his home, though, with a strong door between them and the rest of the world, Phoebe turned to him with a sweet, wicked smile. "You were saying?"

"I was saying," he said, drawing her down the hall, "that I hadn't realized the potential of this mirror until earlier this evening." Standing behind her, he closed his fingers on the zipper tab of her dress and slowly pulled it down. The heavy fabric fell away under its own weight, revealing her smooth, creamy shoulders and arms, the tiny lavender ribbons supporting the silky slip she wore underneath. Adam let the sparkling material puddle at their feet. "You could have worn just this tonight," he suggested, running his hand over the swell of her breast, the plane of her belly, the curve of her hip.

She let her head drop back against his shoulder. "I would have been cold."

"Those of us men who saw you would've been very, very warm." He laughed as he dragged his mouth along the column of her throat. "On second thought, I'm glad I'm the only one who knows how beautiful you are."

"Adam…" She tried to face him.

"N-not yet." He looked into the mirror as he slipped his fingertips under those lavender ribbons and pulled them over the curve of her shoulders. The silk whispered down her body, leaving her wearing the soft light of the hallway and very little else. "S-so b-beautiful." He retraced the path of his hands, shaking with the need to possess.

Phoebe said his name again, and whirled in his arms before he could stop her. "Let's be f-fair about this," she whispered, and reached for his tie. Adam watched the mirror as she undressed him, aroused by the arch of her spine, the strength in her arms and legs, the contrast of his darkness and her light.

Finally, they stood flesh against flesh, and sight became less revealing than sound, less meaningful than scent, less imperative than touch. Passion sent them to his bed, a place where gravity had no real power, a refuge where the physical and the spiritual beings joined as one.

Much later, as they lay together on the verge of sleep, Adam remembered that moment in the garden. "Phoebe?"

"Mmm?"

"You didn't tell me what you were thinking about when I found you."

Again, she hesitated. Again, he felt her searching for the way to say something important.

"Don't w-worry," she murmured, her voice drowsy. "It'll keep till later."

He tried to take her at her word. But he couldn't shake a sense of impending disaster. Whatever might happen in the next two weeks, Adam fell asleep with the overwhelming impression that tonight he'd fought the most important battle of his life.

And lost.

CHAPTER SIXTEEN

DURING ITS LAST WEEK, Adam's campaign reminded Phoebe of a runaway train—horn blaring, brakes screeching, passengers screaming, and a prevailing expectation of imminent doom. Not that Adam seemed destined to lose the election—in fact, the polls showed him pulling ahead slightly, with a good chance of winning.

For Phoebe, though, time was running out. Every day closer to the election was one day less in her time with Adam. She wanted to hoard the minutes, treasure the hours, cherish his voice and his body and his mind, giving herself a wealth of memories to draw on for solace in the lonely days to come.

These memories, though, would mostly recall the hours they spent together shaking hands in parking lots during high school football games and Saturday morning grocery shopping. On Halloween, they walked the streets of downtown, talking with parents about school issues while the kids trick-or-treated at the different shops. Their time alone occurred in the truck, driving from one event to the next, or late at night when they made love if they could stay awake long enough. Which wasn't often.

She met him—and Tommy, of course—for breakfast at the diner on the Friday before the election to plan the final campaign push. "This weekend, we breathe, eat, sleep getting out the vote," Tommy decreed. "Gotta bring people to the polls."

Adam glanced at Phoebe and rolled his eyes. "Like we haven't been d-doing that already? I look in the m-mirror to sh-shave and s-start out with, 'You know, Tuesday is election day. Are you planning to v-vote?'"

"I've got the horses convinced," Phoebe said. "I figure I'll put a hat over their ears and a coat over their tails and nobody'll notice the four hooves."

"Very funny." Tommy had picked up a copy of the daily paper. "I keep waiting for Tate to spring some kind of last minute trap, but I think he's decided that he'll stay in his hole until the shooting's all over."

"Not quite." Sam arrived and scooted into the booth next to Tommy. "Look at the letters to the editor. Tate wrote to announce he's donating the car to an orphanage northwest of here. Says he doesn't need it and wants some good to come of the prize."

Tommy flipped to the back page of the section and hooted with laughter. "Damn. You gotta give the guy credit—he's a canny political animal." When his comment met with cold, offended silence, he looked at Adam and Phoebe and shrugged. "Well, he is."

Tired and stressed, Phoebe didn't bother to mince words. "Since you're such an admirer, maybe you should run that campaign."

Adam put a hand over hers. "It's okay, Phoebe."

"No, it's not." She freed her hands and used them to rub her eyes. "I'm sick of being measured against some mythical political standard and always found wanting. I'm sick of hearing that we're not doing enough, that we could be smarter, quicker, sneakier...whatever. Adam is good enough to be mayor without changing so much as his socks. I'd think you, as his campaign manager, would recognize that fact."

"It's a game," Tommy said. "There are rules—"

"Damn your rules." She slapped her palms on the table. "And it's not a g-game. It's a serious endeavor, the process of choosing the person who will l-lead the community in some pretty desperate times. While you're playing angles and creating sound bites, people are l-losing j-j-jobs and h-health care, wondering h-how they're going to pay for their medicine and buy food, too. Adam went into this campaign to deal with those issues, and you've perverted his effort into some kind of-of pissing contest. Who can shoot f-f-farther?" Using both hands, she pushed on Adam's shoulder. "L-let me out, please. L-l-let me out."

In the ladies' rest room, she locked the door, then leaned back against the panel, crying. Mourning.

"Phoebe?" Abby knocked on the door. "Phoebe, sweetheart, are you okay?"

"No." Phoebe tried to swallow the sobs. "I'll clear out of here in a minute."

"Take your time. And if you want to leave by the kitchen door, be my guest."

"Thanks." She shouldn't sneak out. Tommy deserved an apology…or did he? And what did Adam deserve?

Leaving through the kitchen door a few minutes later, she carried a foam cup of hot tea and the bag of biscuits Charlie Brannon handed her. "I always like a woman who tells it the way she sees it," he said with a wink. "My Abby's as straight-shooting as they come. You, too."

Dry grass crunched under her feet as she walked along the side of the building to the parking lot in front. November had blown in chilly and brittle this year, with unusually low temperatures. Bad weather would keep attendance at the polls down….

"Damn." They had her thinking just like them. Calculating the effect of the weather on the election, instead of accepting what came and being grateful for the beauty in even the worst storm. Jacquie and Erin were seeing more of her animals than she did these days. She hadn't had time to clean a stall in weeks. And she enjoyed cleaning stalls.

The end is near, she promised herself as she started the car. Wednesday, she would once again be simply Phoebe Moss—the speech therapist with a severely diminished practice to build up again and a farm she planned to use for the benefit of battered and abused animals. No more politics, no more campaigns or fundraisers in her life.

No more Adam DeVries.

With that thought, Phoebe pulled off the road and stopped in the parking lot of the Pentecostal Holiness Church...because she couldn't see through her tears to drive.

A GENTLEMAN SIMPLY DID not pound on the rest room door, demanding that a woman emerge before she was ready. His mother had taught him that rule, he was sure.

So Adam waited, even though he figured Phoebe would escape by the back door of the diner. Sure enough, when he glanced out the window, he caught a glimpse of her green Beetle leaving the parking lot.

"You p-pushed too hard," he told Tommy. Standing by the table, he took up the bill for a breakfast neither he nor Phoebe had touched. "She d-didn't want to do this in the first pl-place, and you d-drove her to the breaking p-point."

Tommy set his mug down with a jolt that sloshed coffee on the table. "When you're looking in that mirror in the morning, see if you can't catch a glimpse of the guy who started this whole shebang, who agreed with the decisions and fronted the operation. Then we'll talk.'' His face was closed, his eyes hard, but he couldn't leave with Sam seated beside him on the outside.

So Adam did.

He checked for Phoebe's car at her office, to be sure she'd arrived safely, and was relieved to find the Beetle in its usual spot. Much as he wanted to talk to her, he knew her well enough to accept that she wouldn't want to see him right now. That damn independence would keep her from accepting his comfort, or even his thanks for her defense of him against Tommy's relentless criticism.

Besides, his own work waited—a desk full of papers to be dealt with and projects all over town needing his supervision. Jody had run through a dozen message pads this fall, waiting for him to show up and take his phone calls.

Instead of heading to the office, though, he drove through downtown New Skye and up the Hill, to a street he hadn't visited for more than a month, to a house where he was no longer sure of his welcome.

His mother wasn't sure, either. She stared at him for a speechless moment after she opened the door. ''Come in,'' she said finally, and moved back.

With the door closed, they faced each other across the entry hall. Cynthia looked…small. Beautiful, well dressed, but diminished.

''How are you, Mother?''

''Well enough. Would you like some coffee?''

''Sounds good, thanks.'' He didn't need coffee, but maybe they both needed a minute to get their balance back.

She brought a tray into the living room, where he'd

settled on one of the armchairs, then sat on the end of the sofa farthest away from him. "I'll let you fix your own." As he added sugar and milk to his cup, she said, "Why are you here?"

His mother was nothing if not direct. Adam sat back in his chair, leaving the coffee cup on the tray. "Because I care about you."

"After..." She pressed her lips together and fingered the cording on the cushion beside her.

"Even though I don't like what you did, and I hate the way you treated Phoebe, you're important to me." The words sounded lukewarm, but "I love you" had never been part of the family dialogue.

"Your father is still furious."

Adam grinned. "Ten grand is a lot of money to donate to a political campaign in this town. You should have talked with him first."

"I didn't want to be...dissuaded."

No surprise there. "He'll forgive you. He always does."

Cynthia smiled and Adam recognized the expression as one of his own—a one-sided tilt of her mouth that conveyed her doubts, her regrets. "Do you?"

He thought for a minute. "Yes, as far as I'm concerned. You're entitled to your own political opinions, and you're not required to vote for me just because I'm your son." By the lift of her eyebrows, he saw that she heard his "but" before he said it. "But with respect to Phoebe, I think you have an apology to make. You were cruel and thoughtless, trying to turn people against her with no reason beyond a need to demonstrate your personal power."

His mother sat motionless, staring down at her hands,

folded in her lap. As Adam watched, a tear splashed onto one of her rings.

"If you can approach Phoebe, I believe we can become a family again." He got to his feet and, after a moment, stepped close enough to put a hand on her shoulder. "I hope that's possible." Bending, he kissed her soft silver hair.

He'd crossed the room and reached the front door before she spoke. "Adam?"

"Yes, ma'am?"

"You don't…stutter…much anymore."

He grinned. "Maybe you could thank Phoebe for that, while you're talking."

"I will."

The concession was as much as he could have asked for. "Take care," he told her, and closed the door to his childhood home behind him.

FRIDAY…SATURDAY…Sunday…a hurried, nonstop attempt to reach every citizen with the message. Adam got no time to talk to Phoebe—Tommy had set up schedules that kept the three of them working in different parts of town all weekend long. Monday, they campaigned together, hitting all the shopping centers and the mall as a couple, arms around each other and smiles wide as they posed with the constituents. Otherwise, Phoebe remained out of reach. She didn't answer her phone late at night or early in the morning.

This was some engagement—his fiancée seemed engaged in an effort to avoid talking with him at all.

Election day dawned clear and cold, but Adam had stumbled out of bed even before the stars left the sky. A shower woke him up without restoring his energy, and the search for matching socks—in the drawer he hadn't had time to sort for weeks now—took ten frustrating minutes. He sat on the side of the bed for a long time, elbows on his knees and head propped in his hands, seeking the incentive to get through just one more day. Win or lose, tonight would end the campaign. And he could hardly wait.

On impulse, he took hold of the phone and dialed Phoebe's number. He had no reason to expect this day to be different, but—

"Hello?" She sounded as tired as he felt.

"Hey, there, sleepyhead. You still under the covers?"

"Mmm." He could picture her stretching, as he'd seen her stretch when she lay beside him in the mornings they spent together. "I think I threw the alarm clock at the wall when it rang this morning."

"Don't blame you. It's cold outside."

"And the polls open in an hour."

"Your horses need their grain. And the dogs want to go outside."

"How'd you know? They're standing here beside the bed, panting at me. All right, guys," she said to Lance and Gally and Gawain. "You can go freeze your tails off if that's what you want." The sound of the door opening came through the phone, and the slap of the screened porch door as she let the dogs out. "There. Now everybody's happy. Have you had your coffee yet?"

Adam pulled himself back from imagining Phoebe in her kitchen, wearing that favorite flannel nightgown, her hair down and her feet bare, her face all sweet and sleepy and sexy. "N-nope. I'll get some at the diner."

"I'm having hazelnut cream coffee. You can't get that at the diner."

"There are a lot of things I want I can't get at the d-diner."

Phoebe was quiet for a long minute. He heard her sigh. And then she seemed to switch mental gears. "So today's the big day. Any new surveys out? Are the numbers still good?"

She'd put him at a distance. Again. Adam resolved that this would be the last time. After tonight, they would have the time to work out whatever stood between them and then move forward. Together.

"The numbers that count will come in at the end of the day. You'll be at the party, right?" The candidates and their staffs for all the races would gather tonight in the ballroom of the Highlander Hotel, waiting for the vote count. Adam had reserved rooms for himself and Phoebe and Tommy, so they'd have somewhere private to retreat to if the tension got too high.

"I'll come home to take care of the horses and then drive back," Phoebe told him. "I wouldn't miss watching you get elected mayor of New Skye for anything."

"Then I guess I'll see you tonight." He hadn't said the words before, but this morning, they seemed especially important. "Have a good day, Phoebe. I love you."

Hearing the words, Phoebe closed her eyes against tears. "You, too," she managed to say, though she knew that wasn't what he wanted her to say. "Take care."

Adam had made her day a thousand times harder with those three simple words. She met her campaign responsibilities, saw three new patients in the office, and all the while the sound of his "I love you" burned like a brand on her heart. She voted on the way home from work, taking immense pride in the opportunity to mark her choice for mayor: Adam DeVries.

Out at the farm, she fed the horses and played with the dogs until the light failed, then spent a long time in the barn, dusting, tidying, coiling ropes and straightening halters as they hung on the racks, even going so far as to clean Marian's bridle. Maybe tomorrow she'd get home in time to ride. Both Brady and Cristal were looking a little chubby, in need of more exercise.

Finally, though, a fat white moon rose over the trees and Phoebe knew she couldn't delay the inevitable. She changed into her election-night outfit, a black pantsuit with a sparkly top underneath, and donned her heavy jewelry. There would be pictures, and she wanted the last one of her to be decent.

Heading into town, she noticed L. T. LaRue's construction site, and the huge stack of pine logs left over when his bulldozers mowed down all the beautiful trees. The tobacco field had become an ugly square of flat, bare dirt. She doubted his buildings would be an improvement.

The Highlander Hotel bulged at the doors and windows in an effort to contain the election night crowd. Balloons were tied to every available anchor along the hallway—doorknobs, table legs, potted plants, bobbing in Phoebe's face as she eased through the press of people. Streamers hung in the air, or flew at her from unseen directions.

The crush in the huge ballroom was just as dense, and she began to despair of ever finding Adam.

"There you are." Adam's arms came around her from behind, and he turned her to face him. "I've been watching for you all night, wondering if you'd decided not to come."

He looked more handsome, more alive than she'd ever seen him. His dark blue suit, white shirt and red tie hit just the right patriotic note. "Of course I came. What's the news?"

"Exit polls have me ahead by six percent." His wonderful smile broke over her. "Is that g-great, or what?"

Phoebe threw her arms around his neck and hugged him tight. "Terrific," she lied. "I'm so proud of you."

"P-proud of us all." He managed to swing her off her feet, even in the crowd. "Our command center's over here—we've got food and drinks. Come on."

Insanity reigned as they were swept up in election-night fever. Adam's crowd cheered each time new numbers appeared on the results board, scoring another precinct in his favor. By eleven o'clock, his victory was all but assured.

At midnight, the crowd hushed as Curtis Tate appeared behind the microphone on stage. Kellie stood at his shoulder, her face stiff and marred by tears.

"I am here to concede the race for mayor," Curtis said, his voice shaky. "I congratulate Mr. DeVries on running a successful campaign with dignity and honor. And I thank all the citizens of New Skye for allowing me the opportunity to serve them. I hope that I can find a new venue of public service in the very near future." Deafening applause greeted his statement, both from his supporters and from Adam's crew. The former mayor raised his hand for silence. "I would like to thank my campaign staff for their heroic efforts on my behalf. My wife, Kellie, deserves a great deal of credit for...for supporting me in my campaign and in my work for the city." Kellie smiled, her fingers playing with the flashing necklace at her throat.

"Finally, I would like to thank my good friend L. T. LaRue, who has stood by me for many years. His advice and support have been...invaluable. L.T., come up here." LaRue joined the mayor on the stage and the two men hugged, patting each other on the back. Tate turned to the microphone one last time. "Y'all enjoy the party, now. Hear?"

At that moment, the ceiling full of balloons dropped onto the heads of the crowd and an evening that had been wild exploded into frenzy. Adam had intended to make his acceptance speech, but after watching the chaos, he turned to Phoebe with a grin and a shrug. "Later, maybe. How about some champagne?"

They toasted his staff and all the people who had helped pursue the campaign. The barbecue cook from the Labor Day rally had come to the party, along with those who had stuffed envelopes, posted signs and made telephone calls. Dixon and Kate were there for hugs and handshakes.

"Good job," Dixon shouted at Adam. "You're gonna be a great mayor."

Kate kissed Phoebe's cheek. "Are you all right?" she said directly into Phoebe's ear. "You look pale."

"Just tired. Call me this week so I can see your honeymoon pictures." Phoebe escaped with evasion and a smile, only to run right into Mary Rose and her husband, Pete. More questions, more hugs, more celebration. Miss LuAnn Taylor was there, along with Daisy Crawford and Judge Taylor, but the pandemonium made any real conversation impossible.

Finally, just when Phoebe thought her head would explode from the noise, Adam leaned close.

"I'm going to commandeer the mike. Then we can get away for a while—I've got some rooms upstairs."

She nodded gratefully and gladly followed him as he wove his way through the throng, stopping every stride or two to receive congratulations from people who had never thought he would actually win.

He kept hold of her hand and drew her with him onto

the stage, with Tommy following them. The noise decreased as the crowd caught sight of them, enough that Adam could be heard when he spoke.

"I want to hold with tradition and accept Mayor Tate's g-gracious c-concession of the election." Raising his hand, he quieted the cheers. "I am honored and humbled by the c-confidence of the p-people of N-New Skye in choosing me as their next mayor, and I p-pledge to do everything within my p-power to see that our government operates honestly, morally and responsibly.

"Before I leave you to your celebration, I have thanks of my own to offer. This victory, this opportunity, would not have been p-possible without the energy and dedication—not to mention the sheer c-cussedness—of my friend and campaign manager, Tommy Crawford." Adam motioned Tommy to stand with him and take a bow. "Many, many p-people helped us in this effort, and I can't name them all right now, but you know who you are and you have my d-deepest g-gratitude."

As Tommy waved to the crowd and stepped back, Adam continued. "I also want to thank my family f-for p-putting up with me all these years. My brother, Tim, and my sister, Theresa." He looked down at Tim and Theresa in the front row next to the stage…and then paused. Between Adam's brother and sister stood his father. "And-and my d-dad, who's here tonight. Y'all come up on the stage." The three members of the DeVries family climbed the steps and there were hugs all around. Preston DeVries stood beside Phoebe, wearing a red, white and blue sticker that read I voted for honest government. I voted for DeVries. His smile was teary and proud.

"Finally, I want to acknowledge before all of you how much I owe to the woman beside me, the woman who sacrificed more than any of us will ever understand to make tonight a reality.'' There on the stage, Adam turned away from the microphone and took her in his arms. ''Words aren't adequate to say what I feel.'' His whisper was for her alone. ''Will you marry me, Phoebe? Let me spend the rest of my life showing you how grateful I am for everything you are?''

She couldn't answer, not in front of all of these people, with camera flashes blinding her and the roar of applause stopping her ears. So she smiled and hugged him, and waved to the crowd like a good campaigner should.

And put off the end for a few more minutes, at least.

TOMMY UNLOCKED THE DOOR to his hotel room around 3:00 a.m. He let Sam step in ahead of him, hung the Do Not Disturb sign on the knob and shut the world outside. Then he walked to the bed and dropped facedown, spread-eagled on the mattress.

In another moment, Sam had eased off his suit jacket and somehow, without making him move, managed to remove his tie. His shoes dropped with a thump on the floor. By the rustle of cloth, he deduced that she'd taken off some…all?…of her own suit.

''Damn,'' he said with a groan, ''I'm too tired to roll over and look at you.''

''Don't worry. We'll get there.'' The bed dipped, and she knelt beside him. ''First, I'm gonna get you to relax.''

Her hands took hold of his shoulders, and Tommy groaned again. Muscles that had been knotted for months started to uncoil beneath her persuasive fingers. His neck resembled a tree trunk, until Sam used her knuckles like twin rolling pins. By the time she'd reached the base of his spine, he thought he might actually survive the night.

Until she made love to him, that is, and destroyed him all over again.

"You are incredible," he murmured finally, unable to do more than kiss her hand as he held it between his own. "What do I have to do to keep you around?"

"Show up at the right time, at the right place, with a ring in your pocket and a promise you're willing to make."

Tommy pushed himself up on an elbow and looked down into her sassy, vulnerable face. "That's all, huh? A ring and a promise?"

"Too much to ask?"

He dropped back against the pillow and pulled her closer into his arms. "Nah. I can handle it. Just make an appointment with my secretary. She'll get you on the calendar. I'm a busy man, you know."

"Oh, I know."

"And Sam?"

"Mmm?"

"I'm expecting doughnuts at the reception. Chocolate iced doughnuts."

A chuckle ran through her. "Whatever you want, Tommy. Whatever you want."

COMPLETELY DISORIENTED, Adam awoke in a strange bed and couldn't remember where he was, or why. Reality came in pieces—he recognized the hotel room first, and then remembered the election. He'd won, which brought a grin to his face. Winning felt good.

He recalled proposing to Phoebe, which also felt good.

She hadn't answered, though, and he'd brought her to the hotel room to talk, to celebrate, to plan. So…where was she?

"Phoebe?" He sat up, recognized the pile of his

clothes by the bed. They'd gone a little crazy with that first kiss, hadn't been able to stop or to think or to talk. Adam grinned again, reliving their passion. He'd never known what freedom meant until he'd made love to Phoebe Moss.

"Phoebe, are you here?" Dumb question, since she hadn't answered him the first time, since her clothes were nowhere to be seen. She'd dressed and gone out. For a sandwich? For a newspaper to read about their win? For another bottle of champagne?

Forever, according to the note he found on the table by the window.

Dear Adam,
I wish I could marry you, but I'm selfish, I guess. You've chosen a path I can't follow without giving up myself. Hard as it will be, I'd rather live without you than spend my life trying to be someone I'm not. I'm so very, very sorry.
I do love you.

Phoebe

P.S. This officially breaks our "engagement." I'll let you make the announcement.

Adam sat for a long, long time with the note in his hands. Then he got up, got dressed and went home to listen to the messages of congratulations on his answering machine.

And to start his first day as mayor-elect of New Skye, North Carolina, with the ashes of victory bitter in his mouth.

CHAPTER SEVENTEEN

BY THE WEEKEND AFTER THE election, Phoebe had begun to wonder if she'd dreamed the entire campaign experience. Except for those times when she was unwise enough to turn on local news reports or read the paper—and she'd quickly learned to do neither—she hadn't seen or heard from Adam DeVries, his family or his friend Tommy since Wednesday morning. She went to work, resolutely keeping her gaze averted from L. T. LaRue's construction site, and came home again to take care of herself, her farm and her animals. That was the life she'd desired, had built for herself. Should be satisfied with.

And she was, for the most part. The weather had warmed, giving her golden, if short, afternoons and a beautiful Saturday for riding and working. She cleared the pastures of sticks brought down by the wind and finally coaxed Samson into taking pieces of apple from her hand. The dogs all got baths and the horses received a good brushing.

Saturday night the weather turned wet, and then cold, so feeding the horses on Sunday morning wasn't quite the usual pleasant experience. She'd just dumped alfalfa over the fence rail when a sleek silver car appeared at the turn of the driveway. She only knew one person with a silver Lexus.

"Hi, Tommy." Meeting him without Adam seemed strange. But at least it wasn't too painful.

"Hey, Phoebe. How are you?" He looked more rested than she'd seen him in weeks, more relaxed. She realized suddenly, and with no little guilt, how much the campaign must have taken out of Tommy himself. He'd probably worked harder than any of them.

She invited him inside and poured them both a cup of coffee. "I came to apologize," he said, sitting at the kitchen table in the same chair where Adam had worked on his stutter. "Things got really tense those last few weeks. There were times I should've just kept my mouth shut."

"That makes at least two of us. I'm sorry, too, Tommy. I know you were trying to do your best for Adam's campaign."

"I was. And I could never figure out whether you were an obstacle or a help." He shrugged and gave her his sideways smile. "Guess it doesn't matter now. He won, and that's all there is to it."

"Here's to Mayor Adam DeVries." She lifted her mug and Tommy joined her in the toast. "I hope he can make the changes he thinks are important."

"He's a stubborn cuss. I imagine he'll get just about everything he wants."

She ignored the glint in his eye. "Good for him. How's Sam?"

"She's great, working on analysis articles of the election. Seems that Adam won with a heavy margin of the middle income voters, who got really fed up when Tate won the car in the raffle. They started paying attention to our ads at that point, and sixty-five percent of them decided to try out a new mayor. Combined with the high-income voters and a reasonable percentage of lower income votes, we came out a comfortable fifty-five to forty-five. We really did okay."

Phoebe listened to him ramble, realizing that this was, to a large degree, Tommy's achievement and he deserved to brag about it. When he left, she gave him a hug and a promise to come into town some time for dinner.

Then, ordering herself not to cry and not to look back, she returned to cleaning the house. She was flat on her stomach on the bedroom floor, vacuuming up the dust bunnies under the bed, when she heard the rumble of truck tires on the driveway.

Scrambling clumsily to her feet, Phoebe went to the window, where the sight of the white DeVries Construction vehicle drove her heart into a gallop. As she walked slowly, almost reluctantly, outside, her throat closed with something that felt like fear and hurt like hope.

Adam dropped out of the driver's seat with a thud of his boots on the hardened ground. "Hi." He didn't smile, and he had his arms crossed over his chest in a stiff pose. "How are you?"

"O-okay." Which was more or less true, although she probably had dust in her hair and dirt on her face and these were her oldest jeans and sloppiest sweatshirt. And her heart was breaking, just looking at him. "How are you?"

"Lousy. But I had to bring you something."

"Oh." Had she left a piece of clothing at his house, and he couldn't wait to get rid of it? He should have just thrown it away. "Come on in."

Once he'd followed her onto the porch, though, he stopped. "We might want to do this here. And keep the dogs out."

Turning back to him, Phoebe gave up even trying to figure out what was going on. "That's fine." She didn't know whether to hold out her hand or just stand there.

"I didn't know what else to do with this," Adam said,

unzipping his jacket. He put a hand into one side, and pulled out a small brown ball. "So I brought it to you."

As she watched, the ball moved in his palm. A head emerged, sharp brown ears, two hazy eyes in that peculiar shade of newborn blue.

"Adam! Oh, what is this?" She reached out and cupped the ball of fur, felt slender bones under the fur against her skin. "A puppy? You brought me a puppy?" Backing up, she dropped onto the sofa without jarring the dog. "Why?"

Adam sat down beside her. "I found it. In the middle of the street near one of my housing sites."

"This poor little thing in the middle of the street? Today, in this weather?"

He nodded. "I thought it…he…was a rock…or maybe a turtle…until he moved. And I couldn't just leave him there, sick or starved, or who knows what. The only solution I could think of was to bring him here. To you."

"You brought me a dog." She blinked back tears. And smiled.

Adam gazed at her a moment, then stared down at his hands, gripped together between his knees. "I don't hate dogs. Or cats. I just… See, we had P-Pixie, and she was mine. Tim and Theresa liked her and played with her, but she was my dog. She slept on my bed, waited outside the bathroom door while I took a shower. We did everything together except school. And she waited for me at the end of the driveway each day. The sun shone through the trees in the afternoons, and she liked to take a nap in that spot till I got home."

He cleared his throat. "One day, when I was eight, I came home and she wasn't there. I called, and she didn't come. That hadn't happened since I'd started kindergarten. When I got inside, my mother said…" His deep breath shook. "Said P-Pixie had been run over as she slept. And she was dead. My mother took her to the vet so I wouldn't see. My d-dog just d-disappeared."

"Oh, Adam." In the cup of her hands, the puppy had curled back to sleep.

He shrugged, pretending not to care. "Life g-goes on. I started stuttering. And we n-never got another d-dog. I couldn't."

"I'm sorry. I know how much you must have hurt."

"I grew up, learned how to bury the hurt. But your dogs, your cats…your life…showed me that it's possible to feel the joy without dreading the loss. And so when I found the puppy, I knew he belonged in your world."

"Don't you want him?"

"With my life? He wouldn't be happy living the way I do. Any more than you were."

Phoebe nearly doubled over in pain as the truth hit her. Like his beloved dog, she'd simply disappeared.

But Adam had found the strength to rise above that betrayal, and to come here with an offering she couldn't refuse. Did she have the strength to match his generosity? Could she reject her own fears and become the person she wanted to be?

She set the puppy down in the corner of the couch, where he simply curled tighter, slept harder. Then she turned back to Adam. "How's life as mayor-elect?"

"Slightly less hectic than life as a wannabe. Tommy and I declared a m-moratorium on politics for at least two weeks. He and Samantha are planning a wedding instead."

"That was fast."

"Tommy wastes no time, once he knows what he wants."

"Some of us aren't so smart."

"You have what you want and I..." He dragged in another deep breath and got to his feet. "I do, too."

She wanted to keep him talking. "How are your parents? What happened after the fundraising dance?"

"I had lunch with m-my d-dad this past week. He's still f-furious with my mother, but m-mellowing. They're two halves of a person—I don't think either could survive without the other. I suggested maybe they need some c-counseling. I know how helpful a g-good therapist can be." His smile flashed briefly, then was gone. He looked around the porch, as if he'd lost something and was trying to find it. "I-I guess I'd better get back to town."

"Adam." Phoebe stood, and hesitated yet again as he turned to leave. Leaps of faith could be so terribly hard.

He waited at the door, his back to her. "Take care, Phoebe."

She grasped desperately for something to bridge the gap. "Don't you want to name the puppy?"

"I don't have practice at naming puppies."

"So it's time you started." Grabbing his hand, she drew him around to face her. "Naming puppies gets you ready for naming—" her courage faltered "—other creatures."

The smile returned to Adam's eyes. "You mean cats?"

"Cats." She nodded gratefully. "Horses."

"Fish, maybe."

"People do name fish." She managed a grin and a decent breath. "No birds, though. I don't like birds in the house."

"Kids?" he asked, trying to look innocent.

"You mean goats? We could name goats." He lifted an eyebrow and Phoebe closed the physical distance between them. "Or we could name those children you mentioned, once upon a time."

His arms slipped around her waist. "Children mean marriage."

"Yes." He waited, and she clarified her words. "Yes, that's what children mean. And, yes to your lovely proposal."

Adam squeezed his eyes shut for a few seconds, trying to keep his balance in a world gone suddenly crazy with joy. He hadn't expected this when he came to see her today. Hadn't dared hope.

"We'll make it work," he promised, looking into her face, her sweet gray eyes. "I won't demand you give up this for me." He waved an arm to encompass the farm, the animals, the peace they both found here. "You don't have to be Kellie Tate, or my mother. You don't have to lead the community—that's my job. I want you to be just what you are. Phoebe Moss, the love and light of my life." Adam couldn't repress a chuckle. "It's a good thing you taught me how to manage those *L*s."

"Especially since I expect you to use the L-word frequently."

"L-lust?" He mocked his own stutter.

"That's one of them.

"Ah." The teasing was fun, but he wanted…needed… to be sure. "I love you, Phoebe Moss."

She nestled against his chest. "I wish there was a variation that meant as much or more. But it's really very simple, isn't it? I love you, too. And we will make it work. Together." When she lifted her face to his, Adam was ready with his kiss.

In the corner of the couch, the puppy stirred, poked his head up and yipped. Adam parted his mouth slowly from Phoebe's. "Sounds like he wants dinner."

"Children are so demanding." She kissed his chin, and

the corner of his mouth…and they nearly forgot about the puppy again, who growled this time, reminding them of his presence.

"Okay. Okay." Adam walked over and picked up the handful of fur. "He can't be very old. Do you think he'll get big?"

Phoebe put a finger under the puppy's chin. "His face looks like a shepherd mix. We'll have to get him fed and healthy to be sure." She stared into the blue eyes, bright now with trust. "I'm going to name you…"

"Bo."

"Bo?" She took the puppy out of his hands. "What kind of name is Bo?"

"Spot?"

"He doesn't have any spots."

"Fido."

Phoebe shook her head in disgust. "You, sir, have no romance in your soul."

Adam pulled her back into his arms, dog and all. "Yes, ma'am, I most certainly do." He let his mouth hover a breath away from hers. "Because I have you."

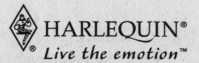

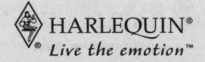

If you enjoyed what you just read,
then we've got an offer you can't resist!

Take 2 bestselling love stories FREE!

Plus get a FREE surprise gift!

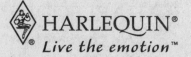

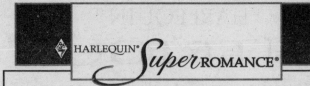

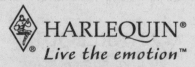